MYANAYMIZ

Arlene Adamo

Cover illustration by Kezia Adamo

The 'gods' know nothing, they understand nothing.
They walk about in darkness;
all the foundations of the earth are shaken.
Psalm 82:5

1

Her eyes opened…just a little at first. What was she looking at? Her ears were ringing…or more like buzzing. Where was she? It was cold. She knew that much. It was cold and damp as in many of her dreams, the kind of cold and damp that seeped into the bones…the kind of cold and damp adored by death itself. "I am not dead," she said aloud. "I am not dead," she repeated, hoping the words alone would bring some sort of life-warmth. "I. Am. Not. Dead."

She blinked her eyes and tried to focus. There were lines in front of her. None of them were exactly straight. Some zigged. Some zagged. Some ended abruptly. Some ended and then started up again. Some faded away slowly into nothingness. What were they, and why did she feel such a mix of emotions to see them there? Were they even real? She could try touching them. That was the test. Touching them would let her know if they were real…but did she even have hands?

Her fingers wiggled. She did have hands! They were almost as cold as death, but they moved. They moved easily, gracefully. They were hands, and they were full of her blood. Hands would let her know if the lines were real.

She slowly moved her arm forward, and gently touched the end of one of the lines. It was cold and hard and damp. She quickly took her finger away. Why could it not be warm? What she needed now was warmth. The cold made her want to go back to sleep. Why did it have to be so disappointing? To wake after such a long time, and see only this meaningless frigidity? Where was the warmth? Hadn't the dreams promised her warmth?

She dragged her finger slowly along another line. A shiver ran down her spine. *I have a spine,* she thought. *But of course, if I can move my hands, I must have a spine. A spine is everything.*

Pressing her palm firmly against the lines she realized that it was a wall, a rock wall. The lines were scratched into the stone. That's when she became aware that she could smell it, that ancient stone smell…the damp, earthless smell of stone all around her.

"Where am I?"

She wiggled her toes. "I am curled," she said. "Just like a baby, I am curled…a baby in a rock womb." She slowly began to stretch out one of her legs, but it did not go far before it was stopped by the stone wall. Her bare foot tapped softly against the surface. A small muffled rhythmic sound broke through the silence, and she smiled to have even this small power. Within this rock womb, she was at least able to make a sound against the stone. Somehow, it made her feel less alone.

Slowly, with effort, she turned over onto her back and stared up at the rock above her. There again were lines. On every side it was covered in lines. She reached up to touch them, and a strange sense of nostalgia washed over her. It was then that she realized how the lines came to be. She had made them. In her restless sleep, she had scratched all of these lines into the stone. Years of tossing and turning, locked in an unconscious prison, she had carved these lines with whatever energy she could muster, a wild chaotic masterpiece of her own creation. Within this living death, she had etched her humanity upon these lifeless walls. "I am human," she said, and then looking at the lines added, "sort of."

She looked at her hand and realized there was a little dried blood on her fingers. This was her blood, and it was in every line on that rock. There was no wind here to remove it or rain to wash it away. She had forced her life upon the lifeless, and it would be there for all eternity. "I have done what I have done."

Taking in a deep breath of air, she began to move her arms and legs. At first, she didn't realize why she was doing this, but then it suddenly dawned on her that she was looking for an exit. "If I am awake, an exit is what I would desire…I think."

Every which way she moved she came up against only stone. If she were stone also, she could live here, but she was alive. "Life needs life," she said, dragging her hand along the wall, searching for anything that might be an opening or a secret latch.

Her fingers, legs, feet, hands searched and searched, exploring every part of that tomb. Over and over again she would feel the rise of some small hope only to have it dashed by cold impervious stone. *There must be a way out.*

After what seemed like a long time and many disappointments, she was ready to give up and resign herself to fate. *Is this place really so bad?* It was then, at that moment, she absently reached up behind her head and felt nothing. She stretched out her arm and wiggled her fingers. There was no wall. There was only open space. *Why did I not find that before?*

Although it was painful, she twisted her head to see what was behind her. There was an opening! The cave had a small opening on this side! *I can be born this way.*

Carefully, as not to hit any part of herself against the rock, she turned once again, this time onto her stomach, and lifted her head as far as she could. It was a dark tunnel, a pitch black tunnel.

She looked deep into the darkness. This was the exit she had desperately longed for…so why now did she hesitate?

It's about facing the unknown, she thought. For now, she was in a place that she knew. A place she had been in for a very long time. There was light in this place. Where it came from, she couldn't tell, but it was some kind of light…dull though it was. She had been here for who knows how long. It was like a home…sort of… if you didn't expect too much from a home.

But the tunnel was pitch black. Anything could be in there, snakes, spiders, monsters of all kinds. Any old thing child-fears could conjure. Wasn't it better to stay where she was? At least here there was some light. She knew the place. She could spend her whole life simply retracing those lines her fingers had forgotten. That was her blood in every last one of them. If she left, maybe she'd never see them again. And perhaps cold and damp were not so bad after all. Surely, it was better than that darkness? And hadn't she been able to stay alive here for a long time…well, sort of alive.

She rested her cheek against the cold damp rock beneath her. "Mother," she softly whispered.

⎯⎯•◆•⎯⎯

     Arlene Adamo

Time had passed. She wasn't sure how long she had remained with her face against the cold stone. She only knew that time had passed, and that her body was feeling numb. Was she returning once again to sleep? Although not all of her dreams had been pleasant, there were many that had been comforting and lovely. Would it be so wrong to return to a life of only dreams? It would certainly be the easiest thing to do. She stared at the lines on the wall.

All at once, she realized there was something new. It was in her stomach. Was it because her stomach was now pressed against the hard stone floor? Maybe, or maybe it was just because she was awake. Was this a part of being awake, this strange pain, this emptiness begging…no demanding…to be filled? *This is hunger*, she thought. *Hunger changes everything.*

She lifted her head and looked straight into the dark tunnel. Was she really afraid of snakes and spiders, she who had scratched an entire blood-filled world of wonder into these stone walls, she who could make rhythms against a rhythmless rock, she who could survive so long in the cold and damp, she whose dreams could rival any reality? Was she really afraid of anything at all?

"I am not afraid!" she shouted, the astounding vibration of her voice filling her with both euphoria and surprise. *Did I really make such a sound?* "I am not afraid!" she shouted again, and with such intensity that she thought she felt the rock tremble. *There is no turning back. The time is now.* Reaching forward with both hands, she began to drag herself into the unknown.

She thought it would take a long time. She was expecting that inching forward through that black tunnel would feel even longer than her sleep, but it didn't. It was fast. Instantaneously fast. So fast, in fact, that it didn't seem like she dragged herself through that tunnel at all, but more like the tunnel swiftly folded back over her body and disappeared behind her. She went from the dull light of the cave into the bright sunlight in the same time it took to take a breath.

Underneath her now was something soft. "Life," she said, pressing her cheek against the grass covered earth. "Warmth," she said, as the sun's rays caressed her back. For a while, she did not move. She only wanted to feel all the new sensations. Sensations that, until now, she had only dreamt of.

3

Rising upon her hands and knees, she looked around. "This world is big," she said.

Directly ahead of her was a thick forest. To the left was a bubbling brook. To the right was a meadow. "Yes. This place was in my dream."

Slowly, she stood up. It felt good to feel so tall. "Freedom," she said, as she stretched and waved her arms in the soft breeze.

She looked behind her at the rock. "You are past," she said, and then turned back towards the forest. That's when she noticed movement.

Quickly, she fell low to the ground. Her dreams had told her of lions and wolves and bears, and how they always hid, waiting in the forest. She wasn't really afraid, but just couldn't be certain if she was ready for such an encounter. Not just yet anyway.

This movement though, was not the great lumbering of some dangerous carnivore. Instead, it was quick and light, little things bouncing and dashing among the trees, funny little sing-song laughter. *Children! I dreamt of children.* She sat up upon her knees to watch them.

They didn't notice her, but instead continued to chase each other around and around the great tree trunks, racing this way and that, bursting out in wild songs that ended as abruptly as they began. *Oh, little free spirits!* She smiled. *Yes, I chose well to leave the rock.*

As she watched, one of the boys suddenly shot out of the forest and ran straight towards her. When he saw her sitting there, he stopped abruptly, just staring in shock and confusion. *What is this?* He looked back at the forest and could see his companions still engaged in play. No one but him had noticed the stranger. "Hey-o!" he yelled to his companions. "Hey-o, come here! Look! Look what I found!" he yelled even louder when they did not come right away.

The children stopped what they were doing, and looked in the direction of their friend. Some of them gasped at the sight of the strange woman in the grass. For a brief second, no one moved, but then they quickly came running over. Once they were all standing together, the boy who had first spotted her, slowly and cautiously began to walk forward. The others followed suit, but stayed alert and ready to run if the woman showed any signs of being dangerous. They stopped a short distance away, and stared in wonder at the sight. Not one of them seemed brave enough to speak first when suddenly, the youngest hollered, "She's naked!", and they all burst out laughing.

The children then circled around her, but kept at a safe distance. One climbed up on the rock to get a different perspective. *Who was this naked Lady with the strange silver hair?*

They whispered and giggled amongst themselves, not knowing what to make of her. It was sort of like the day they found an orange salamander under a rock. That was very exciting. Orange salamanders are rare and hard to find, but this was no salamander. This was far bigger than that.

"Who are you naked Lady?" suddenly quipped one little girl, and they all burst out laughing again.

The Lady did not reply, but only smiled at them.

"Where did you come from?" asked the boy on the rock, feeling less afraid after seeing her smile.

She glanced back at him. "From that rock upon which you sit," she answered.

The children looked confused, and then began laughing. "From a rock, from a rock, a Lady from a rock," one started singing, and three more joined in.

"What's your name?" asked one of the bigger children, interrupting the singers.

"My-a-nay-miz," she answered.

They were puzzled. "Do you not understand? What is your name?"

"My-a-nay-miz," she said again.

"I think she means her name is 'Is'," explained a boy.

"No, she just doesn't understand our language," said a girl. "That's why she keeps repeating 'my name is.'"

"She already told us she came from the rock, so she must understand. What—is—your—name?" one of them asked again, slowly and in a loud voice.

"My-a-nay-miz," she replied. "Myanaymiz."

"Oh, I get it," said the girl. "Her name is Myanaymiz. Is that right? Is that your name?"

The Lady smiled. "I am Myanaymiz."

"Myanaymiz, Myanaymiz, we found Myanaymiz!"

"Myanaymiz, why does your skin twinkle?"

She looked down at her hand. Turning it back and forth, she saw how there were many tiny points of light that appeared to be reflecting the sun. It was subtle, but it was the truth. Her skin did twinkle in the sunlight. "I do not know why."

"And where are your clothes?" one giggled.

"I have none," she replied.

"You need clothes," said another. "You can't walk around like that. That's not proper, and it will also be very cold at night."

"Yes," added a little girl. "You need clothes. Maybe we can make you some."

The little boy on the rock seemed to like this idea. "We could make some clothes out of leaves or grass."

"But how do we do that?" asked the girl. She turned to Myanaymiz, "Do you know how to make clothes from the leaves?"

Myanaymiz looked around at the vegetation. The leaves were small and flimsy, and the grass was short. "It is not possible with what we have to work with."

"But you need clothes," said the girl.

The boy on the rock climbed down. "I know," he said. "Let's go ask Old Jeremiah. He must have some scrap cloth. We can make her some clothes from that."

"But, Axis, what if he is angry at us for finding her?" the girl asked.

"Don't worry. Old Jeremiah never gets angry at us children," replied Axis. "Petal and Dibby, you come with me, and we will ask him. Is that alright Myanaymiz? Would you like us to ask him?"

"Yes," she smiled. "I need clothes."

4

"Old Jeremiah! Old Jeremiah!" shouted Petal, running into the house along with her two companions. The Master Weaver's door was never locked, but always left open for visitors or anyone who might be in need of his assistance.

"Children, I have no time today," Jeremiah said, not bothering to look up from his loom. In accordance with tradition, The Master Weaver neither cut his hair nor shaved his beard, making him look like some old grey lion, whose hunting days were behind him. "You know the Festival of the Gods will soon be upon us."

"But this is important!" exclaimed Petal, jumping up and down. "We found something!"

"You children are always finding something. What is it this time…a ruby, a diamond, a pearl?"

"It's a naked Lady," said Dibby, and they all burst out into giggles.

Old Jeremiah looked up from his work. "Did you say you found a naked Lady?"

"Yes! Yes we did!" Petal proudly proclaimed.

"You are not making up a story, are you?"

"Oh no, Old Jeremiah. We are telling the truth. There is a naked Lady just beyond the forest. She came from a rock," said Axis.

"From a rock?"

"Yes, she said she came from the big rock near the brook, and now we need some clothes for her. We can't bring her into the

Town all naked. That's why we are here. To see if you have any scrap cloth. Do you have any scrap cloth, Old Jeremiah?"

Jeremiah was trying to make sense of it all. Were the children playing with him…weaving a fanciful tale just for fun? As a child, he once heard a story about a Lady from a rock, but these little ones would not have known that. All of the ancient stories have been forbidden since the Great Purification. "You are certain she came from the rock?" he asked.

"Yes, that's what she said. She came from the rock, she is naked, and her skin twinkles in the sunlight," said Petal.

"Twinkles?"

"Yes, it twinkles like millions of tiny stars. Can we have the cloth now?" asked Axis, becoming a little impatient. What if the Lady got tired of waiting, and decided to go away? They needed to get back as soon as possible.

Jeremiah was still not certain about what to make of their story, but he knew they must have found someone…someone who seemed to need clothes. He looked around the room. There was no extra cloth. Preparation for the Festival of the Gods had taken up all of his resources. There was nothing…nothing except the purple and gold gown hanging on the wall, but that was intended for the greatest of the Gods. No one was allowed to even touch that, let alone wear it. Even he was only to touch it while wearing special sanctioned gloves now that it was complete.

"I have nothing children. I have no scraps to give you."

The children looked straight at the gown hanging in the corner. "You have that Old Jeremiah. That will do just fine."

Jeremiah laughed. "That is for the God of Gods."

"But maybe she is a God," said Dibby, wanting more than anything to get his hands on that gown.

"Shhh… child," said Jeremiah. "Such talk could get you in serious trouble. Only the Gods are Gods."

"But maybe they will decide she is a God," piped in Axis. "We cannot leave her alone and naked. What will she do? She needs clothes and she needs them now!"

Before Jeremiah could stop him, Axis ran over to the gown and pulled it down from the hook. He hugged it closely to his chest. "Come with us, Old Jeremiah. Come and see her for yourself."

Jeremiah was frozen in disbelief! The gown had been touched by ordinary human hands! It was now unsuitable for a God! All of his intricate painstaking work had gone to ruin in the blink of an eye! The divine gown of the God of Gods was now being clutched in the unclean little arms of a child…an innocent…a criminal!

"Axis, what have you done?"

From the tone of Jeremiah's voice, the boy suddenly realized that he had committed a serious offense. "Here, take it back," he said, offering the gown to the old Weaver. "I'm sorry."

But it was too late. The child had already broken a law of the Gods. He would face a severe penalty for such a sin as this. The Gods made no allowances for mistakes or for children. Justice was swift and merciless for even minor offenses. A crime on this scale would likely mean death.

It was then that Jeremiah knew he must now break the law also. He must lie to protect this little innocent one from being executed. What else was he to do?

"Listen to me child, there is no need to be sorry," he said. "This gown was intended for the Gods, but I see now that I have made serious errors. The workmanship is flawed because I was sleepy, and as stated in the law, 'no garment may be presented to the Gods that is not perfect.' This gown is certainly not worthy of the God of Gods. Therefore, we shall take it to this Lady you have found."

The children all burst out into smiles. "You will be amazed Old Jeremiah," said Petal. "You will be amazed by this Lady from the rock. She is more amazing than any orange salamander ever could be."

———•◆•———

5

Still sitting in the soft grass, Myanaymiz turned her face towards the blue sky, and closed her eyes. So many sounds! So many sensations! And the warmth! Oh, the warmth! In her dreams she had never felt it like this. The warmth in her dreams had always been like a quick flash…a teasing promise that only hinted at fulfillment. But this was a promise in glorious unwavering fulfillment.

"Is she dying?" asked a child.

"Please don't die," cried another.

She opened her eyes again. "No, I am not dying. I am not sleeping. I am here."

The children were instantly relieved. One of the smaller ones walked over to her, and put a flower in her hair. "There," she said. "You are beautiful."

What a wonderful idea! A second child picked a small blue flower, and placed it on the crown of her head. He then picked another and another and another, tucking each one neatly into her soft silver hair.

All of the children started to join in, laughing as they ran around picking flowers, and bringing them back to Myanaymiz. Soon there were so many flowers in her hair that they began to fall into her lap and pile up around her. When the children had finished it looked as though the sky had rained flowers down upon her. The little artists stood back, and smiled proudly at their beautiful handiwork.

6

When Jeremiah followed Axis, Dibby and Petal out of the trees, he at first didn't see anything but the backs of a group of children standing in the middle of the meadow.

"Hey-o," called Axis, "we have clothes! We have Old Jeremiah! Let us through!"

When the children turned to look, they were relieved to see their friends approaching along with Old Jeremiah. The Master Weaver's presence was always reassuring in times of confusion. The little crowd parted, and for the first time Jeremiah saw the Lady sitting in the grass.

"Look!" said Petal. "Look! There she is!"

For a moment, Jeremiah just stood there staring in amazement. *The children were telling the truth! How is this possible? We have never had a single stranger in Town in my lifetime, and now to have such a one as this?* The woman was naked as the children had said, but he was not quite close enough to see if her skin really did twinkle. Her strange silver hair was covered in colorful flowers that were also puddled in her lap and on the ground around her. He cautiously moved just a little closer.

Dibby decided that he would be in charge of the introductions. "Old Jeremiah," he said, "this is Myanaymiz. Myanaymiz, this is Old Jeremiah, Master Weaver of our Town."

Myanaymiz looked at Jeremiah. His face, his grey whiskers and his long grey hair were all faint memories. He was old, but she knew that in some of her dreams he was young. She also knew that he was a good man who could be trusted.

"Old Jeremiah, Young Jeremiah, I am awake, and can see that here before me, after all this time, is Jeremiah," she said, making the children laugh.

"He brought you some clothes," declared Petal triumphantly.

Jeremiah was so taken aback that he had momentarily forgotten he still held the gown in his arms. "Oh! Oh yes! I have brought this for you to wear." He moved a little closer as he offered over the garment.

Myanaymiz reached out, and took the gown in her hand. The beautiful purple and gold shimmered in the sunlight as she ran her fingers over the soft smooth fabric. It had been seamlessly woven to perfection. "It is as it should be," she said smiling.

"Do you know how to put it on?" Jeremiah asked.

"Yes," she answered. "In my dreams, I have put it on many times."

Myanaymiz gracefully placed it over her head, slipped her arms in, and let the fabric fall down over her body. She then stood up and straightened out the skirt.

"Ahhh!" said the children all together.

"It fits perfectly," said Axis.

"It is meant to fit perfectly on anyone who wears it," said Jeremiah, proud to see his workmanship displayed on such a pleasing form. "That is the magic of the Master Weaver."

Myanaymiz liked the way it felt. Although it now covered her from the sun, the colors worked to attract the heat and trap it against her skin. "This is very good," she said. "I am warm."

Jeremiah had now moved close enough to have a better look at her face. Here and there he would see a small twinkle whenever she moved. *The children are right. Her skin is covered in tiny stars like the sky. But who is she? What is she?* "The children tell me you came from a rock," he said.

"Yes, from the rock that is behind me," Myanaymiz explained.

Jeremiah was familiar with that rock, and knew there was no opening from which this Lady could have emerged. "How is this possible?" he asked.

Myanaymiz took a flower from her hair, and looked lovingly upon it. "When they come to you, Master Weaver, and ask the question, 'how is this possible', how do you answer them?"

It was true. All the time people asked Jeremiah to tell them how he could create such masterpieces for the Gods. What was his secret? 'Please,' they would beg, 'reveal to us the mystery.' But he would never admit to them that it was just as big a mystery for him. Instead, his answer was always the same…three simple words…'I open myself.' It was the best explanation he could come up with.

"Are there others in the rock?" Jeremiah asked, suddenly wondering if there could be an entire world of hidden people he did not know about.

"I was alone," she answered.

"But you're not alone now," chirped Petal, taking Myanaymiz by the hand.

Myanaymiz smiled down at the child.

"What are you?" asked Jeremiah.

"I am human," she said, looking Jeremiah straight in the eye.

Look away. It's too strange. Too powerful. "But you don't seem human. You seem…different."

"I am human," she said again. "I am not alone. Not anymore"

"That's right Old Jeremiah. She is human just like us," said Petal. "She will stay with us. She belongs to us. She is not alone, and the Gods cannot have her."

"She belongs to us!" the children began to chant. "She belongs to us!"

"Shhh, quiet children," said Jeremiah. He would explain to them about their blasphemy later. "Why are you here, Myanaymiz? Why did you come here?"

She looked at him and smiled. "It is the way Young-Old Jeremiah. It is the way that was set for me when God said *'Let there be light.'* It is the way that calls to me. It is the way I must go."

"We do not have God here. We have Gods," said Jeremiah. "You must not talk of God. To do so is dangerous."

"Why is it dangerous, Old Jeremiah?" asked Petal.

"Shush child! Do not speak of such things." He then looked at Myanaymiz and said, "Do you not see what you have done? Such talk could endanger the children. You must be careful. Very careful!"

In this place, there are lions, wolves, bears…and gods. "Do not worry, Young-Old Jeremiah, I will not let them hurt any of the children."

More blasphemy! What was he to do? This woman could not see what kind of a world she had entered. She said things that could get herself and anyone who listened to her into serious trouble. She was dangerous, yet he could not simply abandon her. She was from a rock, and her skin twinkled. His instinct told him she was very important, but how? How did she fit into this world? What was her relationship to the Gods? How angry would the Gods be with him for even getting involved?

"Myanaymiz, will you come and live with me and my family?" asked Petal.

"No! Absolutely not!" Jeremiah blurted out. The idea of allowing this Lady loose in the Town without some guidance was frightening. She could do all kinds of damage. Before that could happen, she must first be taught what is right, and what is not right to say.

Jeremiah then noticed the hurt in Petal's face, and regretted that he had spoken so harshly. He instantly softened his tone. "What I mean to say is that it is not a good idea, Petal" he said. "Your house is already full. I will find a more suitable place for Myanaymiz to stay."

"I must go to the Town," said Myanaymiz. "It was in my dreams. I need to go with or without you. This is the way."

Jeremiah sighed. Where was she to stay? His home was out of the question. No one but he was allowed to live there whilst he created the gowns for the Gods. He must find a place for her, but not with any of the children. She had already spoken blasphemy, and caused them to do the same. He could not have her saying anymore such things in front of them. Suddenly, it dawned on him. *The Cobbler!* The Cobbler had no children and no wife

                    Arlene Adamo

to be influenced. He had a large enough cottage, and he did still owe Jeremiah for a shirt. *The Cobbler is perfect. He is quite capable of understanding this delicate situation, and could even help teach her how not to offend the Gods.*

"Myanaymiz, I know a place where you can stay. If you will come with me, I will take you there."

"Oh you will love the Town," piped in Petal. "There are many people there. Humans like us. The Gods live on the Mount, but the Town is full of people."

"Yes," said Myanaymiz. "I will love the Town. I will love the people. That was in my dreams."

———————

7

The people stopped in the streets and came out of their houses to watch the strange sight of the Master Weaver, the Lady in the beautiful gown and the parade of children pass by.

One man called out, "Old Jeremiah! Tell us, what is this about? Who is that Lady?"

"I will call a meeting later tonight, and speak to everyone about it," replied Jeremiah. "For now, we must go to the Cobbler's house."

The procession carried on through the streets of the bewildered Town.

⎯⎯ ◆ ⎯⎯

As they walked up the path to the Cobbler's cottage, Jeremiah wondered what he would say. It was a highly unusual request to make of the man. It could open the door to all sorts of criticism, but at the same time, the Cobbler had experienced more than his fair share of criticism over the years. He knew how to handle it. Still, this was an entirely new situation, and many of the Towns-folk would likely not approve of her staying there. Some would say it was not proper, and the zealous may even try to claim it is against the will of the Gods. However, this remained the best idea he could come up with under these emergency conditions.

"Jotham!" called out Jeremiah.

The door to the cottage opened, and Jotham stepped outside.

The first thing Myanaymiz noticed when he appeared in the doorway was his long fine yellow hair being caught by a breeze. *Baby hair! This is the one with the baby hair. He was in my dreams.*

Jotham was confused by the strange scene in front of his cot-tage. The children confused him even more when they began to eagerly shout out all the things that were racing through their minds.

"Cobbler, we brought you a Lady from the rock!"

"Old Jeremiah gave her some clothes!"

"She has come to stay!"

"Her skin twinkles!"

"I have a hole in my shoe!"

Jotham stared at this stranger. She wore a garment that could rival anything he had seen the Gods wear, and her strange silver hair was sprinkled with flowers. He watched as a tiny bluebell fell loose, tumbled down her breast and landed upon his front step.

"Children!" shouted Jeremiah, trying to be heard over all of the commotion. "Quiet now! You must return to your homes. I have some things to discuss with the Cobbler."

The children were obviously not happy about being told to leave. "But Old Jeremiah, when can we come back and see our Lady?" asked Dibby.

"Do not worry. She will still be here tomorrow." *I think.* "Now go home to your parents, they will be expecting you to relate to them your adventures today, and you have such an interesting story to tell."

The children no longer objected. Just the thought of sharing this tale in a Town where so very little happened was exciting enough. They all went running off home.

As soon as they were gone, Jeremiah turned to Jotham said, "Now, let us go inside and I will explain."

⸺◆⸺

9

The Cobbler's cottage could only be described as a sincere tribute to the practicality of maleness…the linear singularity of pure man-thought. There was an A. There was a B. And then there was the straight line in between. The workshop took up most of the room with its tools, work stations and shoe molds. The smell of leather filled the air. Everything here was about getting the job done without needless fuss or bother. Even the old ornately carved table and four matching chairs near the window blended in with the piles of cut leather and machinery. On the window sill was the one odd thing that seemed to have secretly infiltrated this man-only place. It was a blue violet in a delicate looking white ceramic pot.

"I would like you to meet Myanaymiz," Jeremiah said. "And this is Jotham, Myanaymiz."

"Hello, I'm happy to meet you," said Jotham, trying his best to be polite under such peculiar circumstances.

"We have met before," she said smiling.

Jotham looked at Jeremiah, his eyes begging the question, 'who is this strange woman?'

"Let's all sit down, and I will try and explain everything to you," said Jeremiah. "A least as much as I understand."

The three sat down around the table.

"Now tell me, what the children meant when they talked of a Lady from a rock?" asked Jotham, eager to clear up his confusion. "Were they talking about you, Myanaymiz?"

"Yes, I am from a rock."

Jotham just stared at her not knowing what to say. *From a rock? This makes no sense.*

"The children found her," said Jeremiah.

"I was naked," added Myanaymiz.

Jotham was now even more confused.

"She claims that she has come from a rock, and when the children found her she had no clothes," Jeremiah tried to explain.

Jotham looked at the beautiful gown she was wearing. Suddenly, he knew where it had come from. It was the one meant for the God of Gods. He looked at Jeremiah as if to ask, *are you mad?*

Jeremiah recognized his concern. "There is no need to worry. That gown was defective. It was not suitable for the Gods."

This was an acceptable enough explanation for Jotham. Whether it was true or not did not matter. He had no great love for the Gods, although he kept it hidden as best he could. He just hoped it would be an acceptable explanation when it came time for Jeremiah to explain it to them.

"I don't even know what she is," said Jeremiah.

"I am human," said Myanaymiz. "I am not alone."

"Yes," said Jeremiah. "You are human…of sorts."

"Why did you bring her to me?" asked Jotham.

"You have room in your cottage, and you can help teach her. She says things…things that could influence the children to displease the Gods. We must teach her that which can be said, and which cannot be said, for the safety of us all."

"You will all be safe," said Myanaymiz.

Jeremiah smiled at her with the same smile he gave when explaining things to the children. "Yes, we will all be safe as long as you stay here with Jotham, and listen carefully to his instructions."

"The Townsfolk will not like it," said Jotham. "A woman staying here with me…alone."

"And when have you ever been bothered by what the Townsfolk had to say?"

Jotham laughed. "Never," he replied.

"Then why would you choose this time to start?"

"And will the Gods allow it?"

"That, we shall have to see, but for now it makes the most sense. We will deal with the Gods when the time comes."

Suddenly, from outside, there came a far off clanging sound. The two men looked at each other in disbelief. It was a sound that Jeremiah had not heard in a very long time. Such a long time, in fact, that he had almost forgotten what it was. But he remembered hearing it once before as a young man. It was the Black Bell that sat atop the Mount of the Gods. And there was only one reason and one reason alone for that bell to toll. One of the Gods was dead!

"Jotham, stay here with Myanaymiz and keep her out of sight for now. I must go and see the Gods." Jeremiah hurried out the door.

Jotham had been too young to remember the last time the bell had rung, but he immediately knew it must be the death knell. This was such a shock! The Gods considered themselves divine and eternal, and even though they did die, an unexpected death would be taken very hard. The Gods were perfect. They did not simply drop dead like humans.

"Such pretty music," said Myanaymiz.

So that's what Jeremiah was talking about. "Myanaymiz, you must not say that. One of the Gods is dead. This is very upsetting for everyone, and saying such a thing could get you in serious trouble. It is alright in front of me or Jeremiah, but in front of other people you must try not to say too much. At least, not until you fully understand this world, and how it works."

Myanaymiz could feel he was afraid. There were many times in her dreams when she had felt fear. She knew what it was like. She knew what it could do to a person…how paralyzing it was. But now that she was awake, she could see everything with her eyes wide open. Fear seemed foolish. "There is nothing to fear," she said. "Do not worry, Jotham. Just enjoy the pretty music."

— · —

10

After they had dinner, Jotham was delighted to discover Myan-aymiz could read. "I can read anything in any language," she told him. "I learned how to read in dreams." He showed her the room where she was to sleep, and left her there with the Stories of the Gods, closing the door behind him. He could already see that teaching her would not be easy. She did not seem to be taking to heart anything he was trying to tell her. How could he possibly teach this Lady who, so far, did not seem interested in learning? *Hopefully, those stories will teach her something.*

By now the bell had stopped. The Townsfolk would all be discussing the situation behind closed doors as they waited for the final ceremonial instructions that Jeremiah was to receive tonight. Among the Stories of the Gods there was one detailing a divine funeral, so even those who were not born or were too young to remember would have some idea about what to expect.

Jotham extinguished all of the lanterns in his workshop, except for one which he picked up and carried into the bedroom. He closed the door behind him, and set the lantern down on the table under the mirror. Looking at his bed, he thought about how good it would feel to finally relax and stretch out. His back was hurting again. It happened by the end of most days, but these days it was especially true. Many Townsfolk wanted new shoes for the Festival of the Gods, and he had been working too hard trying to complete all of those orders on time. All that extra work was taking its toll.

Jotham unbuttoned his shirt, and slid it down his shoulders. He then twisted his head to look at the reflection of his back in the mirror. Usually, he tried to resist looking, but every once in a while he found himself checking just to see if they had faded. He sighed. Nothing had changed. *Why do I even bother when it is just another disappointment?* There they were, those scars, as bold and as ugly as ever…a punishment that lasts a lifetime.

"What has happened to you, Jotham?"

Jotham quickly pulled his shirt back up over his shoulders.

"Myanaymiz, you cannot simply walk into someone's room without knocking on the door!"

Myanaymiz knocked on the open door. "There," she said. "As you require, it is done."

Jotham could not help smiling. She did seem like such a child.

"Now please tell me, what has happened to you?"

At first, he didn't want to tell her. Jotham never liked to talk about it. All of the Townsfolk already knew…some remembering and some just from gossip. Once in a while one of the children would ask about it, but Jotham was always able to steer the conversation onto another subject.

"Did someone hurt you? I do not want you to be hurt."

It suddenly occurred to Jotham that, despite his embarrassment, this would be the perfect teaching moment. Up until now she did not seem to be taking seriously what he was telling her. But here was the undeniable proof. She could not simply ignore this. He slid his shirt down his shoulders and turned to show her.

"I was disobedient to the Gods," he said. "I was a very young man full of pride and not careful with my words. As a result, this was my punishment. And this is not even the worst punishment. No, this was mild compared to what others have been given. Do you understand now what I am trying to teach you? The lashes cut so deep that there was some nerve damage, and I still suffer pain. I will suffer from the pain for the rest of my life. This is not a game, Myanaymiz. This is very, very serious!"

As Myanaymiz stared at his scars, a single tear rolled down her cheek. "But Jotham, you are a kind man. You are a good man. This is not justice." She slowly walked over to him, and gently placed her hand upon his back.

Jotham was not prepared for this. He did not expect that anyone would ever want to touch his ugly scars. He did not expect that when someone did, he wouldn't be able to move away.

"There will be justice," she said, as she began to softly caress his back.

Jotham could not believe the strange deep soothing heat that began to move over his skin…deeper…deeper…deep into the flesh…to the bone…coursing slowly up and down his very spine. Then, suddenly, something overcame him. He was sinking…sinking into a calm deep warm ocean. *Where am I?* The room was no longer in focus. *It surrounds me…engulfs me…the warmth…the warmth…the…floating…I am floating.* His knees began to tremble and give way. To keep from falling over, he reached out and grabbed onto the bedpost with both hands. *Where am I? What is happening!*

Myanaymiz then slowly removed her hand from his back. "It is done," she said.

Jotham felt the heat gently recede like a warm ocean wave. *What just happened?* He turned around and looked at Myanaymiz. "What did you do to me?" he asked. She just stood silently smiling.

All over his back he could feel a soft warm afterglow. He then twisted his head around to check in the mirror. It took him a moment to realize what he was seeing. Still in disbelief, he reached behind and ran his hand in circles over his skin. *It is true! They are gone! The scars have disappeared! Just as I have always longed for! My back is as unmarked as the day I was born!* "Myanaymiz, how did you do that?" He rotated his shoulder blades. *There is no pain! The pain is gone too!*

"This is what I do. This is who I am," said Myanaymiz.

"This is wonderful! You are wonderful!"

"You are a man, Jotham."

He laughed, still staring at his back in the mirror. "Yes, I am a man…a man with a good back!"

Myanaymiz smiled. "Yes, a good man should have a good back. A good back is important. I need a man. You smell right and you are a good man."

Jotham laughed again. "You smell right and you are a very good Lady. Oh, wait until Jeremiah sees this!"

"I need a man and you will do," Myanaymiz said.

What? Jotham quickly pulled his shirt back up over his shoulders and turned to face her. He could see there was now a different look in her eyes…a serious and determined look. This was a look he had not seen from a woman in a very long time. *She couldn't mean…?*

"You will do," she said, moving closer.

"Uh…this is not done…not like this. Jeremiah would not like this. You don't know me, Myanaymiz."

She reached out, slipped her hand into his open shirt, slid it slowly down his chest, and stopped when it came to rest upon his firm stomach. "There is goodness in you Jotham, and you smell right. You will do."

———◆———

11

"Jotham!"

Jotham's eyes flickered open. Jeremiah was calling him. He stretched out his arm, and his hand came to rest on a woman's soft, warm thigh. He then sat up, and looked over at Myanaymiz who was still sleeping beside him. *What have I done?*

"Jotham!"

Suddenly afraid that Jeremiah might get impatient and simply walk in to find him like this, he leapt out of bed and jumped into his trousers. Closing the bedroom door behind him, he hurried to the front door, and swung it open.

"Jotham, you have been sleeping in, and on such an important day too."

Jeremiah looks tired, hopefully too tired to notice anything amiss. "I'm sorry," apologized Jotham.

"How is our guest?" asked Jeremiah.

"She is good…very good. I believe she is still asleep."

"I have been all night in the Palace of the Gods. It was the Goddess Wermungi who has died. As you can imagine, they are all in quite a state. And she was so young too."

"Did you tell them about Myanaymiz?"

"Not yet. It did not seem like a good time."

Jotham felt a sense of relief…and then a little guilt. This was not the time to tell Jeremiah either.

"I suggest you go home, Jeremiah. It's important to get some rest before the Time of Wailing begins."

"Yes, I will need to sleep before this afternoon. You must tell Myanaymiz to remain hidden in the cottage for now. At least until the Time of Wailing is finished. Her presence would only complicate an already complicated situation."

"I think she will understand." *I just hope she will comply.*

———

12

When Jotham returned to the bedroom, Myanaymiz was sitting up. The white sheet was draped across her middle, and her legs and breasts were exposed. Jotham tried not to look at them. "That was Jeremiah. He is planning the funeral for the God."

"Young-Old Jeremiah is a good man…but he is lost."

Jotham laughed. *She does say the strangest things.* "Perhaps we should find him," he joked.

"I will try to find Jeremiah, but not now. Now, I am here with you, and the sun is rising. This is a time for Jotham."

Jotham looked at her and sighed. *What is this? What is any of this?*

"Come here," she said.

He moved close to the bed. *I should not be doing this. It is not right. It could get me into trouble.*

"Do not worry, Jotham."

"I am not worried."

Myanaymiz twisted the edge of the white sheet around her finger. "I know you are worried. Please do not lie to me. It is disrespectful."

"I…I just…it is a strange situation."

She reached over and took his hand. "Am I strange to you?"

"Yes…no…I don't know."

"Do you like me?"

"Yes."

"Do you want me?"

"Yes…oh yes!"

"Then accept what is given with gratitude and respect."

Jotham felt himself being drawn into her eyes. He knew he needed to get dressed…to begin to prepare for the funeral, but those eyes… *What is happening to me? I've never felt like this before. It's so overpowering…making me leave my world…making me forget all of its rules? She's recreating me. That's what she is doing. I am becoming something else. A lover? A man? Was I not a man before this? I thought so, but now I wonder. And why resist? What reason is there to resist? And even if I could think of a reason, what would it matter? There is no holding back when wanting her is all there is.*

"Come to bed, Jotham. You are a good man and morning is a very good time."

———◆———

13

Jeremiah stood looking at his loom. How would he ever catch up on his work now? The God would have to be buried tonight after sunset, and then the Time of Wailing would begin. The Time of Wailing lasted three days, and for those three days no one was allowed to do any work. All effort must be put into prayers for the God to ensure that she would be resurrected. Not that any of them ever were. It was said to only happen spiritually now, but at the time of the Great Revelation it would happen physically. However, without the devote prayers of the people the eternal life of the God could be in jeopardy, and this would lead to the ultimate destruction of humankind. That is why the laws of the Time of Wailing must be strictly adhered to. It was either obey the laws or suffer the Deluge of Death.

Jeremiah looked at the empty hook in the corner, and thought about the beautiful gown he had woven. It had been his best work ever…a perfect masterpiece meant only for the God of Gods. And what did he do with this magnificent creation? He handed it over to a strange naked Lady with a delusional story about emerging from a rock. Thinking about it now, he couldn't help but laugh. *Old Jeremiah, you are going senile. You will be hearing things next.*

"What is the message from the Gods?" a voice suddenly said.

Jeremiah spun around, and was relieved to see the Town Messenger standing in open the doorway. *Thank the Gods, I am not mad. Not yet anyway.* "Tell the people to prepare themselves for the Burial Procession that will take place after the sun has set," he told the man. "When it is done the Time of Wailing will begin. They should consult the Stories of the Gods to remind themselves of the laws that must be obeyed. Any disobedience will be an offense against the Gods and punishment will follow. The will of the Gods shall be done." He felt that old twinge in his back. *I need sleep.*

"The will of the Gods shall be done," repeated the Messenger, and then disappeared.

Jeremiah put his hand on his lower back, and tried to massage the pain away. He must prepare himself for the long night ahead. Although the Townsfolk were not allowed to attend the actual burial, he, as Master Weaver, would be required to journey to the Place of Bones along with the Gods. This is where they kept their dead.

Walking into his bedroom, he dropped his body onto the bed, and sank deep into his soft wool filled mattress. He closed his eyes, and tried to put to rest all of the thoughts that were racing through his brain. *Oh sleep, thou old man's comfort, come to me. I have an exhausting undertaking ahead of me, and now require your relief more than ever.*

14

Myanaymiz sat on a rock in the garden among the flowering vines and mosses. *There are good things in this world…very good things. But there are also things that are not good. There is fullness, but there is also emptiness. Emptiness causes pain to what is full. It threatens what is full. Threatens to pour into the fullness and make it empty. All things grow in fullness. That which is not full should be exiled to the pit of death. This world is for fullness. Fullness is life. Fullness is.*

———•◆•———

15

Leaning in the doorway, Jotham stared at Myanaymiz. She was sitting on a rock in the garden, the sun reflecting off her gown, her hair, her skin. Every time she moved even slightly, there was a beautiful ripple of light that filled him with a strange longing.

He looked away. *How could I have let this get so out of hand? I am supposed to be teaching her…preparing her for dealing with the Gods. Now, I've made it so complicated. What she did to me last night…my back…my scars…my pain…it has left me more whole, but without bearing. What are these thoughts swirling in my head…these feelings? How do I escape this whirlwind?*

He turned and looked at her again. *And on top of everything else, one of the Gods is dead. Would some think there was a connection between her appearance and the death of the God? Would the Gods themselves wonder this? It is so bewildering.*

Jotham took in a deep breath. In all his confusion, he knew one thing as he stared at her. He knew he could not stand by and watch her be hurt. She was vulnerable and lost in a dangerous world she didn't understand. He couldn't leave her without any defences, especially after she had done so much for him. She took away the pain that had plagued him for so long…a pain he thought he would have to endure the rest of his life. No, he must stay on task and continue to do as Jeremiah instructed. He had to make her understand. *Myanaymiz has to know how to get along in this world. She has to be taught the rules…the laws, and learn to fear the consequences of breaking them. And she must certainly know that she cannot simply crawl into my bed. That is not the way of the Town.*

"Myanaymiz!" he called, as he walked towards her.

She looked up and smiled warmly at him.

"Myanaymiz, we have much to discuss."

"Sit please," she said, gesturing to the soft moss near her feet.

Jotham had not sat on the ground since he was a boy. He crossed his legs and lowered himself onto the soft moss. It felt strange. Everything felt strange. "Myanaymiz, you have to learn…I have to teach you…this world is very complicated."

Looking into his eyes, she smiled.

Jotham felt a warm glow run down his spine. *She's muddling my thoughts. Stay focussed.* He looked down at the green moss and tried to concentrate on what he wanted to say. "There are so many things you need to learn, and you must learn these things quickly. First, there will be a Burial Procession after sunset. One of the Gods has died and this is a very serious matter."

"God cannot die," said Myanaymiz. "God is life. Life cannot die as death cannot live."

Why is she is still not listening to me? Desperate to make her see the serious nature of the situation, Jotham looked her straight in the eye and said, "Please understand, it is a very delicate time, and you must be very careful of everything you say. For instance, what you have just said could be interpreted as saying that the Gods are mortals. This would be punishable by death. Do you understand?"

"You have such a pretty mouth, Jotham," she said.

"Myanaymiz, just please tell me, do you understand?"

"Of course I understand. I understand you, and all that you are saying. Understanding is what I do, and who I am."

Jotham sighed in relief. "Thank the Gods! So you will understand that you must be very careful, especially during the Time of Wailing. Tell me you understand this."

Myanaymiz reached over and brushed a strand of hair away from his eyes. "I have read the stories. I understand the Time of Wailing. I understand all that is. I understand all that will be."

"Just please, PLEASE, tell me you will be careful!"

"If you wish this from me, Jotham…I will be careful."

"Thank you, Myanaymiz. This is really all I am asking. There is so much I need to tell you. So much you need to be prepared for."

"You have such a pretty mouth, Jotham. Shall we go back into the cottage now?"

Jotham wanted to look away again, but he couldn't. Instead, he felt himself being drawn in again.

Myanaymiz took Jotham's hand in her own, "Come," she said. "Now is our time together. We must enjoy it while we can. It will not last forever, but it will be written in the Book of Forever."

Jotham stared at his large calloused Cobbler's hand wrapped so tightly in her small soft dove-like fingers. He watched as his hand slowly seemed to melt into hers…becoming one…one flesh…the wondrous undoing of separation…the end of aloneness. *This is not real. It can't be real. Tell her no. Tell her this is not the way to do things. Tell her the Gods would not like this. Tell her….* "Yes," he said. "Let's go back inside."

———•◆•———

16

Jeremiah wanted to check on Jotham's progress with Myanaymiz before the Burial Procession started. It was still a good hour until sundown. On his way to the Cobbler's cottage he came across Petal.

"Old Jeremiah, where is our Lady?" she asked. "I went to look for her at the Cobbler's cottage, but no one answered. What have you done with our Lady?"

"The Lady is fine," said Jeremiah, wondering why Jotham had not at least answered the door to send Petal away. "You must return home immediately. The Burial Procession will begin soon, and you must be with your parents. Remember to listen to them, and follow all of the laws during the Time of Wailing. Will you promise to be a good little girl, Petal?"

"Oh yes! I will do my duty to the Gods, and my duty to the Gods I will do," she said, repeating the last line of the Children's Pledge of Allegiance to the Immortals.

"You are a fine example to the other children. Now go home, and prepare for what is to come."

Petal then scurried off down the road.

———•◆•———

"Jotham!"

"It's Jeremiah!" said Jotham, nervously jumping up from the table. "Please don't tell him…don't tell him about…about what has happened between us. I want to explain things myself."

Myanaymiz was sitting across from him sipping a hot cup of strawberry tea. She looked up and smiled. "This is very good tea."

Good tea? Why can you not simply respond the way anyone else would? Jotham did not press the issue any further, but with the hope that she understood, hurried over and opened the front door. He was shocked to see how tired Jeremiah was looking. The death of a God was a very stressful time for the Master Weaver.

"There you are," Jeremiah said. "Why did you not open your door to Petal?"

"Oh, yes…you see, with everything that has happened I did not want to have to answer any questions, or explain anything at this time. Also, I could not be sure what Myanaymiz might say to the child. I am still trying to teach her what is acceptable, and what is not."

"And that is why I am here. I wanted to check on your progress." Jeremiah entered the cottage, and saw Myanaymiz sitting at the table. "Hello Myanaymiz," he said, as he walked over to her. "How are you doing? Is Jotham teaching you well?"

"Young-Old Jeremiah, you are tired and in pain," she said with concern.

Jeremiah laughed. "So, it is that obvious. Yes, last night was a long night, and tonight will be even longer." He then turned to Jotham. "During the Burial Procession, it is best if she stays inside out of sight. It is a delicate time, and if one of the Gods should see her…well we simply do not need that sort of complication. Eventually they will have to be told, but not just now. Let us wait until the Time of Wailing is complete. I will ascend the Mount myself, and tell them then."

"Do you hear that Myanaymiz? It is important that you remain in the cottage tonight. I will have to stand in mourning at the road as it is written in the laws, but you must not follow me. You must stay hidden until it is time to reveal yourself."

Myanaymiz glanced at Jotham, and then casually took another sip of tea.

"Do you understand?" asked Jeremiah.

"Understanding is what I do. That is who I am."

"She keeps saying things like that," said Jotham. "I'm uncertain what she means by any of it."

"I think it means she understands and will do as we say," said Jeremiah, running his hand through his long beard.

Jotham wasn't so sure. He knew so much more about her than Jeremiah—how unpredictable she could be. But now was not the time to share everything he knew. That would have to wait.

Jeremiah walked over, and sat down in the chair across from Myanaymiz. He rested his elbow on the table, and his placed his chin in his hand. "Did you truly come from a rock?" he asked her. "Once, as a child, I heard a story about a Lady from a rock. I will tell it to you, but not now. There is no time now. After the Time of Wailing is complete, perhaps there will be time then." He looked into her eyes. *What color are they? It's difficult to tell.* He felt himself slowly sinking into them. *Sanctuary…rest…peace…*

"Jeremiah," said Jotham, "the sun will soon set."

"Oh, yes…yes of course…there are things to be done." He jumped up from the table, and headed for the door. Turning back to Jotham, he said, "May the will of the Gods be done."

"May the will of the Gods be done," returned Jotham.

Jeremiah glanced over at Myanaymiz once more. "Good bye," he said then hurried out the door.

———•—•———

                    Arlene Adamo

18

The Townsfolk were lined up and down the road. For most of them, this would be their first time experiencing a Burial of the Gods. As they stood in the darkness, it was both exciting and very frightening. No one even dared whisper a word. They all understood that absolute silence was the law until the holy lanterns were in view. After that, they would be required to begin the wailing.

Jeremiah waited alone at the bottom of the Mount of the Gods for the Burial Procession to arrive. As Master Weaver, it was his job to lead it through the streets. He was worried. The Gods had already expressed their displeasure with him at not having a new gown ready for the burial. He had explained that, had the death not been so sudden and unexpected, he would have woven a masterpiece, but the Gods were never fond of excuses of any kind. Tonight, he had to ensure that everything went smoothly. The last thing he needed was to incur their wrath.

Before he saw them coming around the bend in the Celestial Path, Jeremiah heard the sounds of the carriage and the horses. *This is it! A Burial of the Gods! I may never see such a thing again.*

Six massive black geldings suddenly appeared around the corner pulling the glass funeral carriage. Holy lanterns hung from the sides of the carriage, making the body of the God fully visible. Jeremiah recognized the gown he had woven for last year's Festival. He never imagined he'd ever see her wear it again, and certainly not as a burial gown.

Behind the coach were the Gods who followed on horseback. They sat straight in their saddles, and wore the elegant black shrouds of mourning that had been passed down from generation to generation. Each God carried a long staff with a holy lantern to light the way. *The Way to Eternity will be shown with the light of the Gods.*

Next to come was the High Priest in his formal vestments, followed by thirteen Guardsmen of the Gods marching in perfect unison. Clad in their thick black reptilian skin uniforms, the Guardsmen's faces were covered by black mesh veils that hung from their black steel helmets. Just the sight of one of these men was enough to strike terror into the heart of a Townsperson. These were the guardians against blasphemy…the merciless punishers of lawbreakers. There was very good reason to fear them.

The coach driver brought the horses to a stop in front of Jeremiah. For a moment, everything was silent then Jeremiah heard the sound of a single horse approaching up the side of the carriage. He turned to see a great red steed coming towards him. On the back of the steed sat the God of Gods, Bugiah. He was an impressive figure, tall, strong, and unlike the other Gods, he was dressed in gold as per the divine funeral rites.

"Master Weaver," he commanded, "prepare the way for your Gods to reach the Gate of Eternity!"

Jeremiah bowed low to the ground. "My Gods, I am here to serve you."

⸺•⸺

                                   Arlene Adamo

19

As soon as they could see the light from the holy lanterns, the people began to wail. They were being very careful to follow every detail of the law, and knew the louder they wailed the more it would ensure the safe passage of the God into eternal life. The night air quickly filled with their growing cries and screams.

Jotham's cottage was near the outskirts of the Town. It would be the last house the Burial Procession would pass by. When he heard the distant wailing begin, he knew he needed to get out to the road as soon as possible. If he was even a moment late, it could mean his death.

"Myanaymiz, you must stay inside. Keep the curtains drawn, and the door closed. It is important that they not see you."

"Why, Jotham?"

"They will not under…I mean…it is a delicate time for them, and the Gods do not need to be troubled with anything else but the funeral for now. You would only complicate things."

"I do not know why you say I complicate things, Jotham. Did I not make your life simpler and easier by taking away your pain?"

Jotham sighed, "Yes you did, but please listen to me. Tonight you must stay hidden."

Myanaymiz stared into his eyes. "Everything will be alright. There is nothing at all to worry about."

For a moment, Jotham could feel himself being dragged in again…into those eyes, but he quickly looked away. *I must get outside. Stay focussed.* As he left, he made certain to close the door tightly behind him.

Once out at the edge of the road, he could see the lights of the funeral procession approaching. *Thank the Gods I am not too late.* He tilted his head back, and began to call out into the night sky.

———•◆•———

20

Jeremiah's back and feet were already aching. He was not looking forward to having to lead the Burial Procession up the Mount of the Gods, and wondered if his old body could take it. He continued his duty of chanting the Sounds of Mourning as he plodded on. "Yoo ismee ta." *I must not think of my feet.* "Yoo ismee ta." *I must not think of my back.* "Yoo ismee ta." *Concentrate. Concentrate.*

The wailing of the people continued louder than ever. They were required to keep this up until the Gods had begun the ascent to the Place of Bones.

Jeremiah could now see Jotham's outline in the darkness ahead. At least he assumed it was Jotham, being the only one who would be standing outside of his house. He felt relieved that at least they had made it through to the end of the Town. *Not far to go now.* He tried not to think about the uphill climb ahead.

As he walked past Jotham, Jeremiah did not make any eye contact as per the law. Staring out into the darkness ahead, he felt some relief to know that the procession through the Town was now finished, and everything had gone smoothly. The Townsfolk had fulfilled their duties, and obediently adhered to all of the burial laws. The riskiest part of the ceremony was over.

Suddenly, from behind him came a loud shouting. "HALT! HALT!" a voice yelled over the wailing and his chanting.

That is Bugiah shouting! Oh merciful Gods, what has gone wrong? He knew it was against the law to look back, but what was he supposed to do? Something was amiss, and he had already stopped chanting which was also against the law. Jeremiah turned around, and saw Bugiah riding up beside the carriage. At first, he wondered if the God of Gods was looking at Jotham, but no. He was looking past Jotham. Jeremiah followed his gaze, and his mouth fell open in horror. There in the well lit open doorway stood Myanaymiz. Her magnificent gown was reflecting both the light from the cottage and the holy lanterns from the road. She stood there looking just like a challenger before the Gods.

———◆◆◆———

21

"Who dares to stand before God of Gods and break the law?" Bugiah shouted.

"I am Myanaymiz," she called from the doorway. "I have come from a rock."

Bugiah looked down at Jotham and demanded, "What is this strange woman? Speak!"

Before Jotham could say anything, Jeremiah, who had hurried from the front of the procession, answered, "My God, the children found her."

"What did you say, Weaver?"

"My God, the children found her in a meadow on the other side of the forest."

Bugiah looked from Jeremiah to the woman. "Why did I not know of this?"

"My God, I fully intended to inform you. I merely thought that the burial of our beloved God Wermungi was a far greater priority than the finding of an unimportant waif, and I did not want to bother you with such irrelevance."

Bugiah rode his steed up the cottage path to get a better look at Myanaymiz. He stared down at her, and she straight back up at him. "Where did you get that gown?" he demanded.

"It was given to me by Young-Old Jeremiah."

"Weaver, explain this!"

Jeremiah hurried up the path. "My God, it is true," he said. "I provided the gown. She was naked when the children found her, and was immediately in need of clothing. I wove the gown intending it for you my God, but as you in all your glorious perfection will notice, the gown has flaws. It was not fit for the divine body of the God of Gods."

Bugiah looked at the gown. "Oh yes," he said. "I see the faults. The gown is full of flaws. Such poor workmanship is not like you, Weaver. You must pay more attention to your work."

Turning back to Myanaymiz, Bugiah said, "I should kill you, woman. You have disrupted one of our most sacred ceremonies."

That's when Jotham, who now stood behind Jeremiah, interjected, "Oh My Lord, most merciful God of Gods, she understands very little of our ways. Please spare her life! The children love her, and once she learns the laws, she will make a good and loyal subject. She simply has yet to learn about the goodness and nobility of the Gods."

"And what is she to you Cobbler? And why is she in your house?"

"It was me," said Jeremiah. "I brought her to the Cobbler so that he might teach her all of the wonderful ways set down by the Gods. She is his pupil."

Bugiah looked at the woman and then at Jotham. "You are a poor teacher if this is what you have taught her."

"Forgive me, My God, but she is simple and easily confused. I know that in your glorious divine mercy you would see fit to absolve her of her sins as she is like a child who does not know what she is doing." Jotham's heart was beating rapidly. *I must save her. Somehow, I must.*

"Are you simple?" asked Bugiah of Myanaymiz.

Myanaymiz looked him in the eye. "All things are simple when you are awake."

Bugiah laughed out loud. "She is indeed a simpleton. Cobbler, take her inside and try to teach her something. Weaver, let us return to the Burial Procession. As the God of Gods, by the power that is mine, I declare this interruption to have never happened. All laws were obeyed, and the way is straight for our sister to enter eternity." He turned his steed, and headed back out to the road.

Jeremiah hurried to return to his place at the head of the procession.

Jotham gently pushed Myanaymiz inside then quickly pushed the door shut behind them. The emotions suddenly welled up inside of him, and he began to weep and laugh at the same time. He slid down the door, and came to rest sitting on the floor.

"I am sorry I did not follow your instructions," said Myanaymiz. "But what must be done, must be done."

Jotham ran his hand through his long yellow hair. "You have no idea, do you? You have no idea how close we both came to death."

Myanaymiz kneeled down on the floor beside him. "I would not let them hurt you," she said.

Jotham laughed again. "You would not let them hurt me? Why thank you. How very kind."

Reaching over and straightening his hair with her fingers, she said, "I forgive you your transgressions. Shall we go into the other room now?"

———•◆•———

<h1 style="text-align:center">22</h1>

I t was shuddering cold as the flames from the lanterns did their dance of death on the tomb walls. Long before anyone could remember, this place had been carved out of the rock. It was the Place of Bones where all of the Gods were buried. The original chamber had been filled with bodies a very long time ago, so additional chambers were added as needed. This was chamber number two hundred and thirteen, the last one to be built. It had remained empty….until now.

Jeremiah stood beside the High Priest. It was his job to assist him in the rites. He carefully handed over the crystal vial of sacred oil.

"O' med ee auk risi," chanted the priest, as he dripped the oil onto the head and feet of the body. "The Gods are eternal. The Gods are divine."

Jeremiah next handed over the basket of red rose petals. The priest scattered the petals over and around the body. "All knowing, all seeing, board the boat and sail down the river Broma to the place of Divine Waiting. There, o' great one, shall you repose until the Day of Resurrection when all the Gods will be united once again. Yuu maidius moo nee." Together, the priest and Jeremiah bowed their heads, and then took five steps back.

One by one the Gods approached the body. Each placed a single gold coin on her stomach. Bugiah, as the God of Gods, was the last one to come forward. Placing two gold coins over her eyelids, he then turned his face upwards and called out, "As it is, as it always shall be, our Sister God to eternity!" He next raised his hand to give the signal, and Jeremiah and the priest proceeded to pull the rope that hung from the ceiling, moving the stone slab, upon which the God's body lay, slowly into the vault. When it was fully inside, the two men rolled the stone seal in front of the opening. On the stone was carved the God's name, her dates and her symbol—an eagle in flight, the right talon clutching a small dead bird.

"All hail the Immortal Gods!" said the priest, marking the end of the ceremony. The Gods silently began to file down the passage-way leading out of the tomb.

As prescribed by law, all of the Gods were to exit first, followed by the Priest and then the Weaver. Only the God of Gods should remain at the end. It was he who would be the last one to bid farewell.

Bugiah walked over to the vault then ran his fingers over the symbol of the dead God. "I will miss you, my dear sister," he said.

Jeremiah tried not to hear this sentiment, as the sentiments of the Gods were not something he was supposed to hear. Just as he was about to head down the passageway, he heard Bugiah quietly say, "Weaver, come here."

Jeremiah was confused. *This is against the laws of God Burial. It is forbidden to interact with any of the Gods while in the tomb, other than in the ways prescribed by the rites.* He turned to face the God of Gods.

Bugiah checked down the passageway to ensure that the High Priest had already left, and that they were now alone. He moved in close to Jeremiah and whispered, "That woman at the Cobbler's house, after the Time of Wailing is complete, bring her to me."

Jeremiah bowed his head. "Your will be done, my God," he quietly said, then turned to exit through the passageway. As he walked through the narrow shadowy tunnel, all he could think was, *I do not like this. I do not like any of this.*

—— • ——

23

Jotham kept his door closed and his curtains drawn. He did not want the Townsfolk to know he was not adhering to the laws of the Time of Wailing. He just simply could not bring himself to indulge in what he felt in his heart to be foolishness. One was expected to pray from morning till night. Weeping loud and long was considered a badge of great piousness. *If the destruction of humankind comes about, it will be because they blindly follow laws, not disobey them.* Of course he never dreamed of saying this out loud.

Myanaymiz came in through the back door carrying a bouquet of wildflowers. "Jotham, it is a beautiful day, would you like to go for a walk with me?"

"When the Time of Wailing is finished in two days, we will be able to go for a walk. To walk now would not be proper. The Townsfolk would tell the Gods who would punish us."

"Yes, I know. But we could quietly go out along the back garden path and through the forest. With everyone restricted to their homes, they would not see us."

"But the Gods…"

"I understand that the Gods are required to remain where they are. That means we can go about freely." Myanaymiz walked over to him, and tucked a flower behind his ear. "No one will see us," she said, placing the rest of the flowers in the water jug on the table.

Jotham had never thought of it that way. Of course with everyone confined to their houses, they would not be seen walking in the forest. And how would the Gods' know? For all their claims of special powers, they had no second sight. They only learned of transgressions through Townsfolk snitches or Guardsmen spies. Also, the thought of spending two more days locked inside was too much to think about. He knew he had to get out for the sake of his own sanity.

"Very well," he said, "let us go for a walk, but we must be very careful. We are breaking one of the Gods' laws."

Together they went out the back door and entered the forest behind the cottage. As they walked in the cool shade of the tall ancient trees, Jotham couldn't help but feel protected and hidden. *No one can see us here. We are safe.*

Myanaymiz noticed the beautiful green moss growing on the north side of many of the tree trunks. She stopped for a moment, and pressed her palm deeply into the soft green carpet. When she removed it, the impression of her hand was left upon the tree. She smiled because it reminded her of the lines she had left on the rock.

"Let's go to the place where the children found you," said Jotham. "I'd like to see where that is."

"There is a brook that flows into a river, a meadow and a large rock. Do you know where I mean?" she asked.

"Yes, I know that place well. It was one of the places where I used to play as a young boy." Jotham then gently took her hand in his and led the way.

24

Jeremiah was not supposed to be working at his loom. He was supposed to be wailing in prayer, but who was around to see him? He was so far behind in his work that he needed this time if he was to finish all of the gowns for the Festival of the Gods. At least, he now knew that the Gods could not tell the difference between a flawed gown and a perfect one. This would make his job far easier.

As he tried hard to concentrate solely on his work, he found he couldn't stop from thinking about Myanaymiz. *Why did the God of Gods ask for her? It makes no sense. Perhaps when the Time of Wailing is over, Bugiah will have forgotten all about the order. It may have been only the stress of the funeral that made him say such a thing at all. The Gods never ask for mortal women. They consider this to be beneath them. So likely it was just a mistake of some sort…not that the Gods ever make mistakes. As it is, I will consider the request only a trick of my imagination and ignore the entire thing. And if Bugiah never asks about it again, I will be very content.*

                    Arlene Adamo

25

Jotham climbed up on the rock, looked down at Myanaymiz and asked, "Is this where you came from?"

"Yes."

"I see no entrance. No exit. Are you certain?"

"Yes," she said. "I am from that rock."

Jotham crouched down and hit the rock three times, "Hello! Helloooo! Anybody in there?"

Myanaymiz laughed. "I was alone," she said then turned and started walking in the direction of the brook.

"Where are you going?" asked Jotham.

"I would like some water," she replied

Jotham quickly climbed down from the rock, and followed her to the brook. When she knelt down to take a drink, he immediately plunged his cupped hands into the cool water, and then held them out for her. She smiled, and drank the water from his hands. He did this two more times until she said, "Thank you, but that is all I need."

"Should we sit over there in the soft grass?" he asked.

"That would be nice."

They walked over, and sat close beside each other. Jotham picked a blade of grass, and stuck it in his mouth. For a while, they simply sat together quietly thinking, and soaking in the sunshine.

Suddenly, Jotham threw the blade of grass away and proclaimed, "I like the Time of Wailing!" He then burst out laughing.

"Yes, this is a good time," smiled Myanaymiz. "I am glad you are enjoying yourself.

"Oh Myanaymiz," he sighed, "look what you have done to me! You have turned me from a respectable Cobbler into an outlaw!"

"And do you like it?"

"Yes…yes, I think I do," he mischievously smiled. "I like it very much. Me…the outlaw Cobbler."

Jotham looked up at the bright sky. Not a cloud in sight. *Do I remember it ever looking more beautiful…more blue…more serene?* "I will tell you a secret," he said. "As a child I did not want to be a Cobbler. My father was a Cobbler. My father's father was a Cobbler, but I wanted to be something else entirely."

"I know, Jotham."

"You know?" he laughed out loud. "How could you know? So tell me what was it that I wanted to be."

"A singer."

Jotham's jaw dropped open. "How could you know that?"

"From dreams," she said then asked, "Why did you not become a singer?"

"From dreams?" Jotham laughed. "Myanaymiz, you say the strangest things sometimes. But why, you ask…why not become a singer? Do you not know? A singer is without honour. Even a beggar has more honour than a singer. No one in their right mind would ever want to be a singer. That is for misfits of the lowest kind. My father would have been outraged had I told him. It was my secret."

"I think you would make a fine singer."

"And you would have me be an honourless outlaw singer?"

"Do you not think it would be fun?"

Jotham thought about it and started laughing. "Yes," he said. "I suppose being an honourless outlaw singer could be wonderful fun!"

"Far more fun than fixing shoes."

"But do I have the voice?"

"Sing for me, and I will tell you."

"I don't know any songs."

"Create one."

   Arlene Adamo

"Create one? Alright, let me think…," Jotham was quiet as he thought about what his song should be. "I know!" he suddenly said then began to sing:

You don't have to live as a Cobbler
You don't have to live as a Cobbler
You don't have to live as a Cobbler
When you can be a no good honourless outlaw singer

Myanaymiz laughed. "You sing beautifully, but you must work on your song writing."

"And what about my dancing?" he jumped up, and began to dance wildly around the meadow.

Myanaymiz laughed again. "Jotham, you are wonderful!"

"Thank you," he said bowing. "So are you."

He walked back, and sat down beside her. She reached over, and touched his hand. "Jotham," she said looking deeply into his eyes, "there is no one here to see us."

Jotham looked around, and then smiled at her. "Very true," he said. "There is definitely no one here to see us."

26

Jeremiah examined the three beautiful gowns hanging on the wall. Without having to suffer any interruptions from the Townsfolk, The Time of Wailing had proven to be a very productive time. He carefully inspected each garment closer. They had come out so nicely with all the flaws in just the right places. *None but the trained eye of a Master Weaver would be able to detect these imperfections. But to weave such garments for the Gods, makes me a blasphemer. I should be ashamed. I should be fearful of their wrath. So why am I feeling instead so fearless…and so strangely exhilarated?*

Walking over to the window, Jeremiah threw open the curtains, instantly blinding himself with the bright light. Quickly, he turned his head away. As his eyes began to adjust, he slowly turned his head to look outside again. It was only then that he realized just how late it was. *Oh, I see the sun is already climbing high in the sky. The Time of Wailing ended at daybreak, but I have been so involved in my weaving that time has gotten away from me.*

He stared out at the trees, at the road and then at the Celestial Path in the distance. That's when he was reminded. *Oh yes! The request of the God of Gods!* All through the Time of Wailing, Jeremiah had tried to keep it from his mind. He tried to keep so busy that he would not think of it, but every once in a while the thought would creep back in again, and each time it would make his stomach turn just as it did now. *Why am I feeling this way? And what am I doing? Weaving flawed gowns. Ignoring an order from the God of Gods. I should have gone out first thing this morning, and had it done…had her delivered to the Palace, but just the mere thought of doing it stops me. Why? Who is this Lady to me? She is only a stranger, and I am the Master Weaver. I serve the Gods. That is my duty.*

Jeremiah went to the door, opened it wide, and stood for a moment on the threshold. "Glory to the Gods, Master Weaver," called out a passing Townsman.

"Glory to the Gods," replied Jeremiah. *Do you know I am a disobedient blasphemer?* He quietly watched as the man disappeared around the bend.

Jeremiah then walked over to the kuma tree that grew in his front garden. Over the years it had struggled to produce even a few blossoms, but this year it was magnificent, exploding in its signature red and white flowers! He stood underneath and looked up at the beautiful sight. *In all my years, have I ever seen a kuma tree bloom like this before?* Jeremiah took in a deep breath of the sweet fragrance, and instantly forgot the uneasiness he had felt. *What a wonderful afternoon, and I am wasting it in worry. Since the morning is finished, and I've heard nothing from the Palace, the God of Gods must have lost interest and no longer cares. As I thought before, it was only the grief talking. I have nothing to be concerned about. I'll go to Jotham's now, and think no more about it.*

⎯⎯⎯•◆•⎯⎯⎯

2 7

Myanaymiz sat on a chair in the garden as the children danced and played around her. Jotham leaned against the door-frame watching. The children had arrived early in the morning asking for "our Lady." At first, he hesitated to let them in. It could be risky to let her around them. She could say all kinds of inappropriate things. But when he saw the hopeful determined looks on their innocent little faces, he couldn't help but fling the door wide open. He felt no regrets now as he watched how happy both the children and Myanaymiz seemed to be together.

Suddenly, Jotham had the strange feeling that someone else was watching them too. He turned his head to see Jeremiah standing at the side gate. What an odd sight! For some reason, his old friend seemed so different. He was looking the same…wearing the same clothes, but there was something in the way he stood there, silently staring at Myanaymiz and the children…something Jotham had never seen in him before. "Hello Jeremiah!" Jotham called out.

"Jotham!" Jeremiah opened the gate, and walked over to where Jotham was standing. "How is our pupil doing?"

"She is…she seems to understand what is going on."

"Good," said Jeremiah, "although, we may have a problem. While at the funeral, Bugiah quietly requested that I send her to him."

"She's not going to him!"

Jeremiah was surprised at Jotham's reaction. "For now, I am assuming that Bugiah has had second thoughts, and so far I have ignored the request, but if he asks again, how can I ignore it?"

"You cannot take her there," said Jotham. "I will not let you!"

"Jotham, how can you say such a thing? You know an order from the God of Gods must be obeyed. You, of all people, understand what disobeying him would mean."

Jotham started to laugh.

"Why are you laughing?" Jeremiah asked. He couldn't believe that Jotham would laugh at a time like this.

"She can do things…my back, Jeremiah…my back has been restored!"

"Jotham, what are you talking about?"

"Look!" Jotham turned and pulled up his shirt. "Do you see? Do you see what she did for me?"

Jeremiah was present the day of Jotham's punishment. He knew what sort of damage had been done to his back. Now, he couldn't believe what he was seeing. "She did this?"

"Yes," said Jotham, turning and pulling his shirt back down. "I have no more pain! After all these years of being punished daily, I have no more pain!"

Before Jeremiah could ask anything more, a loud bang and then a shout came from inside the cottage. The two men rushed inside, but stopped in their tracks when they saw a Guardsman of the Gods standing in the front doorway. His thick scaly reptilian skin uniform and black veil made him look more monster than man. Even though they both knew that at one time he was a Townsfolk just like them, Jotham and Jeremiah couldn't help but feel as though they were facing something not quite human. "Cobbler!" he yelled. "Where is the woman?"

"Honourable Guardsman," said Jeremiah, lowering his head. "Please forgive me. It was my duty to inform the Cobbler of the God of Gods' request. As I am old and was so busy this morning weaving the glorious gowns for the Festival of the Gods, my mind was forgetful. Just a few moments ago I remembered the request, and hurried over to make my God's divine wishes known."

"She is not going," said Jotham.

The Guardsman placed his hand on his sword.

"What he means, Honourable Guardsman," Jeremiah quickly interposed, "is that she has yet to eat. She is thin and frail, and could easily faint before the God of Gods if she is not fed. And of course she must eat here. She could not be expected to eat of the sacred food of the Gods. Such a thing would be unthinkable."

The Guardsman paused and thought about it. If what the Weaver said were true, then he would be right to wait until she had eaten. But would the God of Gods approve of this decision? Displeasing him was not something he wanted to risk doing. "Let me see the woman for myself."

"I am here."

Jeremiah and Jotham turned to see Myanaymiz walking in through the back door. A group of children followed behind her.

"Although thin, she looks strong enough to me. Woman, do you require food before we ascend to the Mount of the Gods?"

"Oh my Lady, don't go away," cried one of the children.

"Silence!" shouted the Guardsman, frightening all of the children out the back door.

"I am strong enough to go with you," said Myanaymiz, walking fearlessly up to the Guardsman.

Jotham grabbed her hand.

"It is alright, Jotham. Everything will be alright," she said, trying to reassure him.

Jotham reluctantly let go of her, and then looked helplessly over at Jeremiah. *What can we do? We need to do something!*

"Allow me to go with you, Honourable Guardsman," said Jeremiah. "I would like to discuss with the God of Gods the gown I have been working on for his greatness."

"No Weaver! Just the woman!"

"Do not worry Jotham, Young-Old Jeremiah. It is as it must be," Myanaymiz said. "I will return to you."

"Come!" said the Guardsman, and Myanaymiz left with him through the open door.

"Jeremiah, we must do something!" Jotham cried.

"What can we do Jotham? We have no alternative but to wait. She did say she would return. She told us not to worry."

But Jeremiah's words were of no comfort to Jotham. How could he wait? The thought of her alone and at the mercy of the God of Gods was too much for him to bear. He had to do something. "Oh Jeremiah," he cried. "She is alone in a world she doesn't understand. I cannot wait here and do nothing! She has helped me so much! I must follow after her. I must try to help her!"

28

"You will remain here for now," said the Guardsman to Myanaymiz. He then walked over to the enormous white pillar in the middle of the grand hall, and got down on his knees. "Wash me clean that I might be worthy to be in the presence of the Gods." He made gestures as if he were splashing water over his head. "Eed Dee Aut," he said, concluding the ritual. He then stood up, and ascended a long white marble staircase. At the top, he disappeared through a gilded arched opening.

Myanaymiz looked around at the murals covering the walls. The paintings were elaborate exaggerations of the various stages of victory. Some were of battles being won; some were about gathering the spoils after those battles, but most appeared to be merely about the straight forward glorification and worship of the victors. Myanaymiz felt disgust. *This is an empty place full of lies.*

She then walked over and stared at the white pillar where the Guardsman had performed his cleansing ritual. Reaching out, she placed her hand upon its cold unyielding surface. Quickly, she took it away again. *A simple common piece of rock. Nothing more. Lifeless.*

The Guardsman came back down the stairs. "Get down on your knees before the pillar, woman. You must be washed clean before entering further into the Palace of the Gods."

"I will not."

The Guardsman was not expecting resistance. No Townsperson had ever resisted before. At first, he wasn't certain what to do. He thought about the God of Gods and how difficult and unpredictable he had been since the death of Wermungi. If he punished or harmed the woman, he could be in trouble. But he could not simply allow her to thwart a Sacred Ritual either. *If a Guardsman cannot go through, he shall go around,* he thought then, quickly making a washing gesture over her head, said, "I wash you clean that you might be worthy to be in the presence of the Divine Ones. Eed Dee Aut. Now follow me."

Myanaymiz followed him up the marble staircase. At the top, they went through the archway, and walked down a short hall until they reached an open large double doorway. "Go in," said the Guardsman. Myanaymiz entered, and the doors were closed behind her.

———•◆•———

29

Jeremiah and Jotham stood outside the front door of the cottage. The children had returned looking for Myanaymiz and were upset to learn she had gone with the Guardsman.

"When will our Lady come back?"

"We need our Lady."

"Old Jeremiah, will you find our Lady and bring her back to us?"

"They are right," said Jotham. "We have to go find her. I don't care about the trouble it could mean. We need to go now, Jeremiah!"

Jeremiah could see how determined Jotham was, but he still wasn't sure it was a good idea. "We could both be killed and what use would we be to Myanaymiz then?"

"What use are we to her now, simply standing around fretting with the children? I am the only Cobbler, and you are the only Master Weaver. Even the God of Gods would be reluctant to harm us."

"Old Jeremiah, you are so big and brave. Go find our Lady," said one of the children.

"You see," said Jotham. "You are Big Brave Jeremiah. Why do you not put as much faith in yourself as this child does? Regardless of what you decide, I am going. I simply cannot remain here any longer."

Jeremiah sighed. "If this is the case, I suppose there is nothing I can do but to follow you. You will most definitely require my powers of diplomacy."

The two men then headed out to the road.

30

"Come here!" commanded Bugiah who was lounging on one of the several well cushioned divans scattered throughout the large room. He wore a satiny gold colored robe, and in his right hand he held a half empty silver goblet of red wine.

Myanaymiz began to slowly walk towards him, her bare feet making no sound against the black marble floor. *Cold as death. Death resides here.* She stopped several feet away, and just stared at the God of Gods.

"Come closer," he commanded.

She did not move.

Bugiah sat up, swung his legs around, and put his sandaled feet flat on the floor. He glared at her for a long moment, and then finally asked, "Where did you come from?"

"From a rock," she replied.

"Did you say 'from a rock'!?"

"Yes, a rock."

Bugiah burst out laughing. "You are simple," he said, and then took a drink from his goblet. He looked her up and down. *Simple… yet there is something about you. A secret. A mystery.* "You must tell me more. Are you human?"

"I am human."

"But there is something about you that says this is not entirely true. Are you a hybrid of sorts? Did one of the Gods weaken and impregnate some lowly human, and now you are the resulting outcross?"

She did not answer, but instead turned and walked over to one of the large gothic windows. With her back to him, she stared silently out the window.

"So are you? Are you an outcross? Speak! Do you understand what I am asking?"

"I am human," she said without turning around.

"You are simple…very simple," said Bugiah as he admired her gown. It was a shame the Weaver had made a mistake with such a beautiful gown. Had it been perfect, it would have been his best work ever. Bugiah's eyes came to rest upon the shape of her hips. "Woman!" he said suddenly. "Come here!"

Myanaymiz turned and looked at him, but did not take one step forward.

"Are you deaf as well as simple? I said come here!" Bugiah then threw open his robe. "Come here and pleasure me!"

Myanaymiz turned back to look out the window again. "That is not what I do. That is not who I am," she said.

"How dare you!" shouted Bugiah, slamming down his wine goblet, and jumping up from the divan. "What you will not give, the God of Gods will take!" He was about to march over, and grab her by her hair when he suddenly realized that his blood was fast receding back into the recesses of his body. He looked down at his sorry state then quickly closed his robe. "I will kill you!" he yelled.

Myanaymiz swung around, and looked him straight in the eye. "If you try to harm even one hair on my head, My Lord will strike you down," she said.

Bugiah felt a chill run through his body. "Where is your Lord? I am the God of Gods! I am the only Lord!"

"You are a man like any other. I know God. I know the feel of God. I know the smell of God. I have not seen God's face, but I have seen God's arm. You are not God. God is One, but you and all of you in this house are many."

Bugiah was in shock. He wanted to destroy her. With everything he was, he wanted to destroy her, but he was frightened. There was something in her words that left him feeling paralyzed.

     Arlene Adamo

Never had he felt like this before. The God of Gods was never supposed to know fear.

Myanaymiz looked out the window again. She could see Jeremiah and Jotham at the front gates talking to a Guardsman. "My friends have come for me," she said. "I must go." She then turned back to look him in the eye once again, "But be warned. My Lord loves who I love. You will not touch me, and you will not touch any of my friends. If you try, you have only yourself to blame for what will happen."

Bugiah said nothing, but simply watched helplessly as she walked out the door.

31

Jeremiah was trying the best he could to convince the Guardsman to let him in. "But I must talk with the God of Gods. I have a new idea for his gown for the Festival and would like to get his approval before going forward."

"You know the law, Weaver. An appointment must be made first. If you wish an appointment, I shall submit a formal request."

"But this is an emergency," said Jotham. "The Master Weaver is at a critical point in his work. Surely the God of Gods would be displeased if you were to hold up work on his Festival gown."

Just as the Guardsman appeared to be considering the request Jeremiah cried out, "Jotham! There she is!" Myanaymiz was walking calmly towards them.

Jotham pushed past the Guardsman, and ran towards her. Throwing his arms around her, he said, "I thought I might never see you again."

Myanaymiz hugged him back. "I told you I would be back. Why do you not believe me? I would never lie to you."

Jeremiah stared in shock as he watched the two together. *Was there something going on between them? No it couldn't be. Jotham surely would not have…and if he had, he would certainly have told me about it.*

Jotham and Myanaymiz were now walking towards him. "Hello Young-Old Jeremiah," she said with a smile. "I told you I would return."

Jeremiah looked over at the Guardsman who was obviously annoyed by the chaotic scene these Townsfolk were making on his watch. "Honourable Guardsman, forgive us for the bother. I will submit my request to talk with the God of Gods at a more convenient time."

"Let's go," said Jotham, wanting to get Myanaymiz away from the Palace as soon as possible. The three then turned and headed for the Town.

From the window, Bugiah watched intently. He was the God of Gods, and this woman had distressed him. No one had ever dared do such a thing before. She had defied him, and then calmly walked out as though she had every right to do so. And now, to see her out there proudly walking as though she were not a blasphemer, and to see her openly embrace that Cobbler…it was infuriating. But at the same time Bugiah sensed that there was something about her, and he had to be careful. It was by his keen instincts that he had risen to the level of God of Gods, and it was important to put trust in those instincts now. *She is not like the other Townsfolk. I must not be hasty, but approach this with cautious thought and planning.* He watched as she and her companions disappeared down the hill. *Do not think you can simply walk away, woman. You will pay for your insolence and blasphemous ways, and you will pay dearly.*

32

The children who had returned to the Cobbler's cottage were waiting patiently for their Lady's return. Petal was the first to spot them on the road. "There she is!" she called out.

Myanaymiz found herself suddenly surrounded by the excited children. Axis grabbed on tightly to her hand. "Oh thank you, Old Jeremiah," he cried. "Thank you for bringing our Lady back to us."

"Children you must calm down," said Jotham. "Your Lady must go inside and rest. It has been a long climb, and a long walk back from the Mount of the Gods."

"But she doesn't look tired," said Axis.

"We also need to have a grown-up discussion," said Jeremiah. "You must go now, but I promise you may return tomorrow."

"It is alright children," said Myanaymiz. "I will be here for you tomorrow. Do not worry."

As the children left, Jotham opened the cottage door then quickly ushered Myanaymiz and Jeremiah inside. He shut the door securely behind them. They could now finally talk without the worry of being overheard by Guardsman spies who might be hiding in the trees or bushes along the road. "Did he harm you, Myanaymiz?" asked Jotham, relieved he could at last ask the question that had been burning in his mind all the way down from the Palace. He was surprised at the thoughts that were running through his head. Only yesterday he was terrified of the God of Gods, but today he found himself imagining ways to kill him.

Myanaymiz reached up and gently tucked Jotham's hair behind his ear. "I was not harmed."

Jeremiah tried to ignore this intimate gesture between them. The strange mix of emotions it caused him was too disconcerting. He'd rather not know. "What did the God of Gods say to you?" he asked.

"Nothing of any consequence or significance," she answered.

"Are you certain he did not harm you? You must tell us if he did," said Jotham.

"I am perfectly unharmed. Would you cook me a meal now? I am unharmed, but I am very hungry."

Jotham laughed in relief. "Of course I will. Jeremiah, will you stay and eat with us?"

Jeremiah was hungry, but he also knew he had a great deal of work to finish. "I would love to, but I shouldn't stay when I am so behind in my weaving." He then turned to Myanaymiz and asked, "Tell me this, why did the God of Gods release you so quickly?"

She smiled sweetly at Jeremiah and answered, "Because I gave him no other choice."

"You? You gave the God of Gods no other choice?" Jeremiah repeated in utter disbelief.

"That is correct."

Jeremiah stared at this tiny woman in front of him. *How could she possibly command the God of Gods? She couldn't be telling the truth. Surely she is confused. She couldn't have such power. Could she?* "And Jotham's back? How did you heal him?" he asked.

"That is who I am, and what I do." she replied.

Jeremiah looked over questioningly at Jotham, but he only responded with a simple smile and shrug of his shoulders.

"Shall I make your favorite?" Jotham then asked Myanaymiz.

"That would be very kind. Thank you."

Jeremiah was not sure what to say at that point. There were many things to consider. Never had he found himself in such a strange and complicated situation. Up until recently, his world had been a very structured and predictable place. He needed time alone to think upon it. "I will be back tomorrow. There are still things I need to know, but, please Myanaymiz, before I go answer me one more thing. When you left the God of Gods was he in good spirits?"

"Oh no," she replied. "He was in very bad spirits."

Jeremiah felt the hair on the back of his neck stand up. "I must go," he said as he headed to the door. Before he left, he turned and looked at Jotham. "We must be prepared," he warned. "I don't know what is coming, but whatever it is, the God of Gods is angry, and we must somehow prepare ourselves for the consequences."

33

"**A**aaaah!" Vyx cried as loud as he could, encouraging the tears to flow freely. *C-c-crack! C-c-crack!* The repeated blows of the cane sent searing pain into his leg, arm and back. Curled up on the floor like an infant, his coarsely woven grey tunic pulled down over his knees, he knew there was no sense in trying to be proud or brave. Normally a Guardsman was strictly forbidden from showing such weakness, but in this instance he knew the rules were different. Showing anything other than great suffering could get him killed. If he exaggerated his pain, and pretended to feel the occasional blow that fell weakly or missed it's mark, the God of Gods would get his satisfaction, and Vyx would be able to limp away still alive.

Bugiah madly swung the cane, his eyes blind with rage as he imagined this Guardsman was the woman. *How dare you! I am the God of Gods! No one defies me! No one insults me!*

Vyx felt three more stinging hard blows before Bugiah suddenly let the cane drop to the floor. He then watched as the God of Gods turned, walked over to the divan, and dropped exhausted into the soft cushions. Vyx remained on the floor. He knew not to move until he was given permission.

For a moment, Bugiah just stared with contempt at the crumpled wounded Guardsman. Finally, he commanded, "Get up! Get up and act like a Guardsman of the Gods!"

Vyx moved his arms and legs a little to assess the damage. There was some pain, but it was not as painful as past beatings had been. *Was the God of Gods getting old?* He slowly got up, acting as though he had been almost completely debilitated by the beating. Anything less could possibly anger Bugiah again.

Bugiah, meanwhile, had poured himself a goblet of wine, and was now quickly gulping it down. Almost instantly his veins warmed, and his tension began to ease. He looked at Vyx who was standing, but doubled over in apparent pain, and a sense of satisfaction settled in his stomach. "Oh Vyx, you are my most loyal Guardsman. But look…look what she has made me do. She has made me pull you from sleep, and beat my most dedicated servant. You should hate her as much as I do."

Vyx did not know who he was talking about, but that didn't matter. He knew the duty of the Guardsman was to always agree with the God of Gods no matter what. "Yes My God, she is an evil witch."

"Of course! That is exactly what she is! She is a witch…and the strongest kind of witch…an evil Juju Witch. Why did I not see it before? Yes, a Juju Witch is among us!"

As all Guardsmen were well versed in the Stories of the Gods, Vyx knew well that a Juju Witch was a very powerful creature, but he had never imagined that he'd ever see one in his lifetime. He wondered what such a thing might look like.

"And that evil Juju Witch has infiltrated our Town…putting spells on our beloved and loyal subjects, turning their hearts away from the worship of the Gods!" Bugiah slammed his goblet down on the nearby table.

"I have but one heart to give, and I give it to my Gods," said Vyx, repeating a line from the Guardsman's oath.

"Yes, you are incorruptible. Your heart belongs to the Gods. This is why I am choosing you over all other Guardsmen. You have the strength and loyalty to carry out my will. But we must be careful. Destroying her will not be easy. It will take some planning. The powers of the Juju Witch are very strong."

"But not stronger than the God of Gods. You will be able to defeat her."

"Yes, of course! The God of Gods is superior in every way!" he declared. "I will destroy her! And look," Bugiah pointed to the streak of blood that had soaked through Vyx's tunic sleeve leaving a deep dark red line, "look what she has already done to my most trusted Guardsman. Do you see? Do you see what she has done to you?"

Vyx obediently looked at his arm, and then back up at Bugiah. He silently nodded.

"You know she must be stopped. We cannot let her do this to you again. We cannot let her harm our loyal subjects. We will stop her together."

"I am your obedient servant," said Vyx, carefully getting down on the one knee that had not been hit in the beating.

Bugiah clapped his hands together, "Oh Vyx! How happy you make me! In my divine wisdom, I have surely chosen right. Now, as I said, this will require both care and cunning. I need to first learn all I can about her. That is where you come in. You must move into Town for a time, and become my eyes and ears."

Vyx was shocked! *Move into Town? I, a Guardsman, move into Town?* Such a thing had never been done before. Guardsmen were taken as young children from their families to the Palace of the Gods for training. They were restricted to a life of regiment and isolation. No Guardsman was ever allowed to return home.

Bugiah seemed completely unfazed by the strangeness of what he had just ordered. "You will need to gather as much information about her as possible," he continued. "Pay close attention to anything that may be a weakness. Every Juju Witch has a weakness. The stories tell us that finding her failing is the way to defeat her. You will help me find that hidden flaw so that I may put an end to her."

"It is my honour to serve you, my God," said Vyx who couldn't imagine what it would be like to return home. Would his parents recognize him? Would he recognize them? Were they even still alive?

"Of course the Townsfolk will be confused by your return. We shall simply tell them that the God of Gods has received divine inspiration, and it is my wish that you should be there. They need no other explanation."

Vyx suddenly became aware of the drying blood gluing his tunic to his back. "When does my God wish me to leave?" he asked.

"Today!" Bugiah answered. "There is no time to lose. First, go and clean yourself up. You'll be provided with the appropriate civilian clothing, as you certainly cannot casually walk around Town looking like a Guardsman. You must be as inconspicuous as possible. That is essential if I am to learn anything."

Today? I will walk into Town today? Wearing clothes like any of the Townsfolk? Just simply walk into Town like it had always been that way? Vyx felt disoriented at the thought. The leg he was kneeling upon began to tremble slightly, and for a moment, he was afraid he might fall over.

"Get up now!" said Bugiah "Get up and go prepare yourself. You have work to do."

Vyx slowly stood up. As he did, he could feel the renewed pain of the beating, but it seemed so insignificant now. *I am going to Town!*

Bugiah poured himself another goblet of wine. "Go!" he commanded. "Go and fulfil your duty to the God of Gods."

"As you wish, my God. I am your faithful servant until death." Bowing his head, Vyx slowly backed out of the room.

Bugiah took a long drink of wine. He then stared at the cane on the black marble floor. *How dare she! Evil witch! Evil Juju Witch! She will know what happens to those who disobey the God of Gods! She will know the merciless extent of the Law of the Gods!*

— • —

                    Arlene Adamo

34

Jeremiah stood in front of the Cobbler's cottage. He was about to call out to Jotham, the way he always did, when he heard a strange sound coming from inside. It sounded like singing…it sounded like a man singing? He paused for a moment before he shouted "Jotham!" The singing abruptly stopped.

The door opened, and Jotham stood there looking a little embarrassed. "Oh! Hello, Jeremiah. Please, come in." Jeremiah stepped inside. He decided not to mention what he had just heard.

Myanaymiz was sitting at the table. There was a cup of strawberry tea in front of her. "Hello Young-Old Jeremiah," she said.

"Hello Myanaymiz." He walked over to the table, and sat down.

"Would you like some tea?" asked Jotham.

"No thank you, but we do need to discuss the weeks ahead. The Festival of the Gods is not long off, and I have no idea what we will do with Myanaymiz at that time. Keeping her in the cottage would be best, but the law states that everyone, short of those on their deathbed, is required to attend. Also, for now we have kept her away from the Townsfolk. How should we introduce her to them? They are already talking of course, and know about her visit to the Palace of the Gods yesterday. What shall we tell them?"

"Just tell them to come and see me," said Myanaymiz. "When they see me, those who want to understand will understand."

Jotham sat down at the table and said to Jeremiah, "I think we should do as she says. The children already come to see her every day. Arrange to have some of the adults visit, but not too many at once. It could become too chaotic, and result in misunderstandings.

The situation is already so volatile, and we don't need more complications. It is, however, necessary that the Townsfolk meet her, and perhaps the more people who meet her, the safer she will be from Bugiah. If he is still angry, we do not know what he may try. As for the Festival, we can decide that later. For now, we should deal with this extraordinary situation on a day to day basis."

Jeremiah cringed at that thought of Bugiah, and how angry Myanaymiz said he was. *What exactly happened at the Palace, and if it was something that angered the God of Gods, why was she not killed on the spot? It is all so confusing? I am no longer certain of anything anymore, and a Master Weaver is supposed to be certain of most everything. It is my job to be the rock of the Town and the faithful servant of the Gods. I shouldn't be floundering like this.* He looked over at Myanaymiz, and she smiled back at him. "You worry too much, Young-Old Jeremiah," she said. "You are too tired and have too much pain."

Jeremiah's tension eased as he found himself laughing at her child-like candid ways. "Yes, I have been working hard at my loom. I am tired, I am old and I am in pain."

"Shall I fix you?" she asked.

Jeremiah remembered what she had done to Jotham's back. "No!" he exclaimed. "I...I am fine." But he wasn't fine and he knew it. He was afraid...afraid of the truth. If he did not see these magical powers of hers at work, he did not have to fully believe it was true. Right now it was simply a story belonging to someone else. He was safe from belief. Believing would perhaps sever the line that tethered him securely to the world he knew and understood. If he were to let her touch him, he might find himself floating away...lost and alone. Jeremiah was terrified at the idea of being lost.

Jotham was surprised by his friend's strong defensive reaction, but decided not to try and convince him otherwise. He would never want to deny Jeremiah freedom from pain, but at that moment he also secretly enjoyed being the only one who had received her magic healing. It was something special between the two of them.

Myanaymiz looked sadly at Jeremiah. "I am sorry you do not want my help. I forgive you for your transgressions."

Transgressions? How could refusing help be a transgression? Like a child, she makes no sense. But I must not get bogged down in her confusing ways. I shall keep focussed and plan ahead. That is my job. I am the Master Weaver and the Town depends upon me. "Jotham, I will instruct people to begin arriving directly after the midday meal… if that is alright with you?"

"Myanaymiz, is it alright for you?"

"Yes Jotham, that is fine. I know that some of them will not like me, but it must be done."

"Why would anyone not love you?" asked Jotham.

Myanaymiz softly smiled at him.

Jeremiah looked away. *I don't want to know.*

———•———

35

Vyx carried a small bag on his shoulder as he walked down the Celestial Path towards the Town. The warm breeze blew lightly through his soft civilian clothes. He took in a deep breath of fresh air. How free and light he felt, no longer weighted down by the thick reptilian skin armor that usually covered him. The gentle push of the wind on his back seemed so natural. He must have felt this once…a long time ago…so long ago that he could not remember. *This is something I will never forget again.*

The road to the Town seemed vaguely familiar. He had been down this way in the darkness during the Funeral of the Gods… veiled…under strict instructions not to look anywhere but ahead. Still, he found his eyes wandering beneath the black mask…scanning the houses…the faces…searching for anything even vaguely familiar…searching for something he once knew.

Vyx walked around the bend in the road, and suddenly, there it was! The Town! He stopped for a moment just to take it all in. There was the first house they had come upon during the funeral procession. He remembered it well. How struck he was by such a small and simple the structure, and then the family who stood in front, loudly crying for their dead God…two parents and three children. Did he once know the adults when they were children? Would they remember him, if they saw his face?

At the time, part of him secretly wanted to tear off the veil and scream, 'it is I, Vyx!' but he was a Guardsman. Guardsman took great pride in their professionalism and loyalty. Those kinds of secret thoughts were to be fought and fought vigorously. That was

                                    Arlene Adamo

one of the first things a Guardsman was taught. *Thought must be fought.* A Guardsman had only one purpose in life, to protect and serve the Gods. If he failed to do this, he was nothing. He was less than nothing. *I do my duty to the Gods and will put nothing, including myself, before them. And now, sent by the divine hand of the God of Gods himself, I have a sacred mission to carry out. May the blessings of the Gods be upon me.* Vyx then hitched up the bag on his shoulder, and headed into Town.

36

The first person to arrive at Jotham's cottage was Slemi, a well respected matriarch in the Town. She did not come alone. She was not the alone type. A group of five of her most loyal associates accompanied her. Although Jotham expected that she would be among the first to show up, he was still not entirely prepared when he opened the door and saw her standing there…that accusing look on her face. He hated that look.

"Cobbler, we have come to see this woman who is staying in your cottage."

"Slemi…ladies…Please come in," said Jotham, smiling politely, and standing aside to allow them to enter.

The women stepped inside the doorway, and looked around the workshop suspiciously. The Cobbler had always been a strange one. First, there were his past transgressions against the Gods… why he was alive at all was a mystery, and then there was the way he lived…alone…beholden to no one. It was simply not right. 'He is like a boy who never grew up,' Slemi would tell anyone who listened. 'He should take responsibility for things. He should show more shame for his insult to the Gods. He is a bad influence on the children.'

"So where is she?" Slemi demanded of Jotham.

"In the back garden."

The group, led by Slemi, then headed to the back door, and marched out into the garden. Jotham quickly followed after them.

In the center of the garden, Myanaymiz was seated on the soft grass, her beautiful gown spread out like a fan. The children were dancing and singing all around her:

> *Our Lady from the rock*
> *Our Lady from the rock*
> *She takes us by the hand*
> *And leads us 'cross the land*
> *She killed the monster dead*
> *We feasted on his head*
> *Our Lady from the rock*
> *Our Lady from the rock*

Slemi did not like what she was seeing…or hearing. "Children!" she shouted. "Go home now!" The children, who were well aware of Slemi's influence in the Town and with their parents, immediately scattered and disappeared.

"Why would you allow the children near her?" Slemi asked Jotham. "We do not know anything about her or what kind of an influence she might have on them. And what was that horrible song they were singing?"

Jotham couldn't help smiling even though he knew it would anger Slemi even more. "The children come begging every day to see her," he explained. "Their parents have not complained, so I assumed there was no harm in it. As for the song, one of the boys had a nightmare where he was being chased by a monster. The Lady suddenly appeared in his dream and slew the beast with a golden sword. After that, she cut off the monster's head, and offered the child a piece of the meat which apparently tasted as sweet as honey. All of the children so liked this story that they made up a little song about it."

"The song is appalling!" said Slemi. "And I am certain the Gods would not approve."

To hell with the Gods! "I would never dare speak for the Gods," Jotham replied with a smile. He then proceeded with the introductions. "Slemi, this is Myanaymiz, and Myanaymiz, this is Slemi and the ladies from The Society of Women Servants to the Gods."

Slemi looked down at Myanaymiz who remained seated on the ground. *Her hair? Her skin? And where did she get that gown?* "Have you no manners?" Slemi demanded. "Are you going to stand up, and greet me properly?"

Myanaymiz slowly stood up, and looked her straight in the eye. Slemi found herself feeling suddenly unnerved, and instinctively took two steps back. *Those eyes…she is strange. But…but to look at me like that…so boldly! Who does she think she is?* "They say you came from a rock. How can this be true?" she asked. "No one can come from a rock. It's utter nonsense." The women behind her giggled.

"It is true," replied Myanaymiz. "I came from a rock."

"Obviously, you are a liar," said Slemi. "Only the Gods would be capable of such magic, and you are most certainly not a God. Such a claim would be blasphemy. Are you a blasphemer?"

"She would not even know what that is," interjected Jotham.

"Let her answer the question," said Slemi. "Are you a blasphemer?"

Myanaymiz smiled. "I am from a rock. I am not a blasphemer."

"How possibly could you say you are from a rock, and then claim not to be a blasphemer?"

"A blasphemer disrespects God. I am not a blasphemer."

Jotham did not like where this conversation was going. "Do any of you ladies require new shoes for the Festival? There is still time to create a unique pair just for you."

"Be quiet Cobbler," said Slemi. She looked at Myanaymiz, "You mean 'Gods.' A blasphemer disrespects Gods."

Before Myanaymiz could reply, a large blue butterfly suddenly flew in between the two women. Everyone watched in fascination as it fluttered around and around Slemi's head. *What is that? I've never seen such a thing before.* Three times it swooped in towards her face, making her duck and scream each time.

Myanaymiz stood where she was, then calmly extended her arm, and opened her hand. The butterfly circled above her once, fluttered downward, and came to rest in the hollow of her palm.

No one said a word. Instead, they were all spellbound by the strange and beautiful insect. Not one of them could take their eyes from those majestic blue wings shimmering in the sunlight. They watched in absolute fascination as the wings then began to slowly move. Open…close…open…close…each time like a slow breath. Breathing in…breathing out. They could feel it. Moving closer… closer… It was now within them…deep within their chests… rising…falling. Gently opening…drawing in…closing…pushing out…the slow steady movement of life. *What is within is without. What is without is within. All…is…one.*

"Somebody come quick!" a voice suddenly shouted, breaking the spell. They all turned to look at the excited boy who had thrown open the side gate, and was running towards them. When Jotham glanced back to look again at the butterfly, he could see it was gone. Myanaymiz was not looking at the boy like everyone else. Instead, her gaze was turned skyward.

"There is a stranger in Town!" the boy shouted at the group. "A man! He came from a tree! You must come quickly!"

Slemi looked accusingly at Jotham, "A man from a tree now? First, a Lady from a rock, and now a man from a tree? What is going on here?! May the God of Gods save us all!"

⸻ ◆ ⸻

37

Vyx had already passed by two houses, and had yet to see a soul…no one in the road, and no one around the homes. *Does anyone live here at all?* He had seen the Townsfolk as they lined the road during the funeral. He had heard them wailing in the dark. They were here somewhere. *Could I have frightened them into hiding? Where are they?*

He thought about finding the home of his parents, but couldn't remember where it was. *There's a cottage with white trim. Did it have white trim? That well in the front garden over there looks familiar, but does that mean it's the house of my parents or is it merely a neighbor's well I knew as a child.* He wished he could remember something clearly. Shadowy images in his mind, which may or may not be real memories, were all he had to find his way.

Suddenly, he saw something he recognized. *Yes, I do remember you!* He then ran towards the tall oak tree that stood like a magnificent monument in the middle of a large meadow. It was wide and full of sturdy strong branches, the lowest of which made it perfect for climbing. Long ago someone had carved a peculiar face into its trunk, and although it was not recognizable as either man or woman, the children had always called it Old Man Tree. Vyx now stared into those familiar grey eyes. How strange it was to see them again after all this time…those eyes that still seemed so alive… eyes mysteriously full of both wisdom and whimsy…eyes of a long ago friend. "Hello Old Man Tree," he found himself saying, as he used to do when he was a child.

Dropping his bag on the ground, he then easily pulled himself onto the lowest branch. *This used to be so high off of the ground that I needed to stand on an old crate to reach it.* He stood straight, his feet firmly on the thick bough. Reaching up to the next branch he then pulled himself up again. Quickly he climbed the tree until he found himself up as far as he could go. *I've never been this high before.*

He looked around, and could now see the entire Town. *There are the people!* Some were in their back gardens, and others were scattered about here and there. Three were walking along the road, and over there was a woman drawing water from a well. The Town was full of people! Someone should be able to tell him where his parents were…or if they were even still alive.

Vyx then noticed four boys approaching the meadow from the road. They ran straight to the bottom of Old Man Tree, laughing and chattering like squirrels. *The sounds of children…how strange. I think I remember being like that.*

One boy hoisted himself onto the lowest branch, and then sat there swinging his legs. "This is my branch, and you can't take it!"

Another boy immediately spotted Vyx's bag on the ground, and walked over to it. First, he gave it a suspicious little kick, and when nothing inside moved, he picked it up. "Look what I found!" he cried, as he held it up for the other boys to see.

"That is mine!" Vyx shouted down.

The boy, who had been sitting on the branch, immediately jumped to the ground, and stood close to his friends for protection. All four stared up in wonder.

"What is it?" one of them asked.

"It's a monkey," another answered.

"There are no monkeys around here."

"Maybe it's a monkey that escaped from a circus."

"A circus monkey! A circus monkey!" All of the boys laughed.

"I am not a circus monkey," Vyx yelled down.

"It's a talking circus monkey!"

"I am not a monkey!" Vyx started to climb down.

"Oh no! He's coming down! I think we angered the big monkey! Run!"

The boys all began to run. The one who found Vyx's bag dropped it to the ground as he fled. Once they felt they were at a safe distance, the children stopped, and turned to see if the creature was following them.

Vyx jumped from the last branch, and picked up his bag.

"It's not a monkey," exclaimed a boy. "It's a man…a strange man."

"I'm going for help," said the smallest who then rushed off in the direction of the Cobbler's house.

The other boys remained where they were, and watched uneasily as the strange man began to slowly walk towards them.

———————

38

Jeremiah was hurrying to Jotham's cottage. Once he heard that Slemi had taken it upon herself to be the first visitor, he was hoping he could get there before her. *I have to warn Jotham! Why did I not do this before? Of course Slemi would make herself first.*

Just as he turned up the front path, he saw the whole group of them, led by a boy, heading in his direction.

"Old Jeremiah!" yelled the child, "Come quick and help. There is a man who came from a tree?"

"There seems to be another stranger in Town," Jotham explained.

"Quickly Weaver, the world is falling apart, and you just stand there!" said Slemi as she hurried past him.

Jeremiah joined in with the group. "Where's Myanaymiz?" he asked Jotham.

It was then that Jotham realized that Myanaymiz was not following them. "She must have stayed in the garden," he answered.

Jeremiah looked at Slemi and the other women up ahead of them. They were definitely in a panic. It was never a good thing when the women of The Society were worked up about anything. There were times when Jeremiah dreaded them even more than he dreaded Bugiah. *Perhaps the garden is the best place for Myanaymiz at this moment.* He then hurried to keep pace with the rest.

39

Vyx approached the boys slowly so as not to frighten them off. They could be useful in giving him information. "I am Vyx," he said. "Guardsman of the Gods."

The boys started to giggle nervously.

"You are not a Guardsman."

"You don't even look like a Guardsman."

"Where is your uniform?"

"Where is your veil?"

"Where is your sword?"

"I am a Guardsman. I was sent here by the divine order of the God of Gods. By divine order I am to wear Townsfolk clothing."

The boys looked at each other, wondering if they could believe this ridiculous story.

"Everybody knows Guardsmen never wear ordinary clothes or wander through town or climb trees. You are lying."

"It is by divine order of the God of Gods that I am here, and divine orders must not to be questioned." Vyx stopped a reasonable distance from the boys. He was trying his best not to appear too threatening. Normally, it was a Guardsman's job to be as threatening as possible. This was a completely new experience for him.

The boys could now clearly see the stranger's face. He did speak like a Guardsman…short, quick and to the point, but was that the face of a Guardsman? They had always imagined something far more sinister, perhaps something monster-like hiding behind that veil. But this man didn't look so frightening. He looked a lot like everyone else. Then again, if this man really was telling the truth

A r l e n e   A d a m o

about being a Guardsman, would it matter how he looked or what he wore? He would still be very dangerous.

Suddenly, they heard a woman's voice call out, "The child spoke the truth! It truly is a foreigner!"

The boys turned, and were relieved to see their companion bringing with him many grown-ups.

"Who are you?" demanded Slemi as she boldly walked up to the stranger.

"I am Vyx, Guardsman of the Gods." Slemi took a step back.

"Vyx?" said Jotham.

Vyx looked at Jotham. *That hair. That mouth. I know this man. A faint memory. Laughter. What is his name?*

"Do you mean to tell me you are Vyx, son of Li and Geed? But that makes no sense. Vyx was given over to the Gods a long time ago," said Slemi.

Li and Geed! Yes, those were their names! Are they still alive? "I am here by divine order of the God of Gods," Vyx replied. "By divine order I am here to live among you."

Slemi went silent with shock. The world really was falling apart. A Guardsman living amongst the Townsfolk? Who ever heard of such a thing?

Jeremiah knew this had to be about Myanaymiz. Why else would Bugiah issue such an order? "How long are you to live here?" he asked.

"I do not know. I arrived by divine order and when, by divine order, I am told to leave, I will leave."

"Vyx, do you remember me? I'm Jotham."

Jotham! "I knew you before I was honoured to be accepted into Guardsman training."

"Almost every day, we used to climb that very tree." Jotham pointed to the tree.

Vyx looked at Old Man Tree. *Climbing. Laughing. Swinging from the branches. Dreaming of building a tree fort.* "That was before I was honoured to become a Guardsman," he said.

"Do Li and Geed know you have returned?" asked Slemi.

So they are still alive. "No. I have not seen them. I could not remember where they live."

Slemi smiled. "Honourable Guardsman, they do not live in the same place anyway. After you left, they moved to a new home. We shall all take you there. This will certainly be a big surprise for them."

40

Myanaymiz sat on the ground, alone in the garden. Everything was still and very silent. She took in a deep breath as she basked in the warm sunlight. *This is a very long way from the cold and damp of the rock. I am glad I am here.*

The blue butterfly suddenly appeared again. Myanaymiz watched as it flew in circles around her. Dipping…rising…floating…fluttering. She held out her hand, and the butterfly came to rest once again in her palm. She could feel the soft tickle of its tiny sticky feet. *This is who I am. This is what I do.*

The beautiful delicate wings opened and closed, opened and closed. Suddenly, they opened flat upon her hand, and remained. In that moment, time instantly vanished. There was only her hand, and the fine soft tenderness of those wings upon it. All else was gone, the world, the sky. There was nothing in the entire universe but this. *This is the place…the place of peace…the center of centers… the heart of hearts. I was. I am. I will be.*

Suddenly, the wings closed again; then, after seeming to hesitate for just a moment, the butterfly instantly flew off, and disappeared into the sky. Time and the world rolled in once again. *It is done.*

Myanaymiz stared in amazement at her still open hand, and the imprint of blue powder left on her palm. She watched as her twinkling skin underneath made the mark come alive in the sunlight. *Yes, it is so beautiful, but this is far more than just something beautiful…this is so much more.* She looked closer, her eyes carefully studying the wondrous shape. *What is it I see?* Then suddenly, she understood! *A word! The butterfly has written a word upon my skin!* She stared deeper into the blue lines. *Yes! Oh yes, I know what it says! This is the word I have longed for. The word that I love!* Even though she had never seen it before, she knew she loved it…she knew she had always loved it. *This is that which cannot be spoken. It can be felt. It can be heard. It can be seen. It can be tasted. It has a scent. It can be sensed. But it can never be spoken.* "This is the Word," she said aloud. "The Word is the name of my Lord."

   Arlene Adamo

41

As the odd procession snaked through Town, people all along the road stopped to stare in astonishment. *What is going on?* Whatever was happening, they knew it must be important with Slemi leading the way. But who was that strange man with her? And what did the Master Weaver, the Cobbler and the ladies from The Society have to do with it? It was definitely official and very serious business, but why then were the children with them? Children had no place in the official business of the Town. Many of on-lookers began to join in with the group, trying their best to get answers as they marched along.

"Where are we going?"

"Who is that stranger?"

"Where is that strange woman we heard about?

"Are they connected?"

"What does Slemi know?"

"This is exciting!"

The procession finally came to a stop at the front door of Li and Geed. Instead of a cottage like most of the other Townsfolk, Li and Geed had a large house. The parents of Guardsmen are well compensated for their sacrifice.

Slemi rapped heavily on the door. When it opened, a small grey haired woman stared out in confusion at the strange crowd in her front garden.

"Li," said Slemi, "look who is with me! Your son has returned!"

Li stared in puzzlement at Slemi, and then at the tall stranger who stood beside her. Her eyes grew wider. *That face! It can't be! How is this possible!*

"It is I, Mother. It is Vyx."

A young man suddenly appeared behind Li. "What is this about?" he demanded.

"Konn, this is your brother Vyx," said Li, still bewildered by the fact that her eldest son, whom she thought never to see again, was standing on her doorstep.

"But Vyx is a Guardsman of the Gods. How could this be him?"

"I don't know," said Li. She looked at Vyx and asked, "Have you disgraced us with your conduct? Have they sent you back because you have disgraced us? Must we now give up this house and our other fine things?"

Vyx stared at these two people whose faces bore such a likeness to his own. To think that, while he was required to keep his face strictly veiled in public, these similar faces walked around freely. Feeling the sun. Feeling the wind. Free. It was all very strange.

"I am an Honourable Guardsman," Vyx said. "I am here by divine order. I am here to live among the Townsfolk."

"He can't stay here," Konn said to Slemi. "It would not be right. He is a Guardsman, and is no longer our concern. All familiar ties are to be severed till death. That is the law. We are obedient Townsfolk who follow the law."

A grey-haired man peered out from behind the door. "Vyx?"
Father!

"Geed," said Li, "your son has arrived from the Mount of the Gods by divine order. He cannot stay with us. It is forbidden."

Geed saw the stern looks on the faces of Li and Konn. He silently turned his gaze downward, and stared at the floor.

"As I said before, he is not our problem," said Konn. "We have done our duty. We have sacrificed. I have no brother, and they have no son. There is no more to be said." He then shut the door.

Vyx silently turned and walked through the crowd. Slemi, Jotham and Jeremiah followed after him. He stopped at the road and said, "They are correct. I am a Guardsman. I cannot stay with them."

"Well, you must stay somewhere," said Slemi. "You are an Honourable Guardsman here by divine order, and it is our duty to find you shelter." She then turned and looked directly at Jotham.

Jotham knew she was expecting him to volunteer. "I am afraid that I already have one guest, and my cottage cannot shelter another," he said. "Otherwise I would be honoured to have a Guardsman of the Gods stay with me." *A Guardsman? In my home? That would be impossible at the best of times, and with Myanaymiz there, it would be extremely dangerous.*

"But where else will he stay?" asked Slemi, trying to push the issue. She did not like the idea of the woman and Jotham alone in that cottage. A Guardsman could keep an eye on things.

"I will take him," said Jeremiah.

"But no one is allowed to stay in your cottage while you weave the gowns for the Gods," said Slemi.

"Actually," he replied, "the law states that no Townsfolk are allowed to live there, but a Guardsman is not Townsfolk. According to the holy pyramid of nature, the Guardsman sits above the people of the Town. He is between the Gods and the people, and therefore that law does not apply to him."

Slemi thought about it. She would have preferred Vyx to stay at Jotham's, but she could not dispute Jeremiah's argument. A Guardsman was indeed above the Townsfolk. Besides which, now that she considered it more carefully, the Master Weaver was a far more fitting host for an Honourable Guardsman than was a Cobbler. She could not deny that. It would certainly show greater respect to the Gods for him to stay with Jeremiah, and it was, after all, her sacred duty as leader of The Society of Women Servants to ensure the Gods always received their due respect. "Very well," she conceded, "He shall stay with you."

Jotham breathed a sigh of relief.

— · · —

42

Jeremiah carried out one large roll of thread and placed it on the floor next to the loom. Vyx carried out five rolls, and placed them next to Jeremiah's one. "You are strong," said Jeremiah.

"I am a Guardsman," replied Vyx.

They were clearing out the crowded storage room for Vyx to use. Luckily, Jeremiah had a bench with a straw filled mattress that he kept in his main room. Although a little narrow, it would serve well as a guest bed. He lifted the end and began to drag it towards the door. Vyx then grabbed hold of the bench, picked it up over his broad shoulder, and carried it in.

Jeremiah stood in the doorway, and looked at the small empty room with only the modest bench and Vyx standing next to it. "I am sorry that I could not provide more comfortable accommodation but, as an old Weaver who lives alone, this is all I have."

"A Guardsman is accustomed to austere conditions. This is far more comfort than what I am used to. If I find that I am unable to sleep on this soft mattress, I will simply sleep on the floor."

Jeremiah was surprised. He knew a little about the training of Guardsmen, and certainly it was severe. He was now beginning to realize just how severe it might be.

———◆———

<h1 style="text-align:center">43</h1>

Myanaymiz was sitting on the stool beside Jotham, and watching as he carefully stitched together the pieces of fine brown leather. "These shoes are for a very particular woman," he said. "She will examine every last inch of them before paying me what she owes me. If she finds the smallest defect, she will try to pay me less."

"You do not have to make them for her."

"Yes, I do. That is my job. I am the Town Cobbler."

"You are very dedicated," she said.

"I suppose I am."

"Would you sing for me while you do your work?"

"First, I must talk to you about what happened today. It is important that you understand about the great danger."

"You mean the man from the tree."

"Yes, but he wasn't from the tree. He is a Guardsman of the Gods, and I believe he has come to spy on you or even worse. I'm afraid for your safety."

"Bugiah was very angry," said Myanaymiz. "I expected him to send someone…someone who was not afraid like he was."

Jotham cringed to hear her speak aloud of the God of Gods like that. It was so dangerous, and she did it so casually. "The Guardsman is staying in Jeremiah's cottage. No one knows how long he will be here in Town or what he will do. You should not wander anywhere alone. His name is Vyx, and he cannot be trusted."

"You were children together," she said.

"How did you know that?"

"I know things. That is who I am, and that is what I do."

"We used to play together as boys," he said. "When we were seven years old Vyx's parents offered him over to the Gods to be trained as a Guardsman. He was never supposed to return to the Town again. And certainly not like this. A Guardsman only comes into Town if his face is covered, and he is attending to the needs of the Gods."

"He has returned because of me."

"He is very dangerous, Myanaymiz. Guardsmen are trained killers."

"I will go see him."

"No!" exclaimed Jotham.

"But he has come to see me, has he not?"

"Yes, but…" Jotham realized she was right. He could not possibly keep her from the Guardsman forever. Eventually, Vyx would certainly demand to see her, and all he could really do is to be there when it happened. "It would be better if, when you meet with him, you have me or Jeremiah, or better yet both of us with you."

"Do not worry, Jotham. I will be alright," she said trying to reassure him. "Would you please sing now? I would love to hear a song."

"Why not," he shrugged. "Why worry about a killer in our midst when I can just sing a song. Should I make up a new one?"

"That would be very nice."

As Jotham carefully stitched the shoe, he concentrated on opening his mind. He now knew how to create music by welcoming a song into his thoughts. It was easy as long has he kept his mind focussed. Within a few seconds, a song began to come to him, and Jotham began to sing it as it formed.

Where did you come from
Dream Lady
Where are you going
Dream Lady
Won't you stay a while
Dream Lady
Stay and make me yours
Just a little while longer
Oh dream Lady
Stay and make me yours
Just a little while longer
A little while longer…

44

Jotham awoke to find Myanaymiz gone. "Myanaymiz!" he called, but she did not answer. He quickly threw on his trousers and shirt then searched the cottage. She was nowhere to be found. He checked outside in the garden. "Myanaymiz!" he called, but still no answer. Did she simply wander off? Did someone take her?

He went back inside and quickly put on his shoes. *I must find her. I need to get her back.*

45

The sun was just beginning to rise when Myanaymiz walked up the path to the Weaver's cottage. She knocked on the door. No one answered. She knocked again. Finally, Jeremiah opened the door wearing only his sleeping robe. Being still half asleep, it took a second for him to realize that it was Myanaymiz standing there in the morning shadows. "What are you doing here?" he asked, as he quickly stepped outside, and shut the door behind him. "I have someone staying with me who should not see you. Not yet anyway."

"But I have come to meet the Guardsman, Young-Old Jeremiah," she said. "I have come to meet Vyx."

"Where's Jotham? Does he know where you are?"

"I left him asleep in the bed."

Jeremiah pretended not to hear that. "Please return to Jotham's cottage. We have a very delicate situation here. It is a situation that must be treated with caution."

"Vyx is here because of me. Bugiah has sent him to see me. He will not go away no matter how long you stall."

"Please, Myanaymiz! The sun has not yet fully risen. I am still asleep. Could we at least wait until we have all been dressed and fed?"

Just then the door opened behind him. Jeremiah turned to see Vyx standing fully dressed in the doorway.

"You have come to see me, Guardsman," said Myanaymiz. "Here I am."

Vyx looked at the strange Lady who stood before him. She was wearing a gown so remarkably beautiful he immediately wondered why it did not belong to a God. "Who told you that I was here to see you?" he asked.

"I know things. That is who I am, and that is what I do."

"What else do you know?"

"I know you have not been back here since you were a boy. I know that you used to play with Jotham. I know that it was Bugiah himself who sent you. I know that the day the Guardsmen arrived, and took you from this Town you tripped, and scratched your knee. It was then that you learned a Guardsman was not allowed to cry."

Vyx was shocked! There was no one left alive who knew about his fall, and how he had been severely punished for crying. The Guardsmen who took him that day were dead, having taken their own lives years ago after showing signs of becoming too old to properly serve the Gods. This was the Rite of Death for all Honourable Guardsmen. The only possible way she could know about the fall is if she were indeed a Juju Witch. "Are you a Juju Witch?" he asked outright.

"I am what I am."

"Perhaps we should all go inside and have a cup of tea," Jeremiah said, desperately trying to ease the tension.

"I must go now," said Myanaymiz. "Jotham is worrying about me."

"You must tell me more," said Vyx.

"Not now," she replied.

"Why not now?"

"You will come to the Cobbler's cottage when the sun is already past its highest point. You may ask of me all of the questions you want. I shall answer you truthfully, but I cannot guarantee that you will like or understand the answers."

This was not how Vyx imagined it. He imagined that he would have to slowly, covertly gather the information on her. He would have to trick her…coerce her into telling all of her secrets. Wouldn't a Juju Witch want to try and keep secrets? That's what the witches were like in the stories…very secretive. Why was she not like the stories? "I will be there," he said.

Without another word, Myanaymiz turned and walked back down the path to the road. "You see, she is completely harmless," Jeremiah said to Vyx. "Let us go inside now and have something to eat."

Vyx watched silently as Myanaymiz walked off down the road. *She is not afraid of me…not afraid of the Guardsman of the Gods… like a panther she is not afraid. Is a panther harmless?*

Jotham hurried along the road, peering over fences and gates. *Where could she be?* It occurred to him that perhaps she had returned to the rock, but she had already told him once how happy she was to be free of it. Surely she would not go back there.

Suddenly, in the dim light he saw a figure walking towards him on the road ahead. *Myanaymiz!* He ran to her and grabbed her up in his arms. "I didn't know what had happened to you," he said, setting her down. "Please don't leave without telling me again."

She pushed his hair out of his eyes. "It is alright, Jotham. I had to let Vyx see me. That is what he came here for."

"What? You went to see Vyx? Why? I told you Vyx was dangerous!"

"You care about me because you are a good man, but do you not see that I am alright? No harm has come to me. No harm will ever come to me."

He placed his hand softly against her cheek and sighed. "Oh Myanaymiz, you are so innocent. Like a child. I just want to be able to protect you."

"My Lord protects me. You need only care about me."

"Who is your Lord?"

"One day He will come for me."

"In that case, I hope He does not come for a very long time," he said, taking her in his arms. It was then that Jotham noticed some movement in a nearby window…he could not see anyone, but knew someone was there…hidden…peering out through the slit in the curtains; and although he could not see the face, he knew who it was. It was Slemi. Slemi was secretly watching them.

Quickly releasing Myanaymiz, Jotham exclaimed, "Come, we must get home!" As they walked down the road, he did not look back to see if Slemi was still looking. He did not have to. Jotham knew she would still be there…watching them…gathering evidence. Slemi was like a hungry coyote. Once she had something in her teeth, she would never let go.

47

Jeremiah sat at his loom carefully weaving a new gown for the Gods. Vyx stood nearby closely watching him. "I think I remember this as a boy," he said. "I remember you sitting there. The weaving…I remember the weaving."

"The children have always come to watch me weave. I remember you well, Vyx. I remember you coming in with the other children to watch me weave. You were short for your age, and always laughing."

"Was I?"

"Yes," said Jeremiah. "It's amazing how tall you are now. And as for the laughing, you were sometimes known as Laughing Vyx.

"I do not remember that." Vyx looked at the completed gowns hanging on the wall. He walked over to inspect them closer. "The Gods will be pleased," he said. "Glory to the Gods!"

"Glory to the Gods," repeated Jeremiah.

"Did you weave that dress the Juju Witch is wearing?" Vyx asked as he abruptly turned and stared straight at Jeremiah.

"It was flawed…unsuitable for the Gods," Jeremiah quickly replied without looking up from his work.

"Why did you give it to her? Who is she to receive even a flawed gown from the Master Weaver?"

"She was naked. When the children found her, she was naked. Something had to be done."

"And so it was a convenient coincidence that you just happened to have this flawed gown?"

"Yes, a very convenient coincidence." Jeremiah looked up from his work, and stared Vyx in the eye. "If you are implying that I have done something wrong, Honourable Guardsman, Bugiah has seen the gown, and confirmed its imperfections. The God of Gods himself saw that it was unfit for a divine body."

"The God of Gods is perfect, and should know."

Jeremiah returned to his weaving.

"Did anyone see the Juju Witch come from a rock?"

"No, there are no witnesses. The children found her after the fact."

Vyx walked over to the window, and stared up at the sky. The sun was almost at midpoint. "Has anything unusual occurred since her arrival?"

"No. Nothing."

"Are you certain of that?"

"Yes, there has been nothing unusual."

"The death of our beloved God, Wermungi was unusual," said Vyx, turning to look again at Jeremiah.

Jeremiah kept on weaving and replied, "Surely you would not suggest that she has killed a God? No one is more powerful than a God. Glory to Gods!"

"Of…of course, a Guardsman would never suggest such a thing. The Gods are eternal. They cannot be killed. Glory to the power of the Gods!"

Before Vyx could ask anything more, an all too familiar sound suddenly echoed outside the cottage. *CLANG! CLANG! CLANG!* Jeremiah immediately stopped weaving, and stared at Vyx who stared back at him. The two men were dumbstruck with disbelief. It was the Black Bell! The Black Bell of Death was tolling once again! Another God was dead!

—————•—•—————

48

Slemi was on her way to Jotham's cottage. *I know what I saw. Something must be done about it before it's too late, if it's not too late already. I knew the Cobbler was trouble.*

All morning long, she had thought about nothing else, but the embrace she had seen between Jotham and Myanaymiz. With each passing hour her outrage grew until she finally resolved to go and confront them. *Let them just try to make excuses to cover their shame.* After that, she planned to report it to the Guardsman. *He would know what to do. How they should be punished.* She quickened her pace as she hurried along the road.

The Cobbler's cottage was in sight when, suddenly, she heard a sound that made her stop in her tracks. *No! It can't be. Not again!* The sound of the Black Bell was echoing once more throughout the land. *Another God! How can this happen?* She immediately decided to turn back and go see Jeremiah instead. The situation with the Cobbler would have to wait.

By the time she reached the Master Weaver's cottage, Jeremiah and Vyx were standing outside. "How can this be true?" she exclaimed as she hurried up the path. "How could this happen again?"

"I know no more than you," Jeremiah answered.

"It couldn't mean anything else, could it? It's not possible! It's just not possible!"

"The Black Bell tolls only to announce the death of a God," said Vyx.

In a desperate panic, Slemi turned to Vyx and reached out her hand. "Guardsman," she cried. He immediately stepped back before she could touch him. *No woman touches a Guardsman!* "Tell me what is happening! What can we do? We can't lose another God! Oh what will we do if we have lost another God? And who? Which one of our glorious deities was it this time? Oh, Gods help us!"

Vyx felt annoyed by Slemi's frenzied display. Her chaotic behavior was counter to the important orderly thoughts needed in times of crisis. *A Guardsman must always remain focussed. A Guardsman must always anticipate the needs of his Gods. My Gods will be requiring my immediate assistance. I must go to them.* He then looked at Jeremiah and said, "I shall return to the Mount of the Gods."

"Of course," said Jeremiah.

Without another word, Vyx went into the cottage to collect his things.

Slemi looked at Jeremiah. "It's that woman isn't it?" she said. "Somehow she is making this happen! And she's even put a spell on that Cobbler!"

"How dare you say such a thing!" replied Jeremiah. "The Gods are divine. The Gods are immortal! The Gods are all powerful! You have seen that woman…how small and insignificant she is. How can you say she is more powerful than a God? That is blasphemy!"

Slemi went red in the face. "I…I am sorry. I do not know what I am saying. It is all so very overwhelming. The Gods forgive me."

"I understand," said Jeremiah. "I am also very upset. Be assured, however, I will not report your sin against the Gods."

"Oh thank you! Thank you, Master Weaver!"

Vyx walked out of the cottage with his bag in hand. "I do not know when or if I will return," he said.

"If you do return, you are welcome here again," said Jeremiah, hoping he would not.

"I must go now."

Jeremiah and Slemi watched as Vyx walked off in the direction of the Celestial Path.

“What are we to do now?” pleaded Slemi who desperately wanted any bit of reassurance.

“We will do what we did last time,” said Jeremiah. “We will do our duty. Let us prepare for the Funeral of a God and the Time of Wailing.”

49

Jotham and Myanaymiz sat at the table. He was trying as best he could to prepare her for the visit from the Guardsman. "You must watch every word you say," he explained. "The smallest unintended slip could be used against you. Please understand that I am not exaggerating when I say that this is a life and death situation."

"Yes," said Myanaymiz. "It is very much a life and death situation. That is why I am here."

Jotham ran his hand through his hair. "Your answers are so confusing, Myanaymiz. I never know if you understand me or not."

"I understand you very well."

"Good. I hope so. Let us start with a question the Guardsman might ask. Do you believe that the Gods are divine? Now, how would you answer that?"

"God is One," she answered.

Jotham sighed. "No. You must answer; yes, the Gods are divine. Do you think you can do that?"

"Why would I do that?"

"Because otherwise they will kill you."

"This distresses you, doesn't it Jotham?"

"Of course it does! I don't want you to die!" He reached over, and grabbed hold of her hand.

"You do not have to worry. I have not come here to die. That is not what I do. That is not who I am."

Jotham couldn't help laughing at her naivety. "So who are you Myanaymiz? Who exactly are you?"

"Do you see me, and care for me?" she asked.

"Of course I see you, and I do care for you…very much."

"Then it is a pointless question. If you see me, and you care for me, then you know who I am."

Jotham laughed again. "You're making me dance in circles."

She smiled. "We should dance. It is always good to dance. All we need is some music."

CLANG! CLANG! CLANG! CLANG! Jotham could not believe his ears. He sprang up and ran to the door to listen. *Am I really hearing it again? It is tolling again! The Black Bell is tolling!* He turned and stared in disbelief at Myanaymiz who remained calmly seated at the table.

She looked over at him and smiled. "It would seem," she said, "that another one of your immortal gods is dead."

       Arlene Adamo

50

Jeremiah knelt before the white pillar. "Wash me clean that I might be worthy to be in the presence of the Gods," he prayed, miming the washing of his head. He then stood, turned and stared up the marble stairs in front of him. Bugiah would be waiting up there. Jeremiah never wanted to face him at the best of times, but today? He took in a deep breath. *No point in hesitating any longer. It must be done.* Jeremiah then slowly began to climb the stairs.

By the time he reached the top, he could already hear the weeping. *The Gods are gathered together in mourning as is required immediately after a death.*

Cautiously, he walked down the hall to the doorway and peered in. They were definitely distraught. Some were weeping on the divans. Others walked the floor wringing their hands in despair. Bugiah was sitting on his divan holding one of the Goddesses in his arms. She was crying uncontrollably. He looked up, and saw Jeremiah standing in the doorway. "Weaver!" he shouted, releasing the Goddess. "Come here!"

Jeremiah lowered his head, and walked slowly towards him. All of the Gods had stopped crying, and were now looking at Jeremiah. Bugiah got up from the divan and took two steps forward. Jeremiah stopped in his tracks. He did not dare get any closer.

"Another God dead?!" Bugiah shouted. "This time it was our beloved Dee-Kwad! What is happening Weaver? Dee-Kwad was even younger than Wermungi. These Gods should not be dead! It's that Juju Witch! Nothing like this ever happened before she arrived! She must be killed!"

Myanaymiz killed? Jeremiah felt his heart swell in his throat at the thought. He immediately dropped to his knees and exclaimed, "Oh God of Gods, although I am but a simple Weaver, I know that you are all powerful! So perfect and powerful! Surely there must be something far greater here at work than a simple waif found by children. Even if she is a Juju Witch, what is she when compared to you? When I see you all here in this room, in your wonderful divine glory, I am overwhelmed, and know that something great is coming! Has not the High Priest said that the time of Revelation is near? Surely this is a sign that he is right! Soon all of the Gods will be re-united in all of your magnificent glory! The dead will be resurrected as it is written in the Stories of the Gods, and we shall enter a new and golden age when the God of Gods will reign supreme over the universe. There shall be no more death among you! Your immortality will at last manifest in this world. Why, this is not the death of the great Dee-Kwad. No, this is no tragedy, but rather an affirmation of his wondrous eternal life…of the eternal life innate in the Gods alone…an eternal life that belongs to you and only you. Glory, glory, glory to the immortal Gods!" Jeremiah then bowed his head, and waited nervously in the thick silence that had descended upon the room. His old knees pressed into the hard black marble began to hurt as every second passed by like hours.

Just as Jeremiah was about to give up all hope, two words punctured through the dead air. "Oh, yes!" He looked up, and saw it was the Goddess whom Bugiah had been comforting. "Oh, the Weaver is right," she exclaimed. "Why do we weep, when we should be rejoicing? This is certainly a sign of great things to come, and our brother Dee-Kwad, he simply awaits us at the Gate of Eternity. Eternal life belongs to us…to the Gods! We are now coming ever closer to claiming our divine inheritance! I feel it! I know it is true! This is a wonderful sign of the final Revelation! Do you not see my divine brothers and sisters? Do you not feel it also?"

Bugiah stared suspiciously at Jeremiah.

　　　　　　　　　　　　　　　　　　Arlene Adamo

"We are all powerful!" asserted another one of the Gods. "The Weaver is correct! What would we have to fear from such a tiny Juju Witch? We are superior in every way. The death of Dee-Kwad is not a death at all, but simply a sign that our greatest glory shall at last be realized! We are the Eternal Ones!"

Bugiah looked around the room. All the Gods appeared to be in agreement. They had been given a sign of the coming of the great Revelation. It was not a time to worry or mourn. He looked down at Jeremiah kneeling before him. *The Weaver…always so docile and obedient…always so loyal to the God of Gods.* Bugiah then grinned, and suddenly declared, "Yes! This is indeed the truth! We Gods are superior in all respects, including our heightened sensitivities. Why, in our incredible capacity to grieve, we have been temporarily blinded to the truth. Upon reflection, there is no denying it. We are indeed coming closer to our eternal life. The Juju Witch is unimportant. We are the Gods! And we are on our way to eternal glory!"

Jeremiah breathed a quiet sigh of relief. "Glory to the Gods!" he declared aloud.

———◆———

51

Jotham sat quietly watching Myanaymiz eat. Usually, this brought him great delight. He loved how she praised every meal as if it were the greatest gift she had ever received, and how she would gratefully relish every bite. It was amazing to see someone made so happy by something he had always taken for granted. It gave him a fresh perspective. Now, however, he was too worried to find pleasure in it. *How can she eat so freely at a time like this?* he wondered, as outside the Black Bell continued to toll.

Jotham tapped his fingers nervously on the table. "We will be entering another Time of Wailing," he said.

Myanaymiz smiled at him. "The last Time of Wailing was very enjoyable."

Jotham ran his hand through his hair. "Everything has become so complicated and unpredictable. I have concerns for your safety. They may blame you for what has happened."

"Then they would be correct, Jotham."

Jotham looked at her in disbelief. "Did you just say that you caused the deaths of these Gods?"

"God is One and Eternal. God cannot die."

"But you did cause the deaths?"

"I am the cause, and I am the effect. That is why I was sent here."

"I do not understand. Who sent you here?"

Myanaymiz took a sip of tea and then replied, "My Lord sent me here."

"Who is your Lord?"

"My Lord is."

Jotham stood up and walked over to the window. He pulled open the curtains just a little, and peered out. Because everyone was home busily preparing for another Time of Wailing, the road was completely deserted. For a brief moment, it seemed as if they were the only ones left in Town. Everyone else had simply disappeared. No more Townsfolk, no more Gods, just them together in the cottage. *If only this were true.* "You are very confusing," he said, still staring out into the calm empty street. "Please don't tell anyone else what you have told me. Don't tell anyone that you are the cause. If you did, you would be in serious trouble."

Myanaymiz got up from the table, and stood behind Jotham. She placed her hand gently upon his shoulder and whispered into his ear, "Did I not remove your pain, and did I not make your scars disappear?"

"Yes," he sighed, "you did."

"Then believe in me, Jotham. That is all I ask in return…have faith and believe in me. Give me that, and you have given me everything you have to give."

———•◆•———

52

Jeremiah stood in the darkness at the bottom of the Mount of the Gods. The Burial Procession would be arriving shortly. As he waited, he stared up at the crescent moon. Strange, how large and bright it looked tonight. Had it ever looked that large and bright before? He couldn't remember, but he didn't think so. And there was such a lovely sense of peace and calm in the air. What a shame it would be when the Townsfolk would have to break this beautiful silence with their wailing, and him with his death chant.

He looked towards the Town, and could see the shadowy figures already lined up along the road. He knew they were in shock. Never before had the Townsfolk been faced with so much change, and so fast. Another Time of Wailing would definitely take a toll on them, and afterwards, they would certainly require the counsel of the High Priest.

Jeremiah looked back up at the moon, and thought about Myanaymiz. Why was it that every time she was threatened, he found himself coming to her defence? He had risked so much for her, but why? Even facing the God of Gods himself? What was that about? Certainly, he had always gone out of his way to help the Townsfolk whenever they were in trouble. That's just the kind of person he was. But this was different. There was a strange desperate compulsion within him to protect her. Where did this come from, and why was she becoming all he could really think about whenever he sat at his loom?

Jeremiah stared up the Celestial Path. He could now hear the sound of horses' hooves not far off. He began to rehearse the Sounds of Mourning in his mind. *Yoo ismee ta, yoo ismee ta.*

Within a few moments, the great black geldings appeared around the bend. The coach driver carefully made his way down the hill, and stopped in front of Jeremiah. Bugiah, with holy lantern in hand, rode up on his red steed.

"Master Weaver, prepare the way for your Gods to reach the Gate of Eternity!" he commanded.

As he did once before, Jeremiah bowed low to the ground and replied, "My Gods, I am here to serve you."

53

After walking through the Town in the daylight and seeing everything so clearly, it was strange to be looking at it from behind the black veil once again. The world that had been revealed in bright and vibrant colors had now been washed over in dark grey. It just didn't seem real. It was like a bad dream. *I want to wake up.*

Along with the twelve other Guardsmen, Vyx marched in line behind the horses of the Gods. Every once in a while his boot would land in something soft, and the smell of manure would rise up, and linger beneath his veil. *I must not slip. I must stay sure footed.*

The Townsfolk wailed loudly as the Burial Procession moved forward. Their mournful unrelenting calls pierced through the night air. Vyx tried as best he could to block out the horrible noise, but it was not easy. *One, two, three, foot, foot, foot, one, two, three….*

The smell of manure was growing ever stronger as the fumes became trapped underneath his veil. Vyx could feel it begin to stick in his throat. He tried to get some fresh air by lightly blowing on the black fabric to push it a little from his face, but he had to be careful. If he blew too hard someone might notice that he was not focussing on his funeral duties, and report it to one of the Gods. It was the duty of every Guardsman to report on each others' wrongdoings.

⋯⋅◆⋅⋯

54

Jotham and Myanaymiz stood side by side in the dark. As they heard the wails of the Townsfolk growing ever louder, Jotham reached over and grabbed her hand. "Please remember to begin to wail when the Burial Procession comes into view," he said. "If you do not do this, a Guardsman will pull out his sword and strike you down without mercy."

"You must stop worrying so much, Jotham. It will all be fine," she said, as she moved closer so that her shoulder now rested against his arm. Deep comforting warmth ran through his body.

"Do you see the moon?" she asked. "Is it not beautiful?"

Jotham looked up. The silver crescent looked more than three times its normal size and many more times brighter. "Yes," he said. "It is amazing."

"Then sing a song about it."

"Now? But we are required to remain silent."

"We have already broken the law by speaking, and you are now an outlaw singer, so fulfill your nature… break the law and sing."

Jotham smiled then checked down the road. The Burial Procession was not yet in view. He looked up at the moon once more, paused for a moment and began to softly sing:

Moon, do to me
The thing you do to me
Tear me in pieces
Then sew me

Glue me
Renew me
And make me one
Make me one
Make me one
With you forever more

"That is a beautiful song, Jotham! You are becoming such an excellent writer."

Jotham smiled. "It's magic how these words flow out of me."

"Yes," she said. "Beautiful men shall receive beautiful magic."

"Do you think I'm beautiful?" he laughed.

"Yes, you are very beautiful."

Just then Jotham noticed the lights out of the corner of his eye. "They are coming," he said. He then opened his mouth, and began to wail into the night sky.

⸻ ◆ ⸻

55

As the Burial Procession moved towards to the edge of Town, Jeremiah could now see Jotham and Myanaymiz standing at the side of the road. As he got closer, he thought he could hear Jotham's wailing over his own chanting. But what was Myanaymiz doing? He couldn't hear her, but then again her voice was soft… perhaps too soft to hear from this distance. Jotham would certainly try his best to ensure that she followed the law. Jeremiah knew this. But was he able to convince her to do the one thing that would keep her safe this night? Was he able to convince her to cry like the rest of them? *Please wail, Myanaymiz! This is a life or death situation! Please wail!*

56

Vyx was surprised when the Burial Procession suddenly came to a full stop. He was even more surprised as he watched Bugiah's horse step out of line, and the God of Gods ride up to the front of the procession. *Not again! It must be that Juju Witch! What has she done this time?*

The next thing he saw was the assistant to the coach driver jumping down, and hurrying in the direction of the Guardsmen. "Guardsman Vyx?" he called as he got closer. "Which one of you is Guardsman Vyx?"

"I am he," said Vyx.

"Come with me," he said. "The God of Gods requires your service."

Vyx quickly followed the man towards the front of the procession. He ignored the Weaver, the Cobbler and Juju Witch who were standing at the side of the road, and approached the God of Gods who was still on horseback. Bowing his head, Vyx asked, "My Greatest God, what do you require of me?"

"This Juju Witch has sinned against the Gods by not wailing during the Burial Procession!" screamed Bugiah. "Strike her dead!"

"No!" shouted Jotham, jumping in front of her.

"My God!" exclaimed Jeremiah, moving over beside Jotham to face Bugiah. "Oh my great God, she is so simple, and you are so powerful and all knowing! Give her one last chance! I beg of you in all your divine wonder!"

Bugiah looked at the two men standing so foolishly in front of him. *Had the Juju Witch put a spell on the both of them?* He then looked at Myanaymiz. She did look so small and non-threatening from where he sat. He thought carefully about it. *If I strike her down with the Weaver and the Cobbler begging for mercy, it would make for an impressive Story of the Gods. But if I give her one last chance before striking her down, this would make for an even more impressive story… Bugiah, the omnipotent God of Gods, offering a poor simple Juju Witch one final chance at redemption. And what a fine painting that would make in the Hall of the Gods.*

"Very well," he said. "As the great merciful God of Gods, I will give this simple Juju Witch one last chance to obey the law. If she does not follow through, and follow through in a way that pleases me, then you, Guardsman, will strike her dead."

"Oh thank you! Thank you, great and merciful God of Gods!" exclaimed Jeremiah, as he dropped to his knees.

Jotham turned to Myanaymiz, grabbed her by her shoulders and said, "You must cry, Myanaymiz. Please cry! Do this for me! Please!"

"What am I crying for?" she asked.

Bugiah was beginning to lose patience. "You are crying to open the Gate of Eternity, simpleton!"

"Please!" begged Jotham.

"If you wish me to, Jotham, I will cry as to open the Gate of Eternity."

Jotham's hands dropped from her shoulders as he breathed a sigh of relief. "Cry now, Myanaymiz and cry loudly!"

Myanaymiz then opened her mouth and began to cry out.

THAT SOUND! THAT SOUND!

Jotham immediately put his hands to his ears, and fell to the ground. Jeremiah, who had still been kneeling, fell over, his hands tightly clasped over his ears. The coach driver tried to block the sound with his arms while at the same time trying to gain control over the six black geldings. The Gods' steeds had all reared up, throwing each and every one of them to the ground, their holy lanterns falling and exploding into small fires upon impact. Bugiah himself was now lying in the dirt, hands tightly clamped against his ears. The legs of Vyx and his fellow Guardsman buckled, and they were brought to their knees, now helpless to defend their Gods.

The coach driver, still trying to control the horses, quickly realized that there was only one thing he could do to save his life. He released the reigns, and jumped down to the ground, covering his ears as he did. The black geldings then immediately bolted free, following after the runaway steeds. As they ran, the funeral carriage bounced furiously along the road. The holy lanterns began to fall off one after the other, each exploding into flames as they hit the ground. As the last of the holy lanterns fell to the earth, the horses suddenly veered off the road, and into a field. The carriage twisted over, and was now being dragged on its side. There was glass shattering, and wood splintering as the entire thing was ripped to pieces by the force of the frightened horses. The body of the God spilled out, face down, into a mess of glass, wood and mud. The black geldings ran off into the darkness dragging behind them the axle and a single broken wheel.

———•◆•———

$$57$$

Well hidden by the darkness of the forest, Jotham huddled close to Myanaymiz. "Why are we hiding?" she asked him.

Jotham couldn't help but laugh at her question. He protectively pulled her closer. "Do you have any idea what you just did?"

"I cried as they commanded me to," she replied.

"That was crying?"

"Yes, that was crying to open the Gate of Eternity. That is what Bugiah asked me to do."

"I'm quite sure Bugiah was not expecting that!"

"I know he was not." Myanaymiz stretched out her legs in front of her. "We ran very fast," she said.

"We had to run very fast. Luckily I remembered this secret hiding place that Axis had built for himself. We should be safe here, at least for tonight. I'm not sure what we will do when the sun rises. We will need supplies if we are to flee this Town."

Myanaymiz reached over and caressed his face. "You would do that for me? You would run away from this Town?"

"Yes, I would."

"That is so kind, but you do not have to do that, Jotham. It is not necessary."

"You have turned my world completely upside down," he said.

"And do you like it?" she asked. "Was it exciting to watch the Gods fall from their horses? Did you feel exhilarated when we ran away into the forest?"

Jotham sighed, and then smiled. *Why am I smiling? We are in great danger? I should be worrying right now. This is a real life and death situation.* "Yes," he replied. "It was all very exciting."

"They will not come this way tonight," she whispered into his ear. "We are alone. And although we cannot see it through the roof of our hiding place, the moon is just as bright and beautiful as it was before. Bugiah has no power to pull it down. He has no power to find us. We are safe, and we are alone together." She leaned even closer into him. "You are a good man, Jotham, and I need a good man."

———•◆•———

                    Arlene Adamo

58

Vyx walked very slowly as he led the great red steed through the Palace gates. The horse was limping, and occasionally whinnied in pain. Its right leg had been injured sometime during its flight.

The night has been very long for Vyx. Finding the steed had not been easy, but just as the sun was rising, he spotted him near the river. The creature was still spooked, and tried to bolt. If it wasn't lame, it would have gotten away before he could grab it. Some of the other horses were still missing.

Vyx felt a little dizzy, and exhaustion was beginning to scramble his thoughts. All he wanted to do was to return to the security of his private cell and sleep. He desperately needed to remove his armor along with his veil that was now so heavy with the stink of manure and sweat that he felt like he could hardly breathe.

As he led the horse into the stables, he was greeted by the relieved Stable Master. "Guardsman, you found him!"

"Yes, but unfortunately he is injured in his right leg."

The Stable Master ran his hand over the leg. The look of relief on his face changed to that of concern. "He will have to be examined by the Physician to the Horses," he said. "I am not qualified to deliver a report to the God of Gods."

This was not good news. If it were good news, the Stable Master would have been pleased to deliver a report himself.

"The God of Gods will surely be resting throughout the day," said Vyx, knowing that it would be better if the bad news arrived after Bugiah's long afternoon nap. "Our Lord will not require a report until this evening. Have the Physician come to the Palace after the early evening meal." He then turned and left the stable.

As Vyx walked through the courtyard, he glanced down and noticed his boots were caked in manure and mud. The sight filled him with dread. *Boots must always be shiny and spotless. They reflect the pride of the Guardsman…*this was on the first page in the Guardsman's Rule Book. He then felt a sudden stabbing pain in his stomach, but it was not hunger. He was trained to deal with hunger. This was something else…a pain he had never felt before. He looked up through his veil at the dulled grey sky above. *Oh, the agony of chaos! The body of the God still unburied! Needing to be washed and prepared all over again. So many laws have been broken, and now without a funeral carriage, holy lanterns or even a horse for the God of Gods, how can the Burial Procession proceed according to the law? What is happening? Is this the power of the Juju Witch? Is she more powerful than the Gods?* "Blasphemy!" said Vyx, accusing himself aloud. "The Gods are all powerful! Glory to the Gods!"

       Arlene Adamo

59

Jeremiah paced back and forth across the floor of his cottage. He could not sleep. He knew he should. He knew he had to. The worst was yet to come, and he should be prepared. Sleep was of the utmost importance. He stopped and stared at the partially finished gown in his loom. The Festival of the Gods was not far off. *Would there even be a Festival?* This idea was completely unthinkable only a short time ago. Everything had changed so quickly? *The God of Gods will be filled with anger! And how will the Town get through this? How will I get through this? And where are Myanaymiz and Jotham?*

"Oh, Myanaymiz! Myanaymiz!" he cried aloud. "Things were so simple before you appeared. Where are you now?"

"Old Jeremiah," said a tiny voice. Jeremiah turned and saw Axis standing in the open door.

Jeremiah's first thought was to chastise the child for wandering outside during the Time of Wailing, but then he wondered if the laws of the Time of Wailing were still in place considering everything that had happened. After all, the burial had still not taken place. "Axis, you should probably not be here right now. You should return home."

"But Old Jeremiah, I need a loaf of bread and some water."

In his exhaustion, Jeremiah felt himself losing patience with the child. "So why do you come to me? Go home and ask your mother to feed you."

"But it is not for me, Old Jeremiah. It is for the Cobbler and our Lady."

Jeremiah rushed to the doorway. "Where are they?" he asked.

"In my secret house," said Axis. "I went there this morning, and found them."

"You must show me where your secret house is."

"Will you bring bread and water?"

"Yes," replied Jeremiah. "I will bring them bread and water… and some meat also. You must show me where they are, but we must go secretly so that no one sees us. No one but you and I must know where they are. Can you keep this secret, Axis?"

Axis was so excited. His wonderful secret house suddenly had even more secrets…it was a game of secrets. "Yes Old Jeremiah, no one but us will know where they are hiding."

——•◆•——

     Arlene Adamo

60

As Jeremiah followed Axis to the edge of the forest, he saw in the distance a group of Guardsmen making their way down the Celestial Path. *It must be a search party.* "Quickly into the trees," he told the child. "We cannot be seen. That is the most important part of this game."

Axis happily hurried into the woods. "Just follow me, Old Jeremiah. Try not to get lost."

"I will try not to," Jeremiah smiled.

Axis led Jeremiah on a long and winding route, taking him past areas of the forest Jeremiah never knew existed. "Are you alright, Old Jeremiah?" he asked, after they had walked for a while. "Do you need to rest?"

Jeremiah suddenly realized that he had forgotten completely about his fatigue. In fact, he was now feeling more energized than ever. "I am just fine," he answered.

A little further on, Axis suddenly stopped at a small rocky ledge. "It's here," he said, jumping down. "Follow me."

When Jeremiah climbed down, he found himself standing in front of a peculiar tangle of branches. At first glance, it looked as if several trees had collapsed in upon each other, but upon closer inspection he could see how the many branches had been carefully woven in and out of each other to create what appeared to be a roof and walls. *What an ingenious creation!*

Axis got down on his hands and knees, and disappeared through an opening. Jeremiah got down too, and followed after him."

"It's alright," said Axis, loudly. "It's just me and Old Jeremiah."

"Jeremiah, is it you?"

Jotham! "Hello," answered Jeremiah. He crawled in further, and found that, considering how insignificant the little house looked from the outside, it opened up into a surprisingly large room. The floor was made of old dry wooden planks, and there was just enough light shining through several tiny openings in the walls to fill it with a warm glow. *What a strangely comfortable place!*

Jotham and Myanaymiz were in a corner sitting together upon sheep skins. It was then that Jeremiah remembered the formal complaint lodged months ago by one of the Townsfolk over some missing sheep skins.

"It is good to see you my friend," said Jotham.

"I was so worried about your safety," replied Jeremiah. He looked at Myanaymiz. She smiled at him.

"Welcome! Come in and take a seat in our castle," laughed Jotham.

Jeremiah was not very pleased to hear Jotham make jokes at a time like this. He crawled over, and sat on the edge of the sheep skin in front of Myanaymiz. "I brought you some water and food," he said, taking the bag from his shoulder, and handing it to Jotham.

Jotham immediately opened it and handed the waterbag to Myanaymiz who quickly untied the opening, and took a drink. He then pulled out the bread and the dried meat which were wrapped in white cloths. Spreading out the cloths upon the floor, he then broke the bread and meat into pieces. Myanaymiz took a piece of meat, and began to eat. "Everyone, help yourselves," said Jotham, taking a large bite of bread, and then washing it down with some water.

"No thank you. I'm not hungry," said Jeremiah, while Axis quickly scooped up a piece of bread along with some meat.

"Axis, would you go outside and stand watch for a while," said Jeremiah.

"I will be your Guardsman!" Axis chirped.

"That is right. You are our Guardsman. Now go outside and stand guard o' fearless Guardsman."

Axis put the bread and meat between his teeth then crawled out of the secret house.

As soon as Jeremiah was certain that Axis was outside, he turned to Jotham and asked, "What are we going to do?"

"Myanaymiz and I could run away."

"I have already told you that will not be necessary, Jotham," said Myanaymiz.

Jeremiah looked at Myanaymiz. He had never been this close to her before. "What are we to do then?" he asked.

Myanaymiz looked directly into his eyes. "You will convince Bugiah that I would be of use to him."

Before Jeremiah could respond, Jotham exclaimed, "That would be too dangerous! It's better if we run away from here."

Myanaymiz turned to Jotham. "You cannot leave here. What will the children do for shoes? And I cannot leave here. Not yet. This is where I must wait for my Lord."

"And who is your Lord?" asked Jeremiah.

Myanaymiz ignored his question and said, "You are a very persuasive man, Young-Old Jeremiah. Only you can make Bugiah see that I am of value to him. This is the way."

Jeremiah was surprised by her request. "But even if it were possible for me to do this, he would expect you to serve him in every respect, and if you did not do so, and to his full satisfaction, he would kill you."

Jotham cringed at the thought.

"I have not come here to die," she told them. "Bugiah will not harm me. No one will harm me. My Lord would not allow it. You, Jeremiah, will go to Bugiah and refer to the Book of Zetmi from the Stories of the Gods. In the story, the God Zetmi is threatened with destruction by his enemies, but with the help of a Juju Witch he is able to defeat them. Bugiah already believes I am a Juju Witch. If he thinks I can help him bring about the Resurrection of the Gods, he will not try to kill me. You must persuade him that I can help. I will deal with anything that comes after that. Do not worry."

Jeremiah was surprised by Myanaymiz. Perhaps she wasn't as naive as she seemed. Had he been seeing her all wrong?

"Now go," she said. "Go do what you must. Jotham and I will remain here for now. When you have convinced Bugiah I would be an asset to him, then return and let us know that it is safe to come out of hiding."

"I'm afraid for her," Jotham said to Jeremiah. "But I also know from experience that she will not back down. She is very stubborn. You have no alternative, but to do as she requests."

Before Jeremiah could object again, Myanaymiz reached forward and took hold of his hand. A small wave of heat moved up through his arm, over his shoulder and into the nape of his neck, leaving a strange tingling sensation in the back of his head. "There is nothing to worry about," she said. "It is as it should be. Go and convince Bugiah that he requires the help of a Juju Witch. This is not only about my well-being, but it is about you and Jotham, and the children, and all of the good people who live in the Town. There are some very good people in the Town, Young-Old Jeremiah. You know that. You have risked much over the years to protect and care for them. Now, they are in great danger…a danger neither you nor they can see. And I can save them, but I need your help. If you want to save your people, you must do as I tell you."

Jeremiah was at a loss for words. *Danger…she talks of danger. What kind of danger? She needs my help. She asked for my help. Oh, what is that strange calmness in her eyes! It is confusing me. Should I look away? What is it…that calmness? Is it like a warm sunny day? No. Not something that benign. It is like…like the stillness at the center of a raging fire? …a furious commanding stillness. Drawing me forward… deliciously dangerous…strangely soothing. Making me…making me…* "I…I will do my best," he suddenly found himself saying.

Myanaymiz smiled. "You are a good man, Young-Old Jeremiah. That is who you are, and that is what you do."

———•·•———

 Arlene Adamo

61

Before Jeremiah left the forest, he instructed Axis to exit another way. "It is important that we are not seen together. Return home and remember not to tell anyone about your secret house. If you do, then everyone will want to go there, and it wouldn't be a secret anymore."

"Don't worry Old Jeremiah, I am good at secrets," replied Axis, running off and disappearing behind some trees.

Jeremiah stepped out into the field, and then followed the well trod foot path to the road. As he walked in the direction of his cottage, he saw someone hurrying towards him. It was Slemi!

"Oh Weaver! What has she done! I heard that sound last night! They say she made that horrible sound! Oh, our dear Gods have suffered from her black magic! The great Dee-Kwad left in the mud! Where is that woman now? Dead I hope!"

"You must calm down," said Jeremiah. "The Gods are fine and back in the Palace. They are all powerful, and did not suffer. No one has the power to make them suffer."

"No…of course not," said Slemi. "I did not mean…she broke the laws! She broke the laws of the Burial Procession!"

"She did not understand the laws," explained Jeremiah. "That sound you heard was the sound of her crying. She was obeying the God of Gods. It is simply that no one expected her crying to be so…so forceful. But that is what is required of us all to open the Gate of Eternity. We must all wail during the Burial Procession, and wail as loud as we can. This is precisely what she did."

Slemi was silent. She didn't like any of this, but there was no arguing against Jeremiah's logic. The law was the law. She would need to address her concerns from another angle. "There is something going on between her and that Cobbler," she quickly said.

Suddenly, Jeremiah saw a Guardsman coming out from behind a cottage. "Oh look, a Guardsman comes this way. Glory to the Gods, Honourable Guardsman!" he called out as the man approached them.

"Are you the Weaver?" asked the Guardsman.

"I am."

"Have you seen that Juju Witch?"

"No. I have looked, but I have not seen her."

"I think she is with the Cobbler," said Slemi.

"So, you know where she is! Where is she?" the Guardsman demanded.

"Oh no, Honourable Guardsman!" Slemi exclaimed in fear. "I don't know where she is…I was only saying…"

The Guardsman abruptly turned to Jeremiah. "You must come to the Palace of the Gods after the later day meal," he said. "The funeral of Dee-Kwad the Immortal will be held then. Tell the people of the Town that the Time of Wailing must be adhered to, and will commence immediately."

"Oh yes, Honourable Guardsman! The Time of Wailing is nigh. I will return to my home now," said Slemi who then quickly scurried off.

"I understand Honourable Guardsman," said Jeremiah, bowing his head. "The will of the Gods be done."

"The will of the Gods be done," said the Guardsman who then turned and headed towards the Mount of the Gods.

Jeremiah began to quickly walk in the direction of his cottage. *I must now hurry and re-read the Book of Zetmi. If I am going to have any chance at all of convincing Bugiah to spare Myanaymiz, I will need to be very well prepared.*

———•◆•———

62

Jotham was curled up asleep on the sheep skin. Myanaymiz leaned over and kissed his cheek. "You are a good man," she softly whispered. "My Lord will bless you for the way you have treated me." He stirred a little, but did not wake up.

She then quietly crawled out of the hiding place, and sat on a rock outside of the entrance. It was a beautiful warm night as she breathed in the deep rich scent of the forest. *O' fragrance of life! Glorious fragrance of life! What wonderful promises you hide! And how you defy death at every turn!*

The tree leaves suddenly rustled as a warm moist breeze blew in. It gently caressed her face and pushed back her hair. *O' my Lord! My Lord! You come to me! You reassure me that You are here with me. But when will I see You? When will I see You?*

She sighed then stared down at the shadowy outline of her hands. How alone they seemed without someone to touch. Looking at them now, she couldn't help but think of all the lines they had scratched into the rock. *The lines…so many the lines! Lines carved from my dreams…all my many long and lonely dreams in my long and lonely sleep! Some I remember. Some I forget. Some I will remember again. Some I may sadly want to forget forever.*

"My Lord," she whispered into the night. "I am awake now, and have seen many things from outside the rock. It is not good, but I will try to save what good there is. Be with me. Keep me from harm. Help me to prepare. My battle is beginning. As it always has been…as it always will be, the light will conquer darkness once again."

———•◆•———

<h1 style="text-align:center">63</h1>

Bugiah signalled Jeremiah and the priest to pull the rope. As they pulled, the stone slab holding Dee-Kwad's body moved slowly into the vault. They then rolled the stone seal in front of the opening. The God's symbol carved into the seal was the holy symbol for riches, a serpent devouring a man.

"All hail the Immortal Gods!" declared the priest who then bowed his head. The Gods immediately began to file out of the tomb.

When it was time for Jeremiah to take his leave, he hesitated a moment. *Will the God of Gods expect me to stay behind as he did before?* Bugiah, however, remained facing the vault with his back towards Jeremiah. It quickly became clear that, this time, he intended to follow the burial laws. Jeremiah silently turned and headed for the exit.

Walking down the long dark tunnel with only a lit torch at the end to guide him, Jeremiah wondered, how, after all that had happened, could he ever convince Bugiah that Myanaymiz was someone who could help him. *Has she asked for the impossible? Yes, I am skilled in persuasion, but this? This may be far beyond my talents. Has she placed too much faith in me?*

As he stepped out into the moonlit night, someone suddenly grabbed him by the shoulder. Jeremiah turned and stared up into the empty black veil of a Guardsman.

"Weaver!"

He instantly recognized the voice. It was Vyx.

"You must come with me," he said. "There is an important meeting of the Gods, and they require your presence."

"Of course," answered Jeremiah. "I am here to assist in any way possible."

———•◦•———

64

Jeremiah had waited a long time downstairs, and now he waited again in the open doorway of the Hall of the Gods. He looked at the fine delicacies that were heaped high upon the long rectangular table. He knew this to be in accordance with the law. *Whilst the Townsfolk wail to send the God down the river Broma to the Place of Waiting, the Mount of the Gods shall be filled with feasting and repose.*

Bugiah sat in his place at the head of the table. Every once in a while he'd glance over at Jeremiah standing in the doorway, but otherwise ignored him whilst continuing to eat and laugh with the other Gods.

Jeremiah had not eaten in a long time, and the smell of the food was beginning to get to him. He started to feel a little dizzy, and his legs began to tremble. *Don't fall. Don't fall old Weaver. If you fall, you will fail. You cannot fail. Not this time.*

Just as he thought his legs would surely buckle beneath him, Bugiah raised his arm and beckoned him forward. *Oh merciful Heavens, thank you!*

As he quickly walked down the length of the table, Jeremiah could feel all the eyes of the Gods upon him. When he reached Bugiah, he went down on one knee and said, "My God, you have summoned me."

Bugiah wiped the grease from his mouth. "Weaver, where has that Juju Witch gone?"

"My God, I do not know."

"They say the Cobbler is missing also. Is this true?"

"Yes, my God."

"I have dispatched Guardsmen to search past the parameters of the Town. If they imagined they would escape, they are wrong."

"My God," said Jeremiah. "If I may speak openly, this entire situation has left me with many thoughts."

"What kind of thoughts?"

"I have considered carefully what you have told me about how the Lady's appearance has something to do with the Time of Revelation, and you, oh great God of Gods, are perfect. I know that you are never wrong."

"This is true," said Bugiah. He then took a drink from his wine goblet.

"Therefore, in accordance with my sacred duties as Master Weaver to the Gods, I began reading through the Stories of the Gods in search of clarity, and for the longest time I was unable to decipher the signs. All of the strange events that have happened simply did not make any sense. How was I to piece any of it together? Then suddenly, just as I was about to give up, there it was!"

"What? What was there?" asked Bugiah, perking up with interest.

"The truth," answered Jeremiah. "Oh great God of Gods, with your help I was led straight to the truth. The answers are all there in the Book of Zetmi!"

Bugiah set down his goblet. "What is in the Book of Zetmi?" he demanded. "Explain!"

"My God, just listen to the words," said Jeremiah:

"And Zetmi said, "Everywhere I look, I stare into the faces of my enemies. They have surrounded me." That is when he knew he must call for the Juju Witch. When the Juju Witch was brought before him, he said, "Juju Witch you must help me. My enemies are powerful and threaten to destroy me." The Juju Witch answered, "If I help you, you must promise to let me live out my days in peace, and not be persecuted for being a Juju Witch." Zetmi, in his wisdom, knew that this was the right thing to do, and formed an alliance with the Juju Witch.

…and of course you, my God, know how the book ends. With the help of the Juju Witch, Zetmi's enemies were destroyed." Jeremiah then waited quietly while Bugiah mulled it over.

"But there are no longer any enemies of the Gods," he finally said. "Of what use is a Juju Witch to me?"

"Well yes, this is true," Jeremiah replied. "But in the Book of the Resurrection of the Gods, it states that: *A power shall assist them disguised as the powerless.* And as you, my God, have stated, this is the time of Revelation, and the resurrection of the Gods is at hand. Who would appear more powerless than a woman, naked and alone? And did not her crying reveal the power within her? She is a power disguised as the powerless. And she was certainly following your command at the time she demonstrated this great power, which just shows that her ultimate purpose is to be obedient to the Gods, and to the God of Gods in particular."

Bugiah thought about it, then asked, "If she were here to be obedient to the Gods, why has she caused so much chaos, and broken so many laws?"

"She is a Juju Witch. Her nature is that of the untamed. She simply requires the proper guidance of the wise and great Gods," explained Jeremiah. "As Zetmi once guided the Juju Witch, so you in your great wisdom will guide this Juju Witch. You are the God of Gods during this important time for a reason. No other God possesses the strength that you do. This is divine destiny. The resurrection of the Gods is dependent upon you, but to do this you will require the right tools. The Juju Witch is a tool of great power…a tool meant for your use."

Bugiah looked down the table at the other Gods who stared at him in wonder. "The Weaver is right about one thing," he said to them. "I am the God of Gods who will usher in the Resurrection. But the question is, do I need this Juju Witch or should I kill her?" He remembered how she had shamelessly disobeyed him. How could he trust her? What if she disobeyed him in front of the other Gods?

Jeremiah took in a deep breath and said, "Oh great God of Gods, she is only a servant to you, as we in the Town are all your servants. I weave your gowns. The Cobbler makes your shoes. The farmers and tradesmen work hard every day to ensure that the Gods are kept in comfort. You are the Gods…so powerful…so magnificent! She can and she will serve you. That power is yours! The Gods have always used well their servants. She belongs to you, as do I and all of the others. And we have only seen perhaps one part of the power she holds. What more does she have to offer?"

Bugiah never thought of that. The crying power was impressive, but what if she had more? And what if he were able to learn how to do these things himself? Of course he would be able to learn…he was the God of Gods. He would be able to take her knowledge for himself. She could always be killed afterwards if she displeased him, but if he killed her right away, he would never learn her secrets.

"Weaver, she is indeed a simple Juju Witch in need of divine guidance. She must be taught to do the right thing…just like a child or a dog. Guardsman!"

The Guardsman who was standing by the door rushed over to Bugiah. "My God," he said, getting down on one knee. When he spoke, Jeremiah realized it was Vyx.

"I am repealing my order to kill the Juju Witch. Instead, she is to live, but she must be found. She must be found so that I may instruct her."

"And the Cobbler, my God?" asked Jeremiah. "He was misguided in his attempt to protect her, but he is an obedient subject."

"Kill the Cobbler," said Bugiah. "He has been trouble before."

"But, my God, we have only one Cobbler to make shoes, and also the Juju Witch seems very fond of him. You could use the Cobbler to your advantage. He could be useful in training her. Also, as a loyal subject, he could assist you in uncovering other powers she may possess."

Bugiah carefully considered Jeremiah's points. After a moment, he said, "I am a merciful God, and therefore the Cobbler can live. I think I would also like another new pair of shoes before the Festival. But I do not wish her to stay in his cottage again. She will stay with you, Weaver."

"With me? My God, how can she stay with me whilst I weave the gowns for the Gods? Is that not against the law?"

"It is only against the law for Townsfolk to remain in the cottage. She is not Townsfolk. She is a Juju Witch."

"Of course, my God," replied Jeremiah. "You are so very wise."

"And Guardsman…"

"Yes, my great God of Gods," replied Vyx

"You shall return to the Town, and stay with the Cobbler. That way you may keep an eye on him as well as learn more about the Juju Witch."

"As you wish, my God."

"Now Weaver, all we have to do is find the runaways."

"You are the God of Gods," said Jeremiah. "With you all things are possible."

"Yes they are," said Bugiah. "With me all things are possible. Now both of you, go and find that Juju Witch!"

———•◆•———

65

"I do not want you to worry," said Myanaymiz, as she stroked Jotham's hair. He was lying on the sheep skin with his head in her lap.

"I don't know if I can stop from worrying. This is all so strange. I don't know what to think anymore."

"There are times when the greatest truth is found in dreaming and feeling, not in thinking," she replied, softly caressing his brow.

"It's all so simple here, in a child's secret house, but out there? There is the real danger. There is where Bugiah rules, and you know he wants to kill us."

She ran her finger down the edge of his ear. "Jeremiah has convinced him not to."

"How can you be so sure that Jeremiah will be successful? And if he is, what does that mean for you? Will you now be forced to serve Bugiah until he considers you no longer useful to live? Oh, how I wish we could fly away, just you and me."

Myanaymiz smiled. "You do not understand," she said. "When I first came from the rock, I did not understand either, but now I do. I will never serve Bugiah. That is not what I do. That is not who I am. I did not come here to serve any man. But I do know something now. I do know the truth."

"And what is that?" asked Jotham.

Myanaymiz softly traced his lips with her finger. "That Bugiah will serve me," she said.

———⋅•⋅———

66

Jeremiah hurried past the cottages. As the Townsfolk were all busy adhering to the Time of Wailing, the doors were closed and the curtains drawn. Regardless, he was still nervous that someone might accidently see him as he made his way towards the forest. Even though the execution orders had been repealed, questions would be asked if someone were to spot him, and it could possibly come to light that he knew where Myanaymiz and Jotham were hiding. *Just please don't let me run into a Guardsman.*

Reaching the back gate of Jotham's cottage, he then turned to check that no one was following him. There was no one in sight. From the garden, he could enter the forest without the risk of being seen. Adjusting his shoulder bag containing food and water, he then unlatched the gate and entered.

As he made his way through the tall trees of the forest, he worried that he might not remember how to find Axis' secret house. *That tree with the missing bark…I remember that tree. Was it to the right? No wait. I came in through that direction last time, so it is to the left.* After a couple of wrong turns and some back tracking, he was relieved to see the rocky ledge where he knew the secret house was hidden. Once more he looked around to ensure that no Guardsman had followed him. He saw no one. Climbing down the ledge, he then softly called out, "It is I, Jeremiah."

"Is there any news?" Jotham eagerly asked from inside.

Jeremiah crawled in, and saw Myanaymiz and Jotham sitting close together on the sheep skin. They seemed in good spirits considering their confinement. He sat next to Myanaymiz and answered "Yes, there is news. You will be able to leave here, and return to the Town, but I suggest that you wait until nightfall. I brought something to sustain you until then." He handed Myanaymiz the bag containing food and water.

"So, you are saying that you were successful in convincing Bugiah not to harm us?" Jotham asked, still having a difficult time believing Jeremiah had actually managed to do the impossible.

"I was. He has repealed the death order for both of you. However, we still must be cautious about everything we do. Rather than show up with all those Guardsmen about, I would prefer that you come out only after dark. By that time, they will have already returned to the Mount of the Gods. It is best to reduce the risk of any sort of accidental confrontation. The situation is very fragile and unpredictable."

"And what about Myanaymiz? What exactly will happen to her? She will not have to go to the Palace, will she?"

"Thankfully, the Gods would never permit someone they believe to be a Juju Witch to live among them. She will remain in the Town."

"Good," said Jotham.

"But she will not be able to stay with you anymore. Bugiah has forbid it."

"Where then will she stay?" Jotham did not like this. He wanted it to be as it was before. He wanted her to stay in his cottage with him.

"She is to stay with me," said Jeremiah, glancing for a moment at Myanaymiz who was drinking the water he had brought.

"With you!" Jotham exclaimed. For a moment, he stared at his old friend…the long gray hair, the beard, the lines around his eyes. "I suppose if she is not allowed to stay with me, staying with you is the best alternative."

"Do not worry, Jotham. I will take very good care of her. However, you will have a new guest, I'm afraid."

"A new guest?"

"Yes, your old friend Vyx."

"A Guardsman! I don't want a Guardsman living in my home!"

"You have no choice, Jotham. And it is not forever."

Jotham looked at Myanaymiz. She reached over and gently touched his face. "Do not worry so much. It will be alright. This is the way," she said.

"Bugiah wants Vyx to gather information about Myanaymiz," said Jeremiah. "That is why he was in Town before. If he is with you, this could be useful to us. You can keep an eye on him. Having known Vyx in your childhood could give us added advantage."

"The Vyx I knew is not that Guardsman," said Jotham. He looked at Myanaymiz. The thought of her not being there in his cottage was a little painful. "I will visit you," he told her.

Jeremiah could see that Jotham was becoming far too attached to her. He couldn't help feeling secretly glad of Bugiah's order. Such an attachment could cause serious problems for all of them. "You may visit anytime you like, but remember Vyx will be watching, so we all must be very careful."

⸻ ◆ ⸻

        A r l e n e   A d a m o

67

Since returning from the forest, Jeremiah had been working non-stop at his loom. He knew he should be spending the time praying aloud. It was the Time of Wailing and the Master Weaver was expected to be an example to all others…a model of great piety. Yet, here he was secretly flouting the law once again. *So many laws…so many already broken…nothing is the same anymore…what does any of it matter?*

Suddenly, he heard the soft creak of the front door slowly opening. *A Guardsman! He* jumped up in alarm! "Oh, thank the heavens it is only you!" Jeremiah breathed a sigh of relief upon seeing Jotham and Myanaymiz. They quietly slipped in, and Jotham shut the door tightly behind them.

"With the curtains drawn and working so hard at the loom, I did not realize that the dark of night was already upon us. I thought you might be a Guardsman catching me at my work," said Jeremiah.

Jotham was a little surprised at just how openly Jeremiah now spoke of breaking the law. His friend was changing. "I wanted to bring Myanaymiz here before returning home," he said. "Her safety is my first priority."

"Did you run into any Guardsmen on your way?" asked Jeremiah.

"No one saw us."

"That is good."

Jotham turned to Myanaymiz, "You understand that the Time of Wailing will continue for two more days. I will not be able to visit you during that time, but I will return to see you after it is done."

Myanaymiz smiled at him. "You need not worry. I will not forget you."

Jotham laughed. "I know you won't. I just wanted you to know that I will not forget you."

"I expect that Bugiah will send for Myanaymiz soon after the Time of Wailing," Jeremiah interrupted.

"Will you go with her?" asked Jotham, frightened at the idea of her going once again to the Palace alone.

"It depends on what Bugiah demands. At least, with the Time of Wailing, I have two days to teach her something about the kind of God Bugiah is, and what he will expect from her."

Jotham took her hand in his and said, "Listen to what Jeremiah has to say. I want you to be safe."

She smiled at him. "I always listen, that is who I am, and what I do," she said. "And My Lord always keeps me safe."

"She is consistent, Jotham," said Jeremiah. "Not easy to understand, but consistent."

"Yes, she is that…consistently confusing."

Jeremiah walked over and opened the door. "You should go now," he said to Jotham. "It's best that you not stay here too long. I'll send word up to Bugiah tomorrow that both of you have returned. Now hurry home."

Jotham didn't want to leave without Myanaymiz, but he knew he had no choice. At least she would be safe in Jeremiah's cottage. "I will see you soon," he said, reluctantly releasing her hand, and then slipping out the door. He gave her one final look before closing it behind him.

Jeremiah stood alone with Myanaymiz. He suddenly realized that this was the first time he had ever been alone with her. "You are welcome in my house," he said. "You may take my bed, and I will sleep on the bench in the other room. I wake early to do my weaving, so I will try my best not to disturb you. Let me know if there is anything you need. My cottage is not much, I'm afraid, but you are very welcome to anything I have."

"Thank you Young-Old Jeremiah," she replied. "Your cottage is a good place and you are a good man."

———•———

68

Jotham opened the front door to his cottage and walked in. He lit a small metal lantern that was sitting on the table just inside the door. Holding it aloft, he looked around the room. On his work table was the child's shoe he had yet to finish. Everything was just as he had left it. That was a relief. Part of him was afraid they may have destroyed his place as punishment. He began to unbutton his shirt as he headed for his bedroom.

Before Jotham could enter the room, someone suddenly grabbed him from behind! As he was pulled backwards, the lantern fell from his hand, landing with a *clank* on the floor! He began to struggle, but stopped when he realized there was a Guardsman's sword against his throat! From that point, the seconds dragged on forever as he helplessly waited. *Will I die tonight? I did not get a chance to tell Myanaymiz goodbye. Who will find my body? Please don't let it be one of the children.*

"Cobbler, where is the Juju Witch?"

"Vyx is that you?" Jotham felt the sword drop away, and the arm release him.

Pushing Jotham aside, Vyx then reached down and picked up the still burning lantern from the floor. As he held up the light, Jotham could now see Vyx's face. "Where is the Juju Witch?" Vyx demanded again.

"She is with the Master Weaver as ordered by the God of Gods," he answered, noticing that Vyx still held the sword in his other hand.

"Why did you help her escape?"

"I did it for the Gods," he lied.

"What do you mean?"

"I knew in my heart this Lady was sent to serve the Gods. Glory to the Gods! I was keeping her safe until the time was right, and she was ready."

"Why would you think it was the place of the Cobbler to do such a thing?" Vyx asked.

"I was inspired by the Stories of the Gods. As you know, sometimes the Townsfolk do receive inspiration to serve their Gods in exceptional ways. I believed that I received such inspiration. When she revealed her power, I knew that this must be preserved for the Gods, and felt that Bugiah would soon call for her, just as he has done."

Vyx thought about it for a moment. *Inspirational service to the Gods is an acceptable explanation, but this Cobbler must be watched carefully.* "I am no longer staying with the Master Weaver. I am now staying here with you," he said.

"I know," replied Jotham. "The Master Weaver told me as much."

"I have taken the room that does not have your clothes."

"That is fine."

"I will require only that you feed me at appropriate times. I will observe your work. I will observe the other Townsfolk."

"And you will observe Myanaymiz?"

"Yes, of course. That is why I am here…to assist the God of Gods with the Juju Witch."

Jotham didn't like him calling her a Juju Witch. He wanted to shout, *her name is Myanaymiz!* Instead he said, "Please let me know if you require anything else of me. I am here to serve the Gods."

"Yes, we are all here to serve the Gods," replied Vyx. "The Time of Wailing for you will begin now. I suggest you go into your room, and begin your wailing prayers. You must put in an extra effort to make up for the time lost while hiding with that Juju Witch." Vyx then handed him the lantern.

Jotham took the lantern, and went into his room. He set it on the table, and then sat on the edge of his bed, staring at his reflection in the mirror. *I hate having a Guardsman in my house! Oh Myanaymiz, I wish you were here with me. I miss you.* Jotham then opened his mouth, and began to wail out his prayers. *I hope you hear every last note Guardsman, and I hope every last note disturbs your sleep and brings you terrible dreams.*

 Arlene Adamo

69

Standing in the open field, Jeremiah looked up at the strange black clouds overhead. Instead of moving in one direction, they ominously swirled about...snaking this way and that...coiling then uncoiling. He knew he should be afraid...he understood the great power of those clouds, but he felt no fear. In fact, there was something comforting about them. There was something comforting about everything here... the peculiar colors of the grass...the wildflowers with their mysterious vibrancy...everything familiar and soothing. He could feel the warm moist air enveloping him... wrapping him up like a new born baby. *You are safe. You are protected.*

Something gently nudged his arm, making Jeremiah turn. He was surprised to see Bugiah's red steed standing in front of him. As he stared at the creature, he suddenly realized that it wasn't Bugiah's horse at all. This was a red mare. He held out his hand, and the horse placed its soft black lips in his palm. Jeremiah ran his other hand down her long smooth neck. Instinctively, he then grabbed hold of the red mane, and in one swoop, pulled himself upon her back. Turning his face upwards, he looked again at the clouds. These dark swirling thunderheads now seemed so close. He felt as though they were so close that he could reach up and touch them...but he didn't dare try. He knew that to even try would have meant the end of him. They possessed that much power.

Suddenly, the horse whinnied and then reared up. Jeremiah quickly wrapped his arms securely around her neck. As her hooves hit the ground, she began to run...running faster than Jeremiah had ever imagined a horse could! He could feel the powerful wind rushing through his long hair and beard! *Is this real? Is this true? Yes, it is! I, Jeremiah, am riding the great red mare! O' the freedom! O' the magnificent freedom!* It felt as though he were flying…soaring like a great bird towards the heavens…flying over the earth! But where was the earth? Where did the grass and the flowers go? Where was the horizon? He *was* flying! Flying without wings! Heading up… up towards those beautiful dark clouds…being carried towards a strange and wonderful paradise! Rising! Rising! Jeremiah was riding the great red mare into the very heart of heaven.

———•◆•———

                                        Arlene Adamo

70

Jotham was relieved that the last day of the Time of Wailing was almost finished. With Vyx in the cottage he had been forced to do his wailing prayers for hours at a time. Vyx, as a Guardsman, was not required to pray himself, but as a Guardsman, decided it was his job to ensure that Jotham did.

From the window, Jotham could see that the sun was setting. "Oooonay, Oooonay," he chanted loud enough to keep Vyx from coming out to check on him. As soon as it was dark, he could finally go see Myanaymiz. Thinking about seeing her again had been his only comfort these past two days.

Finally, as the last of the sun's rays had disappeared from view, he officially ended his wailing prayer. "Our magnificent God has entered into the Place of Waiting. Eed Dee Aut." He then immediately got up from the table and headed for the door.

"Halt Cobbler! Where are you going?"

Jotham stopped. With his hand still on the door latch, he turned and answered, "The Time of Wailing is now over, Honourable Guardsman."

"Yes it is," said Vyx. "However, if you are going to the Weaver's cottage, I will go with you."

"You needn't do that."

"I wish to see the Juju Witch. Is that not why you are going? To see her?"

"No," denied Jotham. "I simply wish to speak with my friend Jeremiah."

"Then we shall go together."

Jotham knew he had no choice in the matter. "Very well," he relented, "we shall go together."

71

"You gave your best to me," said Myanaymiz.

Jeremiah was busy working at his loom while Myanaymiz sat watching on a stool nearby. "What do you mean?" he asked.

"This gown," said Myanaymiz. "The gown you gave to me was your best work. Your kindness will be written in the Book of Forever, and my Lord will reward you for what you have done."

"Who is your Lord?" he asked. "And where is the Book of Forever?"

"He is on His way, and the Book of Forever is always being written."

Jeremiah laughed. "I have no idea what you are talking about, and I realize it would be foolish to ask anything more about it. Any answers you give are just more questions for me." He stopped weaving for a moment to stretch out, wincing at the pain in his lower back.

"Shall I fix you?" she asked.

Jeremiah remembered what she had done to Jotham's back. How she had taken away his pain and his scars. "No!" he said quickly. "I am fine."

"But you are not fine," she replied. "You are tired and in pain. If you wish to remain tired and in pain that is your choice, but do not lie to me. It is disrespectful."

"I'm sorry," said Jeremiah. "I did not mean to offend you. It's simply that…" He couldn't think what to say next.

"It is that I frighten you."

"No…I…"

"It makes me sad," she said. "It makes me sad that I frighten you. It means that you do not see me, and it means that you are frightened of yourself. I do not frighten Jotham because he sees me. He is not frightened of himself."

Jeremiah wanted to tell her she was wrong, but that wasn't the truth. He was frightened. He was frightened of her shooting strange magic through his body. He was frightened about how it might change things…how it might change him.

Suddenly, there was a knock on the door "It is I," said Jotham, opening the door.

"Come in! Please come in!" said Jeremiah, getting up from his loom.

"Vyx is with me," Jotham warned.

Jeremiah laughed. "Just like when you were small boys together, coming to watch the Master Weaver."

Jotham found nothing but discomfort in the comparison. This Guardsman was a long way from the fun happy boy who used to run with him. He looked over at Myanaymiz. "Hello," he said, wishing only that he could rush to her, and gather her up in his arms.

"Hello, Jotham," she smiled.

Vyx marched straight over to Myanaymiz, and stood over her. "Juju Witch, what magic do you know?" he abruptly demanded.

Jotham wanted to jump in between them. He wanted to challenge Vyx…to rescue her…protect her, but he knew better. That would only endanger them both. He must have patience, and wait to see how she would handle it.

"All is magic," Myanaymiz responded.

"That is not an acceptable answer," said Vyx. "Tell me, what magic do you know?"

"Ask me what is in your mind," she said.

"Why would you say that?" asked Vyx who was beginning to get visibly frustrated with her. "Is this supposed to be a demonstration of your magic? Very well, tell me, what is in my mind." Vyx focussed on imagining the white pillar in the Palace of the Gods.

Myanaymiz stood up and looked him straight in the eye. "You weep," she said.

"What are you saying? I have a picture in my mind. What is it, Juju Witch? Tell me!" Vyx concentrated again on the image.

"You weep,' she repeated.

"Are you that senseless? If you are magic, then tell me the image that is in my mind!"

Myanaymiz continued to stare into his eyes. Vyx felt unnerved. His instincts as a Guardsman told him to look away, but at the same time his training as a Guardsman would not let him. Such a thing would mean defeat, and defeat was never an option for a true Guardsman.

"You weep because, in here with Jotham and Young-Old Jeremiah, you feel his ghost," she said.

"What ghost? There is no ghost in my mind. What are you talking about?"

"It is the boy," said Myanaymiz. "It is the boy you lost…the boy that was taken from you."

"Guardsmen do not marry. I have no boy. Are you mad Juju Witch?"

Myanaymiz began to cry. "He was slain! He was mercilessly slain…oh dear, dear boy!"

Vyx watched as her eyes filled with tears… tears that began to softly roll down her face…tiny salty streams flowing down her strange skin. It was doing something to him. Something was rising up from deep inside. Where was it coming from? This weight moving up into his chest…heavy…slowing his breathing…crushing his heart. His lower lip started to tremble. His eyes began to water. *A Guardsman is always in control! A Guardsman feels nothing but devotion to the Gods! A Guardsman stands firm like the Pillar of the Gods!*

Jotham and Jeremiah watched in astonishment as Vyx then suddenly ran out of the cottage and out into the dark night.

⚊⚊•◆•⚊⚊

72

Bugiah stretched out on the divan. The Time of Wailing was over and he had eaten far too much. He let loose a loud belch.

"My God, you called?" said a boy, running in from the hallway and kneeling down before his God of Gods. He was dressed in the coarsely woven black tunic of those who were in Guardsman training.

Bugiah laughed. "Are you learning to be a Guardsman, or to be a fool?" he asked.

The boy was immediately afraid. *My first time before the God of Gods and have I offended him? How? I must answer carefully.* "My God…a…a Guardsman, my God," he said nervously.

"Then why do you act like a fool?"

The boy felt sick to his stomach. "I am deeply sorry, my God. Forgive me," he said, keeping his eyes on the floor. He could feel the tears welling up. He tried as best he could to hold them back. *Please don't fall. Don't let him see.*

"Let me see your face!" Bugiah commanded.

The boy did not respond. He could feel the tears rising in his eyes even more.

"Obey your God of Gods, and let me see your face!" shouted Bugiah.

In his mind, the boy tried to convince himself that his tears were invisible. As long as he could keep them in his eyes, Bugiah could not see them. He slowly lifted his face, but as he did so he felt a fresh wet tear teeter at the edge of his lid, and then begin to roll down his cheek. There was nothing he could do to stop it.

"You are crying! You expect to be a Guardsman, and you are crying?"

The boy's shoulders now began to shake. He could no longer even slow it down. His entire body trembled with emotion, and the tears freely streamed down his face. He was completely overcome.

Bugiah casually reached down, and pulled out a sword from under the divan.

"Oh great God of Gods, have mercy upon me!" pleaded the boy.

Bugiah smiled, "Yes, I will show you mercy." He stood up, took three steps forward, and then in a flash, he slit the boy's throat wide open. As the blood sprayed out, the child fell forward, his head making a cracking sound as it hit the black marble floor. A deep black pool quickly grew around his twitching body.

"There now," said Bugiah. "I have bestowed my divine mercy upon you. You will now never face the shame of being a failed Guardsman." He then carefully stepped around the boy as not to get blood upon his shoes, and headed to his private chambers.

———•◆•———

$$73$$

"What did you do to Vyx?" asked Jotham.

"I did what he asked. I told him what was in his mind," replied Myanaymiz.

Jotham looked at Jeremiah. "Do you think she is in trouble again?" he asked.

"What is Vyx going to do? Tell Bugiah he was made upset by the Juju Witch?" said Jeremiah. "I don't think so. As a Guardsman, he will have to keep face."

Jotham turned to Myanaymiz. "Why cannot anything just be simple with you?"

She smiled at him. "Did you miss me?"

Jotham blushed. He still did not want Jeremiah to know about them. "Yes," he quickly answered, and then walked over and pretended to examine the gown on the loom.

"I have progressed quickly with the weaving. I'm much closer to being ready for the Festival," said Jeremiah.

"I am behind in my work because I had to obey the Time of Wailing," sighed Jotham.

"It must be awkward with the Guardsman in your cottage."

"Very awkward," said Jotham. He looked over at Myanaymiz. *How I wish the Guardsman was gone, and you were back with me.* "How has it been with Myanaymiz staying here?"

"She…she is good company, but I've had such strange dreams since her arrival. Sometimes they wake me up in the middle of the night. They are not unpleasant dreams, just extremely strange… and vivid."

"Myanaymiz, do you know anything about Jeremiah's dreams?" asked Jotham.

"His dreams are good because Young-Old Jeremiah is a good man."

Jotham remembered when she had first called him a 'good man.' For a moment, he looked suspiciously at Jeremiah. *No. He's too old. That's just ridiculous.*

"Would you like to go for a walk tomorrow?" Jotham asked her. "After the Time of Wailing, it's good to get outside and enjoy the fresh air." *I need to be alone with her.*

"Vyx will not let us," she answered.

"But perhaps it would not be a problem. Perhaps Vyx would not be bothered."

"It will be a problem. I upset Vyx too much. He will not let us walk. He will insist on questioning me again. I know. I can see what will happen tomorrow. He will make you work. He will come here to speak to me."

"If she can fix your back, perhaps she can see into the future," said Jeremiah. "Maybe you should listen to her."

"Expect me tomorrow anyway," said Jotham.

———◆———

74

Vyx sat in the darkness under Old Man Tree. What had she done to him? Her power was far greater than he had anticipated. What kind of spell was that? In the Stories of the Gods, the Juju Witch is always very straight forward with her spells. The spells are bold and full of magic words. This one came out of nowhere. It came hidden in ordinary words. What kind of a Juju Witch was she?

He touched his eye to see if it was still wet. It was now dry, but he knew that even after the eyes had dried, they would still be tell-tale red. He knew that from seeing those Townsfolk who had committed a sin, and were made to come before Bugiah for punishment. Long after they were numb, and their tears had stopped, their eyes were still red.

Bugiah could not be told about this. Although he was merely a victim of an evil spell, he knew he would still be blamed…he would be called weak, and there was always a punishment for weakness. *It is the Juju Witch's fault that I must now hide the truth from my God. She is the reason I am disobeying the law. It is really her who is breaking the law. Not me.*

Vyx looked at the branches above him. He stood up and grabbed the lowest one. He then swung himself upon it, and began to climb. A short distance up, he stopped. *This is about it. This is where I think I would have stood as a child. Now the ground is so close, but then…then I was touching the sky. What was it I used to say…that I used to call down to those on the ground? It was a little poem I created. How did it start…'I am Vyx.' Yes, that is it. 'I am Vyx, King of the tree,*

Can't you see? Can't you see?' So simple and silly now, but I remember
how proud I was of it. No one got to say it but me. Other boys tried to
make similar rhymes, but mine had already taken root. The others could
only come up with hollow imitations. Mine was real. I was real. I was
Vyx, King of the Tree.

                                          Arlene Adamo

75

Jeremiah opened his eyes and saw the dawn's light peeking in through the curtains. As he slowly sat up, he could feel the dull ache in his back. Sleeping on the bench was not helping his condition. He looked around the small barren room. It had been another night of strange dreams. This time he was in the Palace of the Gods which was floating on the river Broma. He stood at an open window, and commanded it with his mind to sail like a boat triumphantly out into the sea. Despite its strangeness, the dream left him feeling deeply comforted.

As he sat there, trying to remember the details of the dream, he suddenly became aware of a familiar noise coming from outside the little room. *Is that my loom?*

Jeremiah got up and opened the door. It was the loom! Myanaymiz was sitting at his loom and weaving. She did not look up as he walked over to see exactly what she was doing.

"It is almost complete," she said as she expertly worked the machine.

Jeremiah was surprised to see a gown in the loom. But this was no ordinary gown. This was the strangest gown he had ever seen. The myriad of colors were woven this way and that, blending here, contrasting there, forming unrecognizable images that seemed to almost move about. He stared in wonderment. Was this a garment or a colony of beautiful living creatures? Creatures flowing over and under, this way and that, alive in unspeakable complexity. So spectacular! So alluring! It was truly a miracle!

"Myanaymiz, this is amazing!" he exclaimed.

"I watched you and learned. You taught me, Young-Old Jeremiah."

"But I did not teach you to do this! This is well beyond my knowledge of weaving."

"But you still taught me." Myanaymiz then expertly tied the loose threads. "There," she said, slipping the gown off of the loom. "It is finished." She held it up and they both stared at her handiwork.

Jeremiah reached out and ran his hand over the material. "How could it be so soft…so perfectly soft? You used my thread, and yet it is not my thread. It is far more beautiful…more pleasant to the touch."

"It is for Bugiah," she said.

"What!"

"It is for Bugiah, and we will tell him that you wove it."

"The God of Gods will be so pleased. Are you certain we should not tell him that you did the work?"

"No," replied Myanaymiz, folding the garment over her arm. "He must not know that I can do such things. Not yet anyway."

"I simply cannot understand you."

Myanaymiz smiled at him. "You do not need to understand," she said. "You need only have faith."

———————

76

Jotham was up and ready by daybreak. He was hoping to slip out before Vyx saw him. Quietly, he opened his bedroom door, but just as he put one foot over the threshold… "Cobbler!" Vyx was sitting at the table finishing off his regular breakfast of bread and water. "It is good you are up early. The Time of Wailing has left you behind in your work. You must put in an extra effort to catch up. The God of Gods is expecting new shoes that must be fittingly perfect for his divine feet."

"Where did you go last night?" asked Jotham, angry that his plan had been thwarted.

"A Guardsman's work is not for you to question."

"Of course." Jotham then resentfully went over his work table, sat on the stool and began working on the unfinished child's shoe. *He makes me feel like a prisoner in my own cottage. When will he leave?*

Vyx stared silently at Jotham for several moments before suddenly asking, "Did the Juju Witch watch you work while she stayed here?"

"Yes, sometimes."

"And she stayed in the room where I am now sleeping?"

"Yes."

"Why is she so fond of you?"

"She is also fond of Jeremiah…and the children. She is fond of most everyone she meets."

"She is a Juju Witch. Juju Witches do not make emotional attachments."

As Jotham skillfully stitched the sole to the upper, he replied, "Then perhaps she is no Juju Witch."

"Our great God of Gods says she is one. He is divine. He is never wrong."

"Then I have no answer for it."

Vyx got up from the table, and went to the window. He looked out at the road, and remembered the night of the funeral…the frightening noise…the chaos unleashed. "Besides her power to cry," he asked, "what other powers does she possess?"

"That is the only one I have seen."

Vyx suddenly turned around, and stared straight at Jotham. "Has she put a spell on you?" he demanded.

Jotham laughed. "No, I have no spell on me."

"But if you did have a spell on you, how would you know?"

"I suppose I wouldn't, but you have been in my cottage for several days now. You have observed me during the Time of Wailing. Have you seen any evidence of me being bewitched?"

Vyx thought about it. "No. You appear to be an ordinary Cobbler."

"There then. I am an ordinary dull Cobbler. Nothing to be concerned about."

Vyx walked over and picked up one of the finished shoes from the work table. He examined it closely. "You are very skilled at your craft," he said.

"Thank you," replied Jotham. He glanced up at Vyx. Within the sternness of that Guardsman's face, was there was still a hint of the boy he knew so long ago? Jotham looked back down at his work and asked, "Do you remember what you said you would be before you were sent away to be a Guardsman? I remember it well. You used to talk about it all of the time."

Vyx could not remember wanting to be anything. "I assume I always wanted to be a Guardsman. There is no greater honour or a nobler calling."

"I understand," said Jotham. "But as a young child, you were… different. You did not think of being a Guardsman. You thought of being something else."

"What would I want to be other than a Guardsman?"

"You wanted to be a Shepherd."

"A Shepherd!" Vyx was surprised. "Why would I want to be a Shepherd?"

Jotham laughed. "You thought it would be fun herding the sheep everyday, taking naps in the afternoon sun, protecting them from the wolves. You even had names picked out for what you would call them."

Vyx could feel himself getting angry. He didn't like the Cobbler speaking of the past. He was a Guardsman. Whatever kind of foolish boy he was before is gone now. He slammed the shoe down on the work table. "I was a ridiculous child. Thank the Gods I was accepted as a Guardsman."

"Yes," Jotham said. "Thank the Gods."

Vyx walked over to the front door. He opened it wide and stared out. "I will be going to see the Juju Witch. I have many questions for her." He then suddenly turned, looked straight at Jotham and said, "You have a great deal of work to do Cobbler. I suggest you concentrate on that."

Jotham watched as Vyx walked out the door. He then carefully placed the tiny new shoe he had just completed beside its match. "Myanaymiz, stay safe," he whispered.

———•———

77

Slemi was considering going to the Cobblers cottage when she spotted Vyx walking on the road. "Honourable Guardsman," she called from her doorway then rushed over to talk with him. "Honourable Guardsman, I must speak to you about that…that woman."

"What do you have to tell me?" he asked.

"She has been influencing the children to sing strange songs."

"What kind of strange songs."

Slemi couldn't remember the words. "Songs about killing and eating," she said. "Entirely inappropriate for children. And then there is the Cobbler…I saw him embrace her almost exactly where we are standing now. For her to be there…in that cottage alone with him? Well, it is entirely inappropriate also."

"She is now in the Weaver's cottage," said Vyx.

"Oh…yes, that is much better…I guess. Yes, the Weaver, unlike the Cobbler is responsible, sensible and past any such questionable notions. I suppose it is acceptable that she stay with him."

"It was by order of the God of Gods," explained Vyx.

"Thank the great God of Gods for his divine wisdom!"

"Do you know anything else," asked Vyx.

Slemi remembered back to the incident in the garden. "Well, there was this blue butterfly."

"A blue butterfly?"

"Yes, I have never seen such a creature before. It flew into the garden, and landed right in her hand."

"Then what happened?"

     Arlene Adamo

"A child frightened it off when he came running into the garden. He ran in to tell us about you, Honourable Guardsman."

"But she was not with you when you came to meet me?"

"No," said Slemi. "She must have stayed behind in the garden."

"And have you seen this butterfly since?"

"No. It has never appeared again."

"I am on my way now to talk with her. I will ask her about the butterfly." Vyx turned and started walking towards Jeremiah's house.

"Honourable Guardsman," called Slemi after him. "Do you know what she is?"

"She is a Juju Witch," he said as he continued to walk along the road.

"A Juju Witch!" Slemi said to herself. "A Juju Witch in our Town! I must let everyone know."

<hr>

78

"Vyx is coming," said Myanaymiz who sat on a chair close to Jeremiah as he worked at his loom.

Jeremiah was not the least bit surprised when a few moments later, Vyx appeared in the open doorway. He stopped weaving. "Good morning Honourable Guardsman," he said.

"Go back to your work," instructed Vyx. "I need only talk with the Juju Witch."

Myanaymiz stood up, and walked towards him. "Let us talk outside," she said.

As Vyx turned to leave, his eye caught sight of the gown that Myanaymiz had woven the night before. He silently stared.

"Is it not beautiful?" said Jeremiah. "It is truly my best work ever. This is the gown the God of Gods will wear at the Festival."

"It is very strange." Vyx walked over to the gown to examine it closer. "It seems…it seems almost as though it were alive," he said.

"It was the magnificence of the God of Gods that inspired me." Jeremiah looked over at Myanaymiz, and she smiled back at him.

Vyx could not take his eyes off the gown. *Is it moving? Something is moving. What am I looking at? Those colors…what are those colors? I see something but…"*

"Guardsman," said Myanaymiz. "Shall we go outside and talk now."

"Yes…oh yes, of course," said Vyx, pulling his eyes from the garment, and turning towards Myanaymiz. "Let us go talk."

Outside, Myanaymiz sat down on a bench under the blossoming kuma tree. "Sit here beside me," she told Vyx.

Vyx looked at the bench. There was nowhere else to sit. Reluctantly, he sat next to her.

"What are your questions?" she asked.

He looked at her face in the sunlight. "Your skin!" he said. "Your skin sparkles. That is not in any of the stories. The skin of the Juju Witch, we are told, is either pale or grey. Why does yours sparkle?"

"Why does yours not?" she replied. "It is what it is."

Vyx felt strange being this close to her…her skin…her scent. "Are you putting a spell upon me Juju Witch?"

Myanaymiz smiled. "Why would you ask such a thing? You are a Guardsman. Is not a Guardsman stronger than such things?"

"I…never mind. I have questions for you."

"I am waiting."

"What is between you and the Cobbler? Did you put a spell on him?"

Myanaymiz reached up to the tree branch over their heads, and plucked a blossom. She put it to her nose, and inhaled the sweet fragrance. "I do not put spells on people," she said.

"But a Juju Witch casts spells. It is in the Stories."

"Then perhaps I am not a Juju Witch."

"Of course you are a Juju Witch. The God of Gods says you are. Maybe you are a new sort of Juju Witch. That would explain your skin, and other strange behaviour. So now, tell me about the Cobbler."

"Jotham is a good man," she replied. "Do the Gods have a law against being a good man?"

"The Gods do have laws about what a man and woman of the Town may do together. All matches must first be sanctioned by the Gods. An unsanctioned union is a violation of the law."

"But I am not of the Town. According to you, I am a Juju Witch. The laws do not apply to me, so your question is irrelevant."

Vyx thought about it. She was a Juju Witch, and it was true that there were no laws that applied to such as her. In the stories, sometimes the Juju Witch worked with the Gods, and sometimes she was killed for working against them, but there were no laws around the everyday conduct of the Juju Witch. Although it didn't seem right for her to behave like this, what could he say without the law to support him? Deciding it was best to move on to the next topic, he demanded, "Tell me about the blue butterfly."

Myanaymiz looked up into the sky and smiled. "He was so beautiful!" she said.

"That Townswoman, Slemi, said that she had never seen such a butterfly before. Did you conjure it with your magic? Can you conjure up things like butterflies? Is this one of your powers?"

"I wish I had such a power," replied Myanaymiz. "But I do not command the blue butterfly. It is he who chooses to come to me."

"Is the blue butterfly powerful? Does it threaten the Gods in any way?"

"You believe that your Gods are all powerful. How could they possibly be threatened by a tiny butterfly?"

Once again Vyx had no argument he could give. It was no easy matter interrogating this Juju Witch.

"Why do you not ask me what you really want to know?" Myanaymiz said, looking him straight in the eye.

"I am asking only questions which are important to the Gods, Juju Witch. That is my assignment. All else is irrelevant."

"But what does Vyx want to know?" She smiled at him.

"I am a Guardsman! I want to know what the Gods want to know!"

"You were Vyx before you were ever a Guardsman."

Vyx abruptly got up, and took a few steps from the bench. He then turned and demanded, "Are you trying to do to me the same as you did last night? I think you are lying about your ability to cast spells. You cast a spell on me last night, and now you are trying to do it again."

Myanaymiz casually plucked the petals from the blossom in her hand. She then threw them up in the air, and watched as they softly floated to the ground. "You believe what you want to believe. I do not cast spells upon men. I only reveal to them what is in their hearts. What they find in there belongs only to them. How they look at it…what they do with it…that is their decision. Do not blame me for the tumult that is yours and yours alone. I do not make you what you are. You do that."

Vyx did not know how to respond. What did she mean that she revealed the heart? He had the heart of a Guardsman. There was nothing to reveal. It was all very straight forward.

Myanaymiz then got up from the bench, and walked over to him. She gently placed her hand on his cheek. Vyx felt his body tense up. *She is touching a Guardsman! Shout! Stop her! Push her away!*

"When you go to see Bugiah later, to give him your report, be very cautious what you say or he will bring out the cane again. Take care, Vyx. I must go see Jotham now. He is missing me very much, and I cannot see him suffer." Myanaymiz then headed down the path, and out to the road.

Vyx stood where he was, and watched bewildered as she walked away. What had she done to him? How did she know about the cane? Surely she must be lying about the spells. Nothing else could explain any of this…this confusion he was feeling. Vyx put his hand to his face. It did not feel any different to his hand, but why did it feel so strange within his skin? So fiery hot and freezing cold at the same time, yet only in that one place…the place where she had touched him.

79

Slemi watched from the window as Myanaymiz passed by her cottage. She hurried out the door and to the road. O' *the boldness! The unashamed boldness!* Slemi began to follow after her. *She must be going to the Cobbler. Where is that Guardsman when there is something to see?*

As Myanaymiz turned up the path to Jotham's place, Slemi smiled. *I knew it!* She looked around for someone else she could enlist into surveillance, but there was no one else about. She would have to be the only witness. She watched intently as Myanaymiz disappeared into the cottage.

Allowing them ample time to do something incriminating, Slemi then slowly crept up to the window. Carefully, she peered in. There was the Cobbler busily working at his work table, but where was the Juju Witch? She was nowhere to be seen. *Where did she go? I saw her go in. I know she went in.*

"I am here."

Slemi jumped in surprise, and turned to see Myanaymiz standing only about three feet away. She couldn't help but be struck by the beauty of her gown and the sparkle of her skin. At first, Slemi fumbled to find the words, but then quickly regained her composure and exclaimed, "How dare you sneak up on me! What are you doing here at the Cobbler's cottage when the God of Gods has strictly forbidden it?"

"As I understand," replied Myanaymiz, "Bugiah only forbade me to live here, not to visit."

"You have had unsanctioned relations with the Cobbler!" Slemi blurted out, no longer able to control her frustration. Her face was red with anger. "Do not try to deny it. I know it is true, and have spoken to the Guardsman about it. As soon as the God of Gods learns of this, you will be forbidden from ever seeing the Cobbler again, and you will both be severely punished."

"Do you know who I am?" asked Myanaymiz, taking a step closer.

Slemi wanted to move further away, but there was nowhere to go. Her back was up against the cottage wall. "You are wicked!" she exclaimed. "You have disrupted this Town! You have put spells on people…on the children. They say you are a Juju Witch, and I think they are right. You are an evil wicked Juju Witch!"

"A Juju Witch is only in a story."

"That's right! And those are the Stories of the Gods. The Stories are true! Praise be to our almighty Gods! They will destroy you! They will destroy the evil Juju Witch!"

"Your gods are as false as your stories."

Slemi could not believe her ears. *How could anyone say such a thing, and so brazenly? Did she have no fear at all of the Gods?* "Blasphemy!" Slemi shouted. "You will die for your blasphemy, Juju Witch!"

Jotham, who heard the commotion, appeared from inside the cottage. "Myanaymiz? What is going on?"

"She has blasphemed! She has said the Gods are false! There is only one punishment for that! Death!" screamed Slemi.

Jotham looked at Myanaymiz, and then back as Slemi "Surely you must have misunderstood. She would not say such a thing."

"No, she understood," said Myanaymiz. "I said that the Gods were false because this is the truth."

"Do you hear? Do you hear? She even admits it! Without a bit of shame, she admits it! Wait until the Guardsman hears of this! You will be publicly executed, and I will be there to watch! I will gladly watch!" Slemi then skirted cautiously around Myanaymiz, and hurried out to the road.

"Why?" Jotham asked Myanaymiz. "Why would you say such a thing? They will believe her, and put you to death! Oh, what will we do now?"

Myanaymiz moved close to him. "You are upset. That is so very sweet, Jotham…to be upset for me. But do not worry. There is nothing to worry about."

"O' Myanaymiz, of course there is so much to worry about. Slemi will not rest until she sees you put to death."

"That will not happen," Myanaymiz smiled. "Slemi will not report anything she has heard."

"How can you say that? You have seen her determination and her hatred for you?"

"Because, pretty Jotham," Myanaymiz reached over and gently ran her fingers through his fine yellow hair, "Slemi is already dead."

Just then Petal can running up to the cottage. "Cobbler! Cobbler! Come quickly! We have found Slemi fallen on the road, and she is not moving!"

⎯⎯◆⎯◆⎯⎯

80

A crowd of Townsfolk had gathered around the now covered body of Slemi. The children who found her had been told to go home, but still lingered a short distance away. The ladies of The Society of Women Servants to the Gods were weeping loudly. "Oh our dear poor Slemi! How could this have happened? She was such a great woman, and such a wonderful and devoted servant to the Gods."

Vyx helped a Townsman load Slemi's body onto the wagon. He then approached Jeremiah and said, "I shall go report this to the God of Gods." He looked suspiciously over at Myanaymiz who was standing beside Jotham in the crowd. *That Juju Witch must have had something to do with this. I just know she is full of deadly magic.* He then marched off in the direction of the Celestial Path.

As the wagon pulled away, the ladies of The Society followed after it along with several of the other Townsfolk. Jotham took Myanaymiz by the hand, and hurried over to Jeremiah, "We need to talk," he said discreetly.

Jeremiah could hear the urgency in Jotham's voice. "We will go back to my cottage and talk there," he replied.

The three then walked silently to the cottage. Only after the door was shut firmly behind them did Jeremiah speak. "Please sit," he said, offering them both chairs. He pulled up the stool from his loom for himself. "Now, tell me what this is about."

For a moment, they all sat in silence as Jotham wondered where to begin. "S-Slemi...," he finally stammered, "...she was at my cottage before..." He stopped, unsure how to explain it. "She... she threatened Myanaymiz!"

Jeremiah did not like where this was going. He looked at Myanaymiz and asked "Why did she threaten you?"

Before she could answer, Jotham jumped in. "At first she only threatened to expose…," he didn't know how to finish the sentence or if he wanted to. What business was it of anyone else?

"She said that she would tell Bugiah I had unsanctioned relations with Jotham," explained Myanaymiz.

Jeremiah suddenly felt very uncomfortable. Part of him wanted to ask her if it were true, but another part just didn't want to know. In the end, he chose not think about it.

"And it was then I explained to her that your gods are false gods, and she threatened to report that as well," Myanaymiz added.

Jeremiah was completely shocked. How could she have simply blasphemed outright? And in front of Slemi! She had been in the Town long enough to know better than that.

"Of course, to say such a thing is punishable by death," said Jotham defensively. "You know there would be no mercy given to her. Slemi would surely have made certain of that."

"This is true," Jeremiah agreed.

"There is more," said Jotham as he nervously stared down at his hands. "Before the child had arrived to tell us what he had found, Myanaymiz had already told me that Slemi was dead. She somehow knew that Slemi had died."

Jeremiah, at first, did not know what to say. He stared at Myanaymiz who simply stared back at him. Her strange hint of a smile offered no answers. It only raised questions. *Who are you? You heal one moment, and then do you kill the next? How am I to understand?* Folding his hands in front of him, Jeremiah sighed. He knew he must ask. "Did you kill her? Did you kill Slemi?"

"It was her choice, not mine," replied Myanaymiz.

Again with the mysterious answers. How am I supposed to understand that? Jeremiah found himself at a loss for words.

Jotham then asked, "Did you do something that…that resulted in Slemi's death? Did you…did you cast a spell?"

"I did nothing to cause her death, but she did everything."

"What do you mean?" asked Jeremiah.

"My Lord does not like when people get angry at me, or when they threaten me, or try to hurt me in any way."

"So your Lord killed Slemi?" Jotham asked, trying his best to understand.

"Slemi killed Slemi," answered Myanaymiz.

Jotham looked at Jeremiah. "Are we ever going to get a straight forward answer from her?"

Myanaymiz sighed. "I forgive you your transgressions," she said. "But try to understand that there are Laws in this world that are not in your stories, and are not of the kind issued by those you call gods. These are the natural Laws…eternal Laws…not fleeting laws of convenience. When the Law is broken, there are consequences. The Law will naturally correct that which malice breaks. Slemi broke the Law when she threatened me. The correction resulted in her death."

For the two men, there were still more questions than answers. What were these Laws she spoke of? Were they written down somewhere? What was the connection between Myanaymiz and these unseen Laws? "So if you did not kill her, how did you know that Slemi was dead before anyone had come to tell us?" Jotham asked.

"My Lord sometimes tells me things that have happened, and things that are going to happen."

For a while, there was only a palpable silence in the room. It was all so strange, and now all so serious. Finally Jeremiah said, "We cannot let anyone know about this."

"Of course not," agreed Jotham.

Myanaymiz smiled at them. "My Lord will reward you greatly for your kindness and for your caring. And please do not worry that he is coming."

"Your Lord is coming?" asked Jeremiah.

"Not yet," she replied. "It was not my Lord I was speaking of. It is Bugiah of whom I speak. It is he who will be arriving in Town very soon."

———•◦•———

81

"**G**reat God of Gods," said Vyx, lowering his head, and getting down on one knee. "I bring you news."

Bugiah was lying back on the divan looking over the cakes that had been brought to him only moments before. He was trying to decide on whether he felt more like a vanilla or a blueberry today. *Oh the decisions! Why must the God of Gods have so many decisions in one day?*

"There has been a death in the Town," Vyx said. He paused and waited. It was best to be very cautious when breaking such news.

"You came all this way to tell me about a Townsfolk death?" Bugiah snatched up the vanilla cake, and took a large bite.

"My God, it was Slemi, leader of The Society of Women Servants to the Gods."

"Well, what a pity. I don't remember her. Was she old?"

Slemi had been to the Mount of the Gods on many occasions for various presentations of worship. Vyx was surprised Bugiah did not know who she was. "She was not old, at least not old enough to die. There are some mysterious circumstances around her death. Before she died, she approached me to complain about the Juju Witch."

Bugiah suddenly sat up with interest. "Are you saying that the Juju Witch killed her?"

"What I can report is that Slemi was found dead in the road not far from the Cobbler's cottage. The cause of death is unknown.

She had come to me with concerns about the Juju Witch, and it is possible the Juju Witch may have learned of this.”

“Was the Juju Witch near her when she died?”

“There is no evidence of that. Although, she and the Cobbler were the first to arrive after the body was found by some children.”

Bugiah was even more intrigued. “Do you think this Juju Witch killed her? Can she kill with her mind?”

“I do not know, my God.”

Bugiah clapped his hands together. “This would be a wonderful thing! A Juju Witch who can kill with her mind! What I could do with a power like that!” He then added, “Of course, I am all powerful, but a killer Juju Witch would be such a lovely accessory to my divine greatness. Guardsman, I need to see her as soon as possible.”

“Shall I bring her to you?” asked Vyx.

Bugiah thought about it. “No,” he answered, “we don’t want the other Gods to know about this just yet. Let’s just keep it between you and me for now. Go tell the Stable Master to prepare my carriage. I will go to Town, and talk to this Juju Witch. I will ask her myself about the death of…uh?”

“Slemi,” said Vyx.

“Yes, that one,” Bugiah grinned from ear to ear. “I was so right about everything, Vyx.”

“As you always are, my God.”

“Yes, as I always am. The Resurrection of the Gods is upon us, and every sign points to the Juju Witch as being that special power sent here to serve me. It is all falling perfectly into place. I am the Chosen One…the Eternal God of Gods…I am Bugiah.” Leaning back on the divan, he then contentedly finished off the vanilla cake in one bite.

82

Jeremiah was working at his loom, while Myanaymiz and Jotham sat nearby drinking tea. "Is he coming soon?" Jotham asked Myanaymiz.

"He is almost here," she replied.

As soon as she said this, they heard the sound of horses outside. Jeremiah stopped weaving, and went to the door. He opened it just in time to see the God of Gods being assisted down from the carriage by Vyx. As Bugiah walked towards him, Jeremiah got down on one knee and said, "O' great God of Gods, your unexpected presence is my blessing. How may I serve you?"

"Weaver, I have heard that the loyal leader of The Society of Women Servants to the Gods has been found dead. Is this true?"

"It is the tragic reality. She will no longer have the great honour of serving the Gods."

"I have also heard that the Juju Witch may have killed her."

Jeremiah hid the alarm he was feeling and replied, "My God, the sad truth is that dear loyal Slemi was found on the road by some children. She was alone when she died."

Bugiah looked past Jeremiah and into the cottage. "Is the Juju Witch in there?" he demanded. "I will speak with her."

"Yes of course, my God." Jeremiah got up, and stepped back from the doorway. He gave a warning glance to Jotham and Myanaymiz.

Bugiah stepped inside the cottage, and looked around. "How small this is," he said. "But I suppose it is enough for a Weaver."

He looked at Jotham who was now on one knee with his head lowered. Myanaymiz remained seated.

Bugiah walked over, and looked down upon her. "Why do you not bow before the God of Gods?" he demanded.

"That is not what I do. That is not who I am," she replied.

Jeremiah and Jotham were surprised when Bugiah simply laughed at what she had said. He then shouted to his Guardsman, "Bring in my chair!"

Vyx, who had been waiting just outside the cottage, ran to the carriage, and pulled out the God of Gods' red velvet chair. He hurriedly brought it inside, and placed it beside Bugiah. Bugiah then sat down, and stared at Myanaymiz.

Myanaymiz continued to nurse her tea, barely looking at the God of Gods.

"Did you kill that woman?" he asked.

"Great God of Gods, she was with me when Slemi died. She had nothing to do with it," said Jotham.

Bugiah glanced at Jotham who continued to kneel and stare at the floor. He then laughed again, and said to Myanaymiz, "It seems that your Cobbler wants to protect you. It is very touching. Should I have him killed?"

Myanaymiz turned her head, and looked directly at Bugiah. "Do not dare touch a hair on his head!"

Jeremiah and Jotham were shocked that anyone would speak that way to the God of Gods! They were even more shocked when Bugiah responded once again with only laughter. "What will you give me for not killing him?" he asked.

Myanaymiz took a sip of tea then casually replied, "What is it that you want?"

"I want to know if you killed that woman!"

"It was her decision, not mine."

Bugiah looked at Jeremiah. "What is she talking about?"

"Great God of Gods," said Jeremiah, "she is…"

"Slemi threatened me," interrupted Myanaymiz. "It was her decision to take this path, not mine."

"So if someone threatens you, you kill them?" Bugiah was getting very excited.

"Slemi broke the Law, and so there were consequences."

"What law? What laws are there other than those prescribed by the Gods?"

Myanaymiz turned and looked directly at Bugiah. "To understand things as deep as the hidden Laws, you must first be able to feel them."

Bugiah was now completely confused. He felt himself beginning to get angry. "You need to speak clearly! No Juju Witch riddles!"

"But this is no riddle. This is the truth. You need to know how to feel things in order to master them."

"And how do I do this? I demand you tell me!"

"It will take some time and effort to learn such things," answered Myanaymiz.

"I am the God of Gods! I am easily capable of learning some simple Juju Witch trickery! Explain to me what I must know!"

Myanaymiz traced the rim of her cup with her finger then said, "To understand and obtain this power, you must begin at the beginning."

"And where is that? Where is my beginning?"

"Your beginning is in your home, of course. First, you must return to your home on the Mount of the Gods, and there you will devise a special ritual for the Festival. This is the way for you. Meditate upon each and every detail of the ceremony, and pray to your dead immortal gods for guidance. Come to me if you are unsure about anything and I will provide my counsel. This is your journey and yours alone."

Bugiah grinned. "You shall be amazed at my power, Juju Witch! Everyone will be amazed at the power of the God of Gods. I am the one who will bring about the Resurrection of the Gods!"

Myanaymiz smiled. "You will definitely make this the most spectacular Festival the Town has ever seen. And do you see what the Master Weaver has made for you?" She pointed to the wall where the gown was hanging.

Astonished by what he was seeing, Bugiah immediately got up from his chair, and went over to the gown. As he stared at the fabric, he found himself being drawn deep into its strange and wonderful patterns. Every time he tried to focus on one of the mysterious images, it seemed to move…ever swirling…ever changing. As soon as he would catch sight of one small detail, it seemed to morph into something entirely different. The images were turning faster than his mind could fathom. He reached out, and slowly ran his hand down the unbelievable soft material. Chills ran up and down his spine. He then grabbed the gown, and clutched it closely to his chest. Bugiah could feel how much it belonged to him. How it seemed to echo every beat of his heart. "Weaver," he exclaimed, "you have outdone yourself!"

"Thank you, great God of Gods. I was inspired by your supreme and glorious presence," replied Jeremiah.

Bugiah turned to Myanaymiz. "I will do as you suggest Juju Witch. I will devise a new and great ritual that will endure for all eternity…one that will usher in the Resurrection of the Gods."

"Just be certain of one thing," said Myanaymiz. "The ritual must include the four elements—wind, earth, fire and water. Allow your instincts to guide you."

Bugiah glanced at Jotham who was still kneeling on the floor. He didn't like this…this thing between the Cobbler and the Juju Witch, but he needed to keep her on his side…at least for a while. He would still require her to stay with the Weaver, and Vyx to remain in the Cobbler's cottage. That, he figured, was the best he could do for now. "I shall keep my bargain with you, Juju Witch, and not kill your precious Cobbler, but you must serve me loyally. Do you understand?"

"I will serve you as you deserve to be served," Myanaymiz replied.

Bugiah grinned. "Good. I will expect nothing less. Now then, I shall return to the Mount of the Gods, and begin working on my new ritual."

Myanaymiz smiled. "And because of you, this will be the Festival that changes everything," she said.

"Yes," Bugiah pronounced. "I will be the God of Gods who changes everything!"

⸻ ◆ ⸻

83

Jotham set the plates on the table. "Sorry, but it is slightly burnt around the edges. I am usually a much better cook," he explained to Vyx.

Vyx was suspicious that Jotham had burnt the food on purpose. He knew he didn't like him staying there. "This will do. It is superior to Guardsman food," he replied.

Jotham sat down and began to cut away the burnt edges of the meat on his plate. For a long while, the two ate without talking or even looking at each other. Finally, Jotham could no longer stand the heavy silence between them. He was determined to at least make an attempt at conversation. "I remember this game…when we were boys together…this game you made up called Birds. Do you remember that?" he asked.

"No," replied Vyx. "I remember very little from before I became a Guardsman."

"It was actually very simple, but somehow you made it seem so complicated. You would have us each pick a bird of prey to transform ourselves into. You always got to pick first, and every time you picked the same. " Jotham started to laugh. "Every single time you were an eagle."

"What is so funny about being an eagle?" asked Vyx.

"It wasn't your choice that was so amusing. It was how persistent you were at being an eagle. You would run all through Town with your arms outstretched…screeching wildly. Sometimes you'd do this for an entire day. Your parents often received complaints from the annoyed Townsfolk." Jotham laughed even louder.

"I was a stupid child," said Vyx. "It is good that my parents sent me into Guardsman training."

Jotham shook his head. He couldn't help feeling some pity for Vyx. "No, you were not stupid. You were simply determined to be an eagle…swooping down upon unsuspecting Townsfolk…making women shriek in fright…encouraging the other children to do the same. You were funny, and you made us all laugh."

Vyx stirred his food with his fork. He was beginning to lose his appetite. "It is not good to talk about the past," he said.

"Why not?"

"The past is gone. It will never be again."

"I remember the past, so it cannot be entirely gone."

Vyx stood up. "It is early," he said. "But I will retire to my room now. A Guardsman must be up before the sun."

Jotham watched as Vyx silently got up, walked to his room and closed the door behind him.

⸺◆⸺

84

J eremiah was hanging up a newly woven gown for one of the Gods. "Another complete," he said. "My work is progressing well."

"There are imperfections in those gowns," said Myanaymiz.

Jeremiah was surprised she could see the flaws he had taken such care to disguise. "Yes, that is unfortunate," he replied, "but what was I to do? With everything that has happened, there simply is not the time. Had things been different, I could have woven them all to perfection."

"Why do you still lament the imperfections when you know that your gods cannot tell the difference between that which is perfect and that which is flawed?"

"I am the Master Weaver. I weave for the Townsfolk, and I weave perfection for the Gods. That is my job. When I do not do my job to the best of my ability, I suppose, I feel I have failed."

"But you did not answer my question. If your gods are incapable of knowing what is perfect, why feel any need to make excuses for yourself? Why feel ashamed or embarrassed?"

Jeremiah thought about it. "I do not know," he finally answered. "I suppose it's a habit."

"Why do you call your gods perfect when they cannot recognize perfection? Why do you call them immortal when they die?"

"We should not be talking about such things."

"Why not, Young-Old Jeremiah? Why should we not talk of such things?"

"Why do you call me Young-Old Jeremiah?" he asked. "It is strange."

She laughed. "That is all you can think to call strange about me?"

"Alright," smiled Jeremiah, "that's true enough, but answer my question please. Why do you always call me by that odd name?"

Myanaymiz walked over to him and looked into his eyes. "You have been in my dreams a very long time," she said. "I remember you when you were young. When I see you now, I still see Young Jeremiah with you yet."

Jeremiah felt uncomfortable with her standing so close, and looking directly at him. He tried not to let it show. "What do you mean? What kind of dreams? How young was I? I don't understand."

Myanaymiz smiled. "You were only a small boy, and you used to love to play alone in the garden. Your parents worried when you showed a preference for playing alone. When they tried to speak to you about it, you explained that you did have a friend. It was just that they could not see her. This worried them even more. That was a long time ago…a time when you still had an open door between worlds. One day you accidently walked straight into my dreams. I remember finding you there, lost, wandering, searching for the way out. You looked so beautiful to me. I took your hand in mine and kissed you, and then I led you back to the door to your world. Many times you returned to find me again. I was your friend Young Jeremiah. I was the friend who worried your parents so greatly."

Jeremiah looked at her in disbelief. He remembered playing in the garden alone. He remembered his parents being worried. Did he remember her?

"You had been forbidden from climbing the trees," she continued. "Your parents were so frightened that you would fall and be seriously injured. You were never a very agile child, and your mother especially worried. One day you tried it anyway. There was a tree with lower branches that you could reach. As you climbed higher, the branches became thinner and thinner. You had no way of understanding that the thinner branches could not hold your weight. You were too young to understand. When you fell, I had to catch you."

Jeremiah was amazed! He remembered that! He remembered climbing those branches…up higher and higher…the one that suddenly snapped in his hand…falling backwards…and then… and then there he was…standing on the ground as if he had never even climbed at all. High above him was the broken branch attached by a shred of bark, swinging in the wind. He stared at Myanaymiz in confused wonder.

"As a young boy you were never concerned with the gods. You believed in sparrows and ladybugs and blue skies, but never gods. Your mind was yet uncorrupted. You would run around the garden pretending you were a wild animal, growling at insects, tearing up the flowers, making your parents worry that they had created too strange a boy. I loved the days I could spend with you in your garden. They were precious to me…and still are."

Jeremiah didn't know what to say. Undefined emotions were beginning to rise up within him…undefined but powerful…so powerful! What was he to think? How could any of this be real? *Was she truly there with me when I was a boy? Was she my invisible friend? Did she really catch me when I was falling? This is all too confusing! It simply does not make any sense! I feel as though I've been cut open! Everything inside of me revealed…so…so vulnerable! I must get out of here!*

Myanaymiz watched as Jeremiah, without so much as a word, ran out the door. She sighed. "Young-Old Jeremiah, you are lost just like when you were a boy. Do not worry. Just as I did once before, I will help you find your way back."

$$85$$

The High Priest hesitated in front of the tall elaborately carved doors. He did not want to ring the bell. He wanted to turn around and go back to the simple tranquility of his temple. The eulogy for the funeral of Slemi still had to be written, and the demands that had been placed on him lately left him behind in his daily rituals. However, when the God of Gods calls for you, everything else is secondary.

Knowing he had no choice but to face what was to come, the Priest finally pulled the chain, ringing the bell. In a short time, the door opened, and a servant to the Gods ushered him in. The High Priest then walked alone down the long hallway of the private chambers of the God of Gods. When he reached the open entrance he stopped, bowed his head and waited to be summoned.

"Priest!" called Bugiah from somewhere inside the room. "Come in here now!"

The Priest walked into the room, but was surprised when he could not see the God of Gods anywhere. *What magic is this?*

"Here Priest! Come here!"

Cautiously walking further into the room, he then spied the God of Gods kneeling on the floor behind a divan. Papers were scattered all around him.

"O' great God of Gods, how may I serve you?"

"Come here, and give me your counsel."

The High Priest walked up closer to Bugiah. He could now see that the papers on the floor were pages from the Stories of the Gods. "My God, tell me what I must do."

"I have had a divine inspiration!" declared Bugiah. "For this Festival we shall have a new ritual! It shall be a ritual like no other…a great ritual set down by Bugiah, God of Gods!"

"It is indeed a year of great blessings!"

"Yes, it is. It is the year of Bugiah! Now get down here, priest, and assist me with my ritual."

The priest stepped closer then painfully knelt down on the floor. *My joints are too old for this.* "Guide me o' great God of Gods, that I may know how best to serve you."

Bugiah shuffled through the various pages in front of him. "I must devise a ritual that involves the four elements…wind, earth, fire and water. I need only see the way to begin, and you must help me with that. Pray with me to the immortal Gods who have gone on to the Place of Waiting."

"Let us pray," said the Priest. "O' great Gods in the Place of Waiting, glory be to your immortality. Be with us this day. Show us the way. Guide your brother and Lord, Bugiah, who has been given divine inspiration. He is chosen among the Gods, chosen to rule over the children of the Town, and chosen to provide them with a new and great ritual. Eed Dee Aut."

Bugiah was very pleased with the prayer. He then stared down at the mess of papers before him. *Where o' where is my inspiration?* Suddenly without warning, the word 'earth' jumped out at him from one of the pages. "The prayer worked! It is a miracle!" he said as he triumphantly picked up the paper and read the sentence aloud. "After the victory, the God plunged his sword into the earth." Bugiah thought about it a moment and then exclaimed, "That is it! Part of the ritual shall involve me plunging my sword into the earth. You have done a fine job of praying, High Priest."

"Thank you, my God. All miracles come through you, and I am but your grateful servant."

"Go now," said Bugiah. "I can manage on my own from here."

"As you wish, my Lord." Then, with some effort, the High Priest got to his feet, and quickly as he could, backed out of the room.

Bugiah remained on the floor, hunting through the papers around him. *Now, where is my next revelation?* Suddenly, he spotted one with a bent corner that had fallen off to the side. *A sign!* He eagerly snatched it up, and ran his finger down the page, scouring the text for any words that would offer further enlightenment. *Damp, spin, sick, death…no, not a single word of inspiration!* Violently crumpling the paper then throwing it down, he screamed, "Where is my divine inspiration! I am the God of Gods! All things should come easily to me!"

 Arlene Adamo

86

Jeremiah sat on the bench in the tiny room. The door was closed shut, and the early morning sunshine was gently streaming in through the window. He thought he could hear Myanaymiz moving in the other room. *Why am I hiding here? I'm an old man not a child…a Master Weaver, and yet here I am huddled in this closet, afraid to even open the door?*

The night before, he had returned to the cottage only after he was certain she had gone to bed. He did not want to face her. He still did not want to face her.

Suddenly, there was a tiny knock on the door. "Jeremiah!" He sighed to hear her soft voice call his name. "Jeremiah, come out and have something to eat. I know that you are awake."

Jeremiah got up and went to the door. He opened it slowly. Myanaymiz was standing there, smiling at him. "On the table, you will find bread, jam and tea. Please, come and eat," she said. Jeremiah looked over to see that the table had been nicely set for him. There was even a vase full of wild flowers placed in the center. He recognized the small white vase as the one he had long ago tucked away in the back of his cupboard. It was a present he had once given to his mother.

Without a word, he walked over and sat down. Myanaymiz followed after then pulled up a chair across from him. "I did not mean to frighten you," she said.

"You didn't…I mean…I wasn't…what you said was so… It brought back memories in strange clarity. It evoked powerful emotions."

"I understand," she said.

"Was I really in your dreams?" he asked. "It is not a trick?"

"I would never trick you, Jeremiah."

"You're not calling me Young-Old Jeremiah, today."

Myanaymiz smiled. "No," she replied. "There is now only one Jeremiah. Do you feel it?"

Jeremiah thought about it. *Do I feel different?* "Yes," he answered, suddenly aware that something had indeed changed. "I do feel different. I'm not certain what it is exactly. Perhaps, I do feel restored in some way…put back together. I suppose, it is true that young Jeremiah was intentionally left behind. Long ago I put him aside… locked him away in a cupboard along with all of his laughter and freedom. There was simply no place for a carefree boy in the life of a Master Weaver. I had many responsibilities, and he would have made it very difficult for me. Did you somehow release him? For a moment, I felt what it was like to be him again, wildly running through the garden, not caring about anything but the glory of the present. I was taken back in time. How can that be?"

"All good things are ours forever when we make room in our hearts," she replied.

Jeremiah laughed. "All good things are ours forever when we make room in our hearts" he repeated.

Myanaymiz stood up, "I will go see Jotham now. He misses me."

Jeremiah wanted to say, *but I'll miss you too.* Instead he said, "Yes, it is good for you to go see Jotham. He will not be finding it very comfortable having to share his cottage with a Guardsman. It will ease his burden to see you." He then sadly watched as she walked out the door.

 Arlene Adamo

87

Vyx stopped Myanaymiz at the open door. "The Cobbler is making new shoes for the God of Gods, and cannot be disturbed."

"Let me see him for just a moment," she replied.

"She is my inspiration!" Jotham suddenly called out from inside the cottage. "Please let her in, Honourable Guardsman, and I will be able to craft the greatest shoes ever made."

Vyx looked suspiciously at Myanaymiz as he considered the request. *It is true that the God of Gods has not said that she is forbidden from seeing the Cobbler. And if her Juju Witch magic really can help him create a superior pair of shoes then such a thing would be to the delight of the God of Gods. And after all, she is now working with my God. But yet, she is still a Juju Witch, and I have seen the strange things she can do. She cannot be trusted entirely. I must deal with this situation cautiously.* Not taking his eyes from her, Vyx then slowly moved aside and said, "You may go in, but only for a brief time. I will remain right here…listening."

Myanaymiz quickly went inside while Vyx remained outside. She saw Jotham seated at his work table. He smiled warmly to see her.

"Jotham, I am so glad to see you," she exclaimed, hurrying over, putting her arms around him and kissing his cheek. "Do as I tell you," she whispered into his ear. "We do not have much time. Take that nail by your hand."

Jotham looked down and saw there was a shoe nail close to his hand. He picked it up.

"Now measure with your thumb one length from the bottom of the heel and one length from the edge, then place the nail there and hammer it in, but leave the head sticking out. Do not allow the nail to penetrate the inside of the shoe. Only take it to the very edge. Be certain to cover the head with leather after you are done so that it may not be detected." Myanaymiz pulled back from him, and looked into his eyes. "Trust me," she said.

Jotham carefully measured with his thumb, and hammered the nail in exactly as she had told him. Myanaymiz then affectionately ran her hand down the side of his face. "You are making such beautiful shoes," she said. "The God of Gods will be well pleased."

Vyx appeared in the doorway. "That is enough! The Cobbler must get back to work!"

"I shall see you later," she said to Jotham, and then kissed him on the mouth. Vyx looked away.

Once outside the cottage, Myanaymiz walked down the path and to the road. Vyx followed behind her. She then suddenly spun around and demanded, "Why do you follow me? Do you have more questions?"

Vyx felt flush with anger. *How dare this woman speak to a Guardsman so! And how dare she shamelessly kiss the Cobbler in front of me!* "What kind of evil Juju spell did you put upon me the other night?" he blurted out. "Tell the truth!"

"I have already told you the truth. That was no spell," she said.

"It must have been. A true Guardsman could not lose his control without the influence of powerful magic."

"Then perhaps you are not a true Guardsman."

Vyx found himself reaching for his sword, but then remembered it was not there. "I am a Guardsman true of heart. I serve my Gods with a loyalty that knows no bounds."

"You are a fool!" exclaimed Myanaymiz. "Bugiah beats you in a way that most would not even beat a dog. You take it even though you know you do not deserve it. You are loyal, and it means nothing! If all you have is your loyalty to that cruel man, then you have nothing."

For a moment, Vyx went silent with shock then through his clenched teeth he uttered, "You will die for that!"

Myanaymiz laughed. "I have not come here to die. Tell Bugiah what I have said, if that is what you wish, but it will only result in you being severely beaten. Bugiah desperately wants the power of the Juju Witch. He will not kill me for my words. But you, on the other hand, he will beat you severely if you bring him news that annoys him. You will be the one who is punished not me." Myanaymiz then turned and headed in the direction of Jeremiah's cottage.

Vyx watched in fury as she walked away. At that moment, he was wishing he had his uniform to cover him…that heavy, stifling uniform. He felt so naked standing alone in the road with only flimsy Townsfolk clothing to protect him. As he watched her walk further and further away, he considered running after her… catching her…frightening her into admitting to her magic and her lies, but what would that help? Of course she was right. He knew that. If he said those words out loud…if he told Bugiah that she had called him a mere man, the cane would come out and smash down on him. It would be more than a simple beating. It could mean his death. *I am a Guardsman. A Guardsman's loyalty is everything.* Yet what would loyalty bring him in this instance? Loyalty would bring him only an unwarranted severe punishment. "Blasphemy," he hissed under his breath wishing he had not had those thoughts. *I am a Guardsman true of heart. I serve my Gods with a loyalty that knows no bounds.*

⸺•◦•⸺

88

Jeremiah looked up from his loom, surprised to see Myanaymiz had returned so quickly from Jotham's cottage. "He is very busy crafting a new pair of shoes for Bugiah," she explained.

"Oh, I see," said Jeremiah, looking down again, and pretending to concentrate on his weaving.

"Will you walk with me?" she asked.

"I am busy weaving the final gown, and the funeral for Slemi is tomorrow. It would not be appropriate."

"You have plenty of time to finish the gown, and there are no laws of mourning around the death of Townsperson. Come and walk with me. It will clear your head, and do you good."

Jeremiah stopped weaving, and looked up at Myanaymiz. She was standing in the sunlit doorway wearing that gown…the most beautiful gown he had ever created. He could hear the birds singing outside, and could feel the warm scented breeze blowing in through the open door. Perhaps a walk would not be such a bad idea. His back had been giving him trouble, and stretching it out might be just the thing he needed.

"Alright," he agreed. "I will walk with you."

Once outside, Myanaymiz exclaimed, "The sun is so very hot today. It is best that we walk in the shade of the forest."

It was true, the sun was hot, and getting hotter. "Very well," said Jeremiah. "We shall walk under the cool of the trees."

By the time they reached the edge of the woods, Jeremiah was already feeling too hot. The forest would indeed provide relief. "It is a good idea to get out of the sun," he said.

"Yes, it is," said Myanaymiz.

As they walked along through the cool damp forest, Jeremiah couldn't help but think about the other night…the things she had told him…the emotions she made him feel. "Walking is good for an old man," he said.

"You are not as old as you look," she replied. "Why do you wear your hair and beard so long?"

"That is the way of the Master Weaver. I cannot cut my hair."

"Is it forbidden?"

"Well, no…not exactly. It is more like a tradition. People expect the Master Weaver to look this way."

"And do you like it?"

Jeremiah thought about it. "I…I'm not sure. It's something I never considered before. It's simply the way it is."

"Like how you worship your gods. You worship them without thought or reflection. You simply accept it as given. You believe they do magic, even when it is obvious that you do far more magic with your beautiful weaving than they ever will."

"We must not talk of the Gods."

"Why? There is no one here to hear us."

"It's…it's just not done."

"It is done all the time in whispers, but no one has the courage to ask these questions out loud."

"What do you mean, it's done all the time?"

"You whisper about it with Jotham. Other Townsfolk whisper about it. I hear them late at night in my dreams. There are some like Slemi, who would never whisper about such things, but they are very few."

Jeremiah was surprised. *Could it be true? Were people really whispering about the Gods?*

"They hate living in fear," she continued. "They hate it, but they continue with it because it is like your beard and hair. It is a tradition…it provides security. The gods are their objects of worship, and that gives their lives meaning. It is far easier to do this… to live in a fantasy and suffer, then to face life for all that it is. Life, the unpredictable. Life, the uncertain. It is easier to cling to these worthless idols than to seek out the one true God who does not lock up the mind, but opens it freely. And freedom is frightening… at first…but only at first. After that, you cannot bear to live without it."

"This God, is this the one you call your Lord?" asked Jeremiah.

"Yes, but it is more complicated than that," said Myanaymiz.

"What do you mean, more complicated?"

"God is not simple. My Lord is my God, but He is also only a part of my God…at the same time within the part is the whole and within the whole are the parts. Spoken words are very limited when it comes to God. God is in the words, but at the same time, words distance God."

"This is very confusing," said Jeremiah. "Can you explain what you mean?"

"It is like when you stand very close to something very large. You can touch it, smell it, sense it, absorb the details of it, hear its breathing and maybe even its heartbeat…but you cannot fully see it. You must create distance to see something that size. Once there is distance, you lose that closeness. You can no longer feel it, but now you see it…but only from afar. So, you see it, but you do not fully experience it. Something essential is lost. Spoken words are like that. They give the illusion of bringing God closer, but really they distance God…make God smaller. Talking about God is distancing God. That is why it must be done very carefully or else something terrible happens."

"What happens?"

"People start to do things like worshiping objects or other people. And then they end up living like the Townsfolk, which is a terrible way to live."

Jeremiah said nothing. The pain had begun to creep into his back again.

"Why do you not allow me to help you with your pain?" she asked. "You know I can make it go away."

"So, you know I am in pain. I cannot hide much from you, can I?" he nervously laughed.

"You did not answer my question. Why do you not allow me to help you?"

Jeremiah thought about it…about what kind of excuse he could make. *Don't be such a coward. Just tell her the truth.* "To be honest," he said, "there is a small voice inside of me that says, 'don't be a fool, old man, let her heal you.' But something is stopping me, Myanaymiz. I do not know what it is, but something is holding me back. Perhaps, it is fear of change, but for some reason I'm just afraid to let you heal me. I wish I understood why I feel that way. It's very confusing."

"Thank you for being honest," she said. "It means a great deal. It hurts when people lie to me. The truth is a gift even when it is not what I would prefer to hear."

"The last thing I want is for you to be hurt," Jeremiah replied.

Myanaymiz looked at him, and softly smiled. "You are a good man, Jeremiah."

The two continued to walk along, but now in silence. Above them, the birds on the branches were singing such strange sweet songs that Jeremiah wondered if they were the same birds he had heard all his life. *Where have you come from beautiful creatures? What wondrous sounds do you make? How the wind rustles the leaves as if in applause for your music. It's all so perfect, so peaceful, so harmonious…* Jeremiah had momentarily forgotten about everything that was troubling him, including his back. There was nothing else in the world but this paradise…this awe-inspiring spectacular miracle. Then suddenly, something leapt out from behind a tree! "BOO!" shouted Axis, making Jeremiah jump.

"You startled us, Axis," scolded Jeremiah.

"I am sorry Old Jeremiah. I was only playing."

"You did not scare me," said Myanaymiz.

Axis ran over and grabbed hold of her hand. "My Lady, my Lady, come and play with me! I am alone, and the birds are too busy, and the insects don't care!"

Myanaymiz smiled at the child. "He reminds me of you, Jeremiah…a free spirit. What shall we play little one?"

Axis could not contain his delight. He jumped up and down, exclaiming, "Lions! We'll play lions! You and Old Jeremiah will be the lions, and I will be the hunter. I will count to ten, and you will run away. If I find you, I will shoot you with my bow and arrow."

"I am too old to run," laughed Jeremiah.

"You are not," said Myanaymiz. "Do not worry, I will run with you."

"I will now count to ten, so run away lions!" Axis turned and hid his face against a tree. "RUN!" he shouted once more before he began counting.

Jeremiah began to run, and Myanaymiz ran along side of him. They darted this way and that, through the trees…jumping roots…dodging rocks…once even frightening up a wild turkey. Soon they changed their pace to a fast walk. "I cannot believe that I ran," said Jeremiah. "It has been so long."

"Did you enjoy it?" she asked.

"Yes, very much! Although, I am now short of breath."

"You just need more practice."

From a distance they heard Axis calling, "Lions, oh lions, I am coming to hunt you!"

"Let us hide," said Myanaymiz.

"Where?"

"Axis' secret house is nearby. Let us go in there."

Jeremiah followed after Myanaymiz. When they arrived at the secret house, Jeremiah looked back to see if he could see Axis. He was nowhere in sight.

"Quickly," said Myanaymiz. "We must hide from the hunter." She crouched down, and disappeared into the small opening.

Jeremiah took one last look back before he too vanished within the strange tangle of sticks and branches. He crawled over, and sat beside Myanaymiz on the sheep skin. The daylight gently bled in through the tiny openings in the walls, giving the place a magical dusk-like glow.

"I don't hear him," said Jeremiah. "Do you think he gave up, and returned home?"

"No, he is still there. He is still searching."

Jeremiah laughed. "I cannot believe I am spending the day pretending to be a lion, and am now hiding in a child's make-believe house. If the Townsfolk could see this, they would think I had lost my mind."

"It is a lion's den, and we are the lions," Myanaymiz reminded him.

"Alright, it is a lion's den. Roooaaaar!" They both started to laugh. "At least I look like a lion," he said, running his hand through his beard. "An old grey lion."

For a while they simply sat together silently, the only sound being that of the birds chirping outside of their refuge. Jeremiah closed his eyes. It was so peaceful and relaxing, but at the same time he could feel his back start to protest sitting on the ground. He shifted a little to try and take the pressure off.

"Why do you not let me fix that for you?" asked Myanaymiz.

Jeremiah opened his eyes. Why not indeed? She had fixed Jotham, and he didn't seem to have any adverse effects, so why did he not allow her to fix him also? *I should not be afraid. I am the Master Weaver, revered by the Town. Why should the Master Weaver be afraid of a woman's touch? If I have the choice of living without this pain, what am I waiting for?* "Alright," he agreed. "Please heal me." He turned his back to her and waited.

"Aha! Pichoo! Pichoo! Arrows straight through the heart!" Axis was crouched in the doorway, his hands raised as he launched his invisible arrows from his invisible bow.

"Oh, this lion has been successfully hunted!" cried out Jeremiah, as he fell over into the soft sheep skin.

Axis crawled up to him and ruffled his hair. "What a fine warm coat you shall make for me."

Jeremiah laughed. He looked up at Myanaymiz and said, "Perhaps we should return now."

Myanaymiz smiled. "Yes, we will fix your problem later, but for now we should return."

"Can't you play just one more time," pleaded Axis.

"Not today," said Myanaymiz. "The Master Weaver has work to finish."

"Yes," said Jeremiah, sitting up. "It's getting late, and we had best return to the Town."

"That's alright. I'm hungry anyway," said Axis, as he quickly disappeared through the exit.

Jeremiah looked at Myanaymiz. "Thank you for encouraging me to go on a walk. It has made me feel better. In fact, it has made me feel young again. Imagine, an old Weaver playing lions! What a thing I have done," he laughed.

"Do not be fooled by yourself, Jeremiah. You are still young," she said to him. "Even when you are tired and in pain, Young Jeremiah is always there in your eyes."

⎯⎯•◆•⎯⎯

89

Jotham carefully polished one of the golden wings that graced the heel of the God of Gods' new shoes. Once it was polished to perfection, he set it down beside its mate. He then stared in amazement at his own incredible craftsmanship. Never had he made a pair that magnificent before…the shining silver of the tops, the beautiful golden wings on the heels and the mirror like black sheen of the soles. "You have outdone yourself this time, Cobbler," he said to himself.

"Yes, you certainly have."

Jotham turned to see Vyx standing behind him. The Guardsman walked over, and ran his finger along the edge of a golden wing. "The God of Gods will be greatly pleased. I suppose that Juju Witch truly has inspired you after all."

The thought of Myanaymiz filled Jotham longing. He considered going to see her, but it was already getting late. Besides which, he was certain that the Guardsman would surely follow him. It was awkward enough with Jeremiah there. Having Vyx there, watching his every move…his every glance…would only be torture.

Instead, he decided to try and annoy Vyx with more talk of the past. It was the one thing he now knew could get under his skin. If he annoyed him enough, perhaps the Guardsman would keep his distance. "Actually, the idea for the wings came from you," Jotham told him.

"From me?"

"Yes, from you. When we were boys, and I told you that I was going to be trained as a Cobbler, you said that was a good thing because then I would be able to make you a pair of shoes with wings. With those wings, you would be able to fly anywhere…like an eagle…over the Town…over the forest…even over the Mount of the Gods."

Vyx went a little red in the face. "I was a silly child. How did you tolerate me?" he said, not looking at Jotham, but instead staring at the shoe.

"We were both children, and you were my friend. A very good friend from what I can remember… entertaining, funny, loyal."

"I am a very loyal Guardsman," said Vyx now looking up at Jotham. "How was I a loyal friend? I remember very little of my life before."

Jotham was surprised by Vyx's seemingly new found curiosity about the past. Before he answered, he thought about it for a moment. What memory would best describe Vyx's loyalty? There were many times when he had shown his loyalty…mostly in small ways, but would Vyx the Guardsman fully understand the subtly of those stories? He had to think of a memory that was bold and obvious. Suddenly, it came to him. "There was this one time," he said, "when one of the older boys was holding me down, slapping my face, and putting mud in my hair. He was calling it girl hair, and saying that he was changing the color to a proper boy color. You came up behind him and, even though he was twice your size, you whacked him across the head with a big stick." Jotham started to laugh. "The poor boy was knocked unconscious, and we both panicked thinking he was dead. As we were preparing a story about how he had killed himself by hitting his own head with the stick to prove his strength, we saw his eyes begin to flicker open. That's when we both ran as fast as we could."

Vyx scratched his head. "Yes…yes, I think I do remember that. That terrible boy. Very cruel. But what was his name? That I do not remember."

"His name was Oodoo, but we used to call him Poo Doo," said Jotham. "Never to his face of course because he was so much bigger and very mean."

"Yes, I remember now," said Vyx. "He was very mean. He would hide and he would wait. And then, as you walked by, he'd jump out and frighten you. If you didn't manage to get away, he'd then push you down to the ground, and beat you mercilessly." Vyx was silent for a few seconds, and then added, "I should go see him now. See what he thinks of Vyx the Guardsman. Is he still in the Town?"

"No," answered Jotham. "He died many years ago. He was walking along the edge of the river where the current is swift, and he slipped in." Jotham then began to laugh aloud.

"Why is that so funny?" asked Vyx.

At first, Jotham could not get the words out for laughing. Finally, he managed to utter, "He…hmmmf…he was said to have slipped on horse poo! Poo Doo was killed by poo!" Jotham then burst out in uncontrollable laughter again. He wasn't even sure why he was laughing over such a childish joke. It just felt so natural, and the laughter just kept coming. In the midst of it, he glanced over at Vyx and could not believe what he was seeing. Never in his wildest dreams did he ever imagine such a thing was even possible, but there it was. The Guardsman of the Gods was actually grinning.

90

Jeremiah quickly cleared away the dishes. "That was a lovely meal. Thank you, Jeremiah," said Myanaymiz. "I enjoyed it very much."

"You are very welcome," he replied then disappeared into the kitchen. He soon returned with a bowl full of strawberries. "These are fresh from my garden," he said as he held them out in offering.

Myanaymiz smiled then took a plump red one from the top. She put it to her lips, and took a bite. "How very sweet and delicious it is," she said.

"The trick is in the watering," explained Jeremiah, as he set the bowl on the table then sat down on the chair opposite. "It is easy to water too much or not enough. It is an art to water just the right amount."

"You are an amazing artist."

"As are you," said Jeremiah. "The gown you wove for Bugiah is the most incredible thing I have ever seen."

Myanaymiz smiled. "There are far more incredible things to come."

Jeremiah wondered what she meant by that…what kind of incredible things? Part of him wanted to know everything. She had secrets. He could feel it. But another other part of him preferred not to know. Ignorance is a comfort not easily given up, and in the end, he decided to stay comfortable. "Perhaps I should now return to my weaving," he said. "A Master Weaver who spends the day playing in the woods has some catching up to do. I must fulfill my responsibilities."

"Did you not want me to fix your back first?" asked Myanaymiz. "You know it will begin to give you trouble again after an hour at your loom."

Jeremiah looked at her, and then quickly looked away. Of course he wanted that. More than anything, he wanted her to heal his back. He had already told her he did while they were hiding in the secret house. But when he agreed to it, they were in a fantasy place. He was a fantasy lion living in a fantasy world…momentarily lost in a silly child's game. Here, on the other hand, in the cold reality of his cottage, his responsible adult cottage with the gowns of the Gods hanging upon the walls staring accusingly at him, it no longer seemed such an easy decision.

Myanaymiz smiled softly. "Are you still afraid?" she asked.

"I suppose…I suppose I am," he confessed.

"I will not do what you do not wish me to," she said. "That is not what I do. That is not who I am. However, what if instead, you let me fix your hair?"

"Fix my hair?!" Jeremiah laughed. "I'm a Master Weaver. A Master Weaver allows his hair and beard to grow naturally."

"Which certainly did not help you when you accidently wove your beard into that priest's vestment, and then had to spend hours trying to untangle yourself from the fabric," she laughed.

Jeremiah was shocked. "How did you know about that? That was last year. You were not here."

"My dreams have taken me many places, Jeremiah. Now, about your hair, if you let me trim it along with your beard, you would not have that problem again. I promise I will not cut it too short, just enough. Like watering strawberries, Jeremiah…not too much… not too little…just enough."

Jeremiah ran his hand down his long beard. What a strange idea! Master Weavers never cut their hair. For as long as anyone could remember, this was the tradition. But what if he did decide to break with tradition? What would that mean? It was not against the law. It was simply something that always was. But it was something that identified him…protected him. In that way, it was similar to a Guardsman's veil, something that signified who he was.

"Are you also afraid of losing your hair?" asked Myanaymiz. "You are afraid too often, Jeremiah."

Jeremiah did not like to hear her say that. He was not afraid. Yes, he was afraid of the healing, but that was different…that was something strange and foreign. He was certainly no coward, having lived a long time, and having seen many things. He was not easily frightened. People looked up to him…came to him for advice. He was the Master Weaver. He had faced the God of Gods at the most difficult times. Why would he be afraid of a simple haircut? "I am not afraid of you cutting my hair," he said, defiantly.

"Then let me do it," replied Myanaymiz. "If you do not like it, simply grow it back. No harm done."

As Jeremiah carefully thought about it, the idea started to seem oddly exciting…a Master Weaver with shorter hair? How different! How shocked the Townsfolk would be to see him show up at Slemi's funeral with a haircut! How they would talk! Gossip at the graveside…a perfect send-off for Slemi. "Alright," he said, surprising himself. "Why not? I shall make you my barber." He sat down on the chair, adding, "My scissors are by my loom."

Myanaymiz walked over, and picked up the scissors. She then returned, and stood behind him. "Just enough," Jeremiah reminded her, "and no more."

"I will cut no more than just enough," she agreed.

Jeremiah watched as strand by strand, his grey hair began to softly fall down around him. As more and more hair fell to the floor, he found himself beginning to worry. *Is she planning to make me bald? Had I made a terrible mistake thinking that a Master Weaver could get a haircut? It would be one thing for a Master Weaver to have shorter hair, and quite another for him to have no hair. The Townsfolk would not only be talking. They would be laughing.*

"Are you certain that is just enough?" he nervously asked.

     Arlene Adamo

"Do not worry, Jeremiah. Just one more…" *snip* "There. That is enough. Now for your beard."

Myanaymiz walked around, and stood in front of him. As she began to work on his beard, Jeremiah was not sure where to look. She was now so close to him, he could see every line of her face… every beautiful line. He closed his eyes, and tried to think of other things…Bugiah…Vyx…Jotham…dead Slemi. *Oh her scent! What is that scent? Something fresh and pure…air…water…fire or is it the rich scent of life-giving earth?* Just as he thought he could no longer keep himself from reaching out and touching her, Myanaymiz took a few steps back and announced, "It is complete. Old Jeremiah is now New Jeremiah."

Jeremiah opened his eyes, and ran his hand through his new beard. He then ran his hand through his new shorter hair. He felt so light…so free! *Is this a dream? Did I really let her cut my hair and beard?* He stood up, and walked over to the mirror. There looking back at him was a man he had not seen in many years…a younger man…a spirited man…a man full of life and passion. "This is wonderful!" he said, shaking out his hair. "I am so glad I let you talk me into this."

"Would you like me to fix your back now?"

"Yes, please!" he exclaimed, no longer feeling hesitant. "I would be so grateful if you would heal me."

Myanaymiz walked over, and stood behind him. "Are you ready?" she asked him.

With her standing so close once again, Jeremiah found himself wavering. It was all just so suddenly real. What would this do to him? She was already so much a part of his everyday thoughts. Would this make it even worse? Was he truly ready for this? He looked down at his grey hair on the floor. *I cannot waver like this forever. I am getting older. And for all I know, she could disappear just as quickly as she appeared. Could I live with the regret if she left without healing me? If not now, then when, Master Weaver? When?* "Yes," he finally said, "I am ready. Please restore me."

She then gently placed her hand on his lower back, and instantly he felt a strange warming sensation spreading throughout his body. The intensity of it started to grow, until it felt as though his veins were being infused with liquid fire…a life giving fire…a beautiful comforting, living fire! His entire body was now ablaze with a powerful energy! *How could this be real?* Jeremiah reached out to steady himself on the wall.

When Myanaymiz removed her hand, the intensity slowly subsided, leaving a strange satisfying peaceful feeling. Jeremiah carefully reached behind, and ran his fingers over the place where she had touched him. Was it any different? He straightened his spine then twisted it this way and that. There was nothing. No more sharp pain. No dull ache. No pressure. Nothing. She had healed him!

"Thank you, Myanaymiz!" he said, turning to face her. "Thank you so much!"

Myanaymiz smiled at him. "You are welcome," she said, looking into his eyes.

Jeremiah could not look away. "My God, but you are so beautiful."

Myanaymiz reached over, and ran her hand down his newly shorn beard. "You are a good man, Jeremiah, and I need a good man."

Arlene Adamo

91

"Master Weaver!?"

Jeremiah quickly stepped outside, closing the cottage door behind him. "Your Holiness," he said to the High Priest. "Why have you come so early?"

"I have not come early! Why are you still in your night robe? You should be ready for the funeral, and, great Gods, what has happened to your hair and beard?"

"I…I did not wake up. I must have been working too late on the gowns for the Gods. And yes, my hair…my beard…they are trimmed. Please forgive me."

The High Priest shook his head disapprovingly. "The God of Gods says that he intends to pay his divine respects to the Townswoman. This is a great honour for everyone…and you have slept in! And cut your hair! But there is no time to discuss this now, we must prepare!"

"The Gods forgive me," said Jeremiah. "I will only be a moment. Please go to the graveside, and I will join you there shortly."

"Very well, but hurry!"

"Yes," said Jeremiah. "I will hurry." He waited until the High Priest had turned, and was already walking down the lane before he opened the cottage door, and slipped back inside. He closed it tightly behind him.

"I'm late," he called out, as he walked over, and opened the cupboard. He took out his formal trousers then quickly put them on. "The God of Gods is coming. This is highly unusual even for someone as important to the Town as Slemi."

"He is not coming for Slemi."

Jeremiah turned and saw Myanaymiz standing in the bedroom door. His white sheet was draped around her body.

"He is coming for me," she said. "Slemi is merely an excuse for him. He wants to try and learn more about me as well as to get my counsel for his new ritual."

Jeremiah looked away. "Where is my shirt?" he said, checking the cupboard. "Oh, here it is." He quickly took off his night robe, and pulled on his shirt. He then grabbed his official's coat that hung on a hook near the cupboard. As he slipped his arms in, and turned around, he came face to face with Myanaymiz.

"Do not worry, Jeremiah. Everything will be alright," she said, straightening his lapels.

"I have to go," he said, as he rushed past her, and opened the door.

"Jeremiah!" she called. He stopped, and looked back at her. "You look wonderful. Do not ever forget that, Master Weaver."

He blushed and smiled. "I have to go," he said, as he hurried out the door.

⎯⎯•◆•⎯⎯

92

By the time Jeremiah arrived at the graveside, people had already begun to gather. The High Priest gave him a stern look, but said nothing. Jeremiah took his place next to him on the platform then stared down into the grave. The polished wooden coffin was decorated with the elaborate crest of The Society of Women Servants to the Gods. *She's really in there. Slemi is really dead.*

"Look at Old Jeremiah! Old Jeremiah what happened to you?" shouted Petal, who was standing in the viewing area on the other side of the grave. Her father quickly quieted his child, but then turned and whispered to his wife. Jeremiah suddenly realized that they were not the only ones whispering. All of the Townsfolk, who were present, appeared to be staring and whispering about him. Only then did he remember about his hair and his beard. *Don't be surprised. You knew to expect this.*

In preparation for the ceremony, the High Priest handed Jeremiah the tin box containing all of the items required for the Funeral Rites of Mortals. Jeremiah took it in his hands then silently waited as more and more Townsfolk gathered. He was trying hard not to pay any attention to all the staring, the whispering and the giggling of the children.

"You are causing a disruption," the High Priest discretely whispered to Jeremiah. "What kind of Master Weaver trims his hair and beard?"

"It is not forbidden," said Jeremiah.

"When the God of Gods sees it, perhaps it will be."

As the crowd around the graveside grew, it eased Jeremiah's sense of discomfort just a little. Surely a larger group would make him seem less conspicuous. What he didn't realize was that those at the front were whispering about him to those behind and so on and so on. The entire crowd was abuzz with news that the Master Weaver had cut his hair.

When it seemed as though all of the Townsfolk were finally present, the High Priest proudly announced, "We shall begin the proceedings just as soon as our glorious God of Gods arrives!"

Everyone was immediately atwitter over the exciting news.

"The God of Gods is coming here? Oh what a blessing this is!"

"Slemi was such a good woman that the God of Gods himself is attending her funeral! If only she could see this, how proud she would be!"

"I hope the God of Gods walks close to me! I've never seen him up close before!"

"The God of Gods is so magnificent!"

It was not long before the sound of an approaching carriage made everyone turn their heads. "Oh heavenly Gods, it is him!" They all watched with excitement as the large gilded carriage, pulled by six black steeds, stopped at the cemetery gates. Many rushed over to get a closer look, but no one dared get too close for fear of offending their greatest God. They fully understood the rule of distance, and the consequences for breaking such a rule.

Jeremiah watched as Vyx hurried up to the carriage and stood at attention. It was such a strange and comical sight to see some-one dressed as a Townsperson, acting like a Guardsman. For a moment, he felt an urge to laugh out loud, but his strong sense of decorum and responsibility kept him in check.

Another Guardsman in full uniform, who had been riding beside the driver, jumped down, pulled out the step, and opened the door. When Bugiah, dressed in a magnificent black silk formal gown, stepped out, everyone fell to their knees. The Townsfolk all bowed their heads as he walked by to the graveside.

"My God," said the High Priest, kneeling before him.

Bugiah ignored the priest, and instead stared down at Jeremiah. "What has happened to you?" he asked.

"It seemed...appropriate, my God. I pray it does not offend you," Jeremiah replied without looking up.

Bugiah began to laugh. "It's that Juju Witch, isn't it? I send her to live at the cottage of the Master Weaver and next thing I know, he shows up with his hair cut. Where is that Witch?" Bugiah looked around, but could not see her.

"She must be here somewhere, my God,' replied Jeremiah. "Perhaps, she is somewhere at the back of the crowd."

"Never mind now," said Bugiah. "Let's just get on with the ceremony. High Priest, get up and begin!"

———•◆•———

93

Myanaymiz put her head on Jotham's chest. "I like the sound of your heart," she said. "May it beat strong for a very long time."

Jotham ran his hand through her silver hair as he stared up at a tiny drop of sunlight peeking in through the tangle of twigs and branches that made up the roof of Axis' secret house. "We are missing Slemi's funeral, and I know they will eventually notice that we are gone, yet here am I thinking, I don't even care. Let them gossip. Let them report us to the Gods. What concern is it to me? Not long ago, I would have been filled with fear over this. I would have been lying here filled with worry, but not anymore. You've changed so much for me, Myanaymiz."

"I am glad of that. You are now a stronger man."

"Yes, I suppose I do feel much stronger…more certain of myself."

"And when I leave, I will be leaving a Jotham who is stronger and happier."

Jotham had not forgotten that she said she would eventually leave, but he had just pushed the idea to the back of his mind. He didn't like being reminded now. "Why do you have to go? Won't you please stay? I will not be happy if you go."

"When my Lord calls me, I will have to go to Him. That is what I am waiting for."

Jotham held her tighter. "But I don't know if I can live without you."

Myanaymiz laughed. "You will never live without me. I will leave a part of myself in your heart. It will give you power and a long life. You will do great things with it, and be known forever as Jotham the Great."

Jotham laughed. "Jotham the Great? Perhaps, I should make a song about it."

"There will come a day when such a song will be sung," she replied. She then ran her fingers over his firm stomach. "There is also one more thing I must tell you. I have loved Jeremiah as I have loved you."

Jotham was shocked! At first, he didn't know what to say. *Does she understand what she has just said? Jeremiah? She loved Jeremiah?* "What do you mean, 'as you loved me?' Does that mean…?"

"Yes, it does. I loved Jeremiah as I have loved you. He is a good man."

Jotham stared at a small collage of dried wildflowers Axis had placed in the wall for decoration. He was feeling both confused and hurt. "I…I don't understand. Why was I not enough for you? And Jeremiah? He is such an old man."

Myanaymiz gently caressed his arm. "Jeremiah is younger than you think," she said. "And it is not a question of you not being enough. You are beautiful and plentiful, Jotham. But you know I am different. I came from a rock. This is what I do, and who I am. I love good men. For those who are most worthy, I will leave them the secret power. Both you and Jeremiah are worthy men. You will both be left with the secret power."

It was then that Jotham realized he was involved in something more complicated than he had ever imagined. This was no ordinary relationship. What was between them was something well beyond common Townsfolk knowledge and experience. It was something entirely new. This sudden realization left him no longer feeling hurt, but he was now more confused than ever. "What is this power I will receive?" he asked. "What will I be able to do with it?"

"Many things," she answered. "You will see when I bestow it upon you. It is something that can only be felt, not described in words. Now, will you please sing a new song for me? I need to hear your beautiful voice. It helps to strengthen me."

Jotham sighed. *I have unintentionally become a part of something so much greater than just myself. It's becoming clearer now.* He gently stroked her hair and said, "You have already given me the power of song. For that I am truly grateful. Of course I will sing to you. I will do anything you wish." He then paused, and waited for the first words to come to him. As soon as he had them, he knew the rest would quickly follow. Jotham opened his mouth, and sang with all of his heart,

When you go
When you leave me
I ask just one thing
Leave me a piece of your heart
But not just any piece
Leave me the piece that I touched
The piece that I know
The piece that I loved
The piece that I tasted
In your kiss; sweet kisses
Leave me the piece
Where I found my peace
This is all I ask
This is all I ask

     Arlene Adamo

94

"And as we conclude this very sad and solemn ceremony, let me say again that Slemi was not an ordinary Townswoman. She was a law-abider, a Gods worshipper, the eyes and ears of our community. Weep today, for we have lost a great role model for our children. She taught them total obedience to the Gods. Surely there has never been a…"

"Speed it up," whispered Bugiah into the High Priest's ear.

"…never been a woman as devoted to glorifying the Gods as she. Eed Dee Aut. Now Townsfolk, please return to your homes, and, in your prayers to the Gods, always remember our dearest Slemi." The High Priest then reached over to the open box in Jeremiah's hands, and placed the Funeral Rites back inside. He carefully closed the lid, bowing as he did.

Bugiah stood looking over the crowd. *Where is that Juju Witch?* He could not see her anywhere, and it was beginning to frustrate him. *How will I find that Juju Witch with all of these fools lingering here?* "You have received the blessing of seeing your God of Gods today, be thankful for that. Now go home! Immediately!" he loudly declared. "Except for the Juju Witch. Where is the Juju Witch, Master Weaver?"

Jeremiah looked at the dispersing crowd. There was no sign of her. "I do not know, my God," he said, wondering himself where she could be. He thought surely she had arrived after him. *Where are you Myanaymiz?*

"Guardsman!" Bugiah called to Vyx, who was standing close by. "Did the Cobbler come with you?"

Vyx rushed over, and knelt before Bugiah. "No my God, I left before the Cobbler."

Bugiah looked at Jeremiah. "Must we have someone watching them at all times?"

Jeremiah clenched his teeth, and looked to the ground. "Perhaps, my God."

"In the meantime, what am I supposed to do? Wait around this miserable Town for them to be found? I am the God of Gods!"

"My God, I shall find them quickly," said Vyx.

"Then don't just stand there, go!"

Vyx ran off in the direction of the Cobbler's cottage.

Bugiah then yawned and said, "I have been through so much today. The duties of the God of Gods are very demanding. I shall return to my carriage now, and rest there. This has been such a tiring day. It was no pleasure having to bury…uh?"

"Slemi, my God," said the High Priest.

"Hmm," said Bugiah "It's just such a shame she could not see and appreciate my great sacrifice. Very few mortals have such an honour."

"Yes, my God," replied the High Priest. "You have once again demonstrated the greatness of your divine generosity. It is a shame she was not here to see it. Shall I walk you to your carriage?"

"What am I, a child? Don't be a fool! Get out of my sight! You should be in your temple praying for my victories to come, not standing here in the Town babbling!" said Bugiah who was beginning to lose patience with everything. The God of Gods had never been kept waiting before.

"Forgive me, my God. Forgive me. I shall go immediately," said the High Priest, backing up slowly, turning, and then scurrying off in the direction of the Mount of the Gods.

"Great God of Gods, I should go help Vyx look for them," said Jeremiah.

"Good idea, Master Weaver. Make yourself useful."

Jeremiah bowed to Bugiah then started walking in the direction of the Jotham's cottage. As he got closer he suddenly veered off, and headed into the woods. He knew where they were. He just wasn't sure what he'd do when he found them.

———•••———

A r l e n e   A d a m o

95

Axis' secret house was just up ahead. Jeremiah could now easily recognize the tangle of branches that were previously so camouflaged from view. *What should I say? Am I angry? Am I jealous? This is ridiculous. I'm not a foolish love-stricken teenage boy. How did I come to this?*

"Jeremiah!"

Myanaymiz? He turned to see her sitting a few yards away, alone on a large rock. A stream of sunlight was slipping in through the thick tree branches, and drenching her in a soft warm glow. Her gown was brilliant with color, and even from this distance, he thought he could see the sparkles of her skin. *She is so beautiful!*

"Jeremiah, please come here."

As he walked slowly in her direction, he wondered where Jotham could be. *I know they were together. Perhaps he is hiding in the secret house.* Jeremiah stopped a few feet away.

"Come closer," she said. "Come closer to me, Jeremiah."

Jeremiah wanted to say no, but instead found himself cautiously approaching her. When he was close enough to reach out and touch her, she stretched out her arm, and took his hand in hers. "Sit down with me a moment," she said, pulling him closer.

"The God of Gods is waiting for you," Jeremiah responded, taking his hand away, and trying not to look into her eyes.

"That silly man is in a deep sleep," she said. "He will not awaken for some time. Now, sit and talk with me a moment."

Jeremiah reluctantly sat down close beside her on the rock. He didn't want to talk. He just wanted to silently walk back to the cottage. He wanted everything to be as it had been before last night. He would be the Town's reliable, sensible Master Weaver, and she would return to being just a woman from a rock…a curiosity…a distant stranger.

"Where is Jotham?" he asked.

"I sent him back to the cottage because I wanted to talk with you alone," she said, gently tucking his hair behind his ear.

"You knew I was coming?" *Don't touch me like that…please.*

Myanaymiz laughed. "I do not know why you keep asking me questions you know better than to ask, but I love you Jeremiah."

Jeremiah jumped up from the rock. "You think that's funny? Saying such a thing to an old man like me! You love me?"

"I love good men, Jeremiah. I love you. I love Jotham. I cannot help but love good men. That is who I am, and what I do."

Myanaymiz stood up, and moved close to him. She slid her hand softly over his shoulder, and let it come to rest firmly on his arm. "Do you not want my love anymore?"

Jeremiah closed his eyes. All he could feel was the heat where she touched him…the comfort…the peace…the strange knowing. It seeped into his blood and flowed up his arm, into his shoulder and then down deep into his spine. "Yes," he answered. "Yes, I want your love. I want it more than anything."

"Good," she said. "Because I have much love to give."

⸻✦⸻

96

Bugiah stood at the bottom of the Mount of the Gods. He looked hopelessly up at the steep road ahead. "Do they expect the God of Gods to climb that? Where are my Guardsmen? They should have come for me by now. Someone will be severely punished for this."

He turned and looked towards the Town. There was no one in sight. No one at all. He was completely alone. "They must all be busy burying that dead woman. Why don't they hurry? Don't they know I am waiting?"

Above his head the dark clouds were rolling in, and he heard the sound of distant thunder. "The rain is coming, and they have left the God of Gods at the side of the road as if he were a mere mortal. Someone will pay dearly for this." He looked back up the hill, hoping to see someone coming…anyone at all. He had never felt so alone.

Suddenly, BOOM! FLASH! Bugiah jumped in terror. Lightning had struck very close by. Such an incredible and frightening power…and so close! "Where are those fools?"

From behind him, he heard the click clack of hooves against the cobbled road. Turning around, he saw his red steed walking slowly towards him. He let out a sigh of relief. *Finally, help has arrived.* "There you are, boy. Your leg is all better, I see. Come this way now. Come and take your master back home. Come here now."

The horse slowly came closer and closer, and then stopped directly over him. As it stared down into his face, Bugiah felt a chill run up his spine. *There's something different…something very different.* "What is it boy? Do you not know me? Why…?" *No wait! This is wrong! The colour of your coat…the height of your shoulder… the heat of your breath. You are not my horse! You have fire for eyes!*

In an instant, the horse reared up, and all Bugiah could see were the enormous powerful black hooves coming down on his head. "Ahhhhhh! No! Nooo!" His eyes flashed open only to see a black featureless face bearing down on him. He violently thrust out his fist, knocking the concerned Guardsman straight out the carriage door. *That red horse! That terrible red horse! Where is it? Where did it go?* He looked at the gold walls around him…the crimson curtains on the windows. *Oh…my carriage! Oh glory of the Gods, I am in my carriage! Yes…a dream…only a dream.* He sat up, trying not to think about the image of the fiery eyes that still burned in his mind. *Just a dream. Nothing more than a foolish dream.*

Outside the carriage the Guardsman was moaning in pain. He had landed on his back on the hard ground. "Get in here!" Bugiah shouted.

The Guardsman, as quick as he could, showed up at the door. He was trying his best not to let the God of Gods see the agony he was in.

"Where are we?" demanded Bugiah.

"My God, we are still on the road near the cemetery."

"Of course…I was waiting for the Juju Witch to be found. Have they found her?"

"My God, while you were asleep, the Town Messenger informed me that the Juju Witch has returned to the cottage of the Master Weaver."

"And how long have I been asleep?"

"Three hours, my God."

"Three hours?" Bugiah was not happy about learning he had been asleep so long, but he also knew that it was against the law to disturb a sleeping God without permission. "Well then, take me to the Master Weaver…and hurry!"

"Yes, my God." The Guardsman then shut the door of the carriage.

Bugiah wiped his hand across his sweaty forehead. *That dream…that frightening dream. In all my life, I have never had such a terrible dream. Why should it come now? What did it mean? It must be a sign…a sign to remind me that I must continue my work on the new ritual. Everything, of course, depends upon me…the God of Gods. I have great work ahead, and must keep my divine focus. That's all it was, a sign to remind me of the great things to come.*

———•———

97

Myanaymiz stood behind Jeremiah, combing his hair with her fingers. "How am I to weave with you doing that?" he asked, as he worked on a new shirt for himself.

"I think it should help you weave even better," she replied.

He laughed. "You're probably right."

"It is still only 'probably' for you? When will I be a sure thing?"

He turned, grabbed her around the waist, and looked up into her face. "You are a sure thing. I know this now. One of the few things I do know."

Just then there was the sound of the latch. Jeremiah dropped his arms from around Myanaymiz, and turned just in time to see the door fly open. "The God of Gods is blessing you with his presence! On your knees!" commanded the veiled Guardsman.

Jeremiah got down on his knees, and bowed his head. Myanaymiz remained standing. He tugged at her hand, trying to get her to follow his lead.

"Do not bother," laughed Bugiah who was now standing in the doorway. "There is nothing more stubborn than a Juju Witch."

"Glory to my God," said Jeremiah.

"You may get up and go. I wish to talk to the Juju Witch alone."

Jeremiah stood up and looked at Myanaymiz. He didn't want to leave her alone with Bugiah.

Myanaymiz gave him a reassuring smile and a gentle squeeze of his hand to let him know everything would be alright.

"My God, with your permission I take my leave," Jeremiah said, releasing Myanaymiz's hand. On the way out the door, he passed by a Guardsman carrying in the God of Gods' red velvet chair.

"Set the chair right here by the open door," Bugiah commanded. "The Townsfolk are beginning to gather outside, and I shall bestow upon them the blessing of seeing their greatest God."

The Guardsman did as he was told. Bugiah then strolled over and sat down with his back to the doorway. "Pull up a chair and sit here, Juju Witch," he said.

Myanaymiz picked up a chair and placed it directly facing Bugiah…but not too close. "You have some questions for me," she said as she sat down.

"O' Juju Witch, you will be amazed," he began, "My plans for the new ritual are well beyond anything you could ever imagine. I have the most magnificent idea for how to use the earth. But now, I am in need of inspiration to help decide how to involve the other elements. You must inspire me, Juju Witch. That is your duty."

"Tell me what you have devised so far," Myanaymiz said.

"I envision taking my sword and triumphantly thrusting it into the earth! Can you imagine how in awe the Townsfolk will be at such a sight? But where do I go from there? What should I do to include the other three elements? I realize the way of the God of Gods is very difficult, and I, Bugiah, am faced with the greatest of challenges ever faced by any God. So I have come to you, my servant, for inspiration. Inspire me, Juju Witch! Serve your God as you were born to do!"

Myanaymiz smiled. "The secret of power is in union," she said. "It is the taking of what is separate and making it one. Within union is the greatest magic."

"Union," said Bugiah. "And how do I attain this union?"

"To achieve this, you must meld the parts. For instance, plunging your sword into both earth and water at the same time would bring about the union of these two elements. This would give the ritual greater strength."

"Hmmm…so thrusting my sword into just the earth is not enough. Yes, this makes sense. It must involve the earth and the water! The power of union…" Bugiah paused a moment to think about it. He then suddenly exclaimed, "Yes…of course! The river bank! The river bank will be the place where I will perform this miracle! The river bank is also where Zetmi performed his greatest miracle! It fits perfectly! O' I have such divine intuition! Does it not fill you with wonder, Juju Witch?"

"Yes, you are a wonder."

"That's much better. You are finally coming to appreciate the magnificence of the God of Gods. It has taken awhile, but I believe you have come to see it. Why, I would even consider allowing you the honour of pleasuring me had you not already soiled yourself with the Cobbler and perhaps the Master Weaver. Really, you Juju Witches have absolutely no shame."

"What have you considered for fire and air?" she asked.

"I have envisioned setting something very large on fire…a great fire like the Town has never seen before. Burning down a huge swath of forest would produce a great and wonderful inferno worthy of the God of Gods."

"Then where would the Townsfolk find enough wood to build all the things you need, and to warm your palace?"

"Hmmm…this is true. The God of Gods needs the forest. Perhaps instead, I should burn down the Town itself. The people could always build new houses, and it would be a wonderful expression of the extent of my power." He looked around the cottage imagining how easily it would go up in flames.

"But if the people are busy rebuilding the Town, how could they properly attend to the needs of the Gods? They would not be able to grow your food or bring you offerings."

"So true! O' Juju Witch, this is proving far more difficult than I imagined. What can I burn?"

"There is a simpler way than burning things."

"Tell me, what is it?"

"You need only command the wind with magic words. Command the wind to bring with it the fire. Are not such things written in your Stories of the Gods? Did not those who came before you command the wind and lightning? And it would be another mighty union of the elements. Two such unions would forge a very powerful ritual."

"Yes, of course! Command the wind! Command the lightning! This is the power of the God of Gods! I shall command the winds with my words…my magic words! I need only devise an incantation…an incantation forceful enough to herald in Eternal Life. That, I certainly can and will do." Bugiah leaned back in his chair and smiled. "Do I amaze you even more, Juju Witch?" he asked.

"Yes, it amazes me," she answered. "But there is only one thing missing."

"What? What is missing?"

"Mathematical movement. To make anything come to pass, mathematical movement is required."

"Hmmm…what kind of mathematical movement?"

"If you were to create…say, a dance to accompany your incantation…a precise and calculated dance…that should be just the thing to tie it all together. Its strength will reinforce the two unions."

"A dance? Hmmm…Zetmi was renowned for his magnificent dancing. This makes sense, Juju Witch! In fact, as I think about it, it gives me a good feeling…a very good feeling. This dance shall be a glorious expression of my divinity! Every step in perfect harmony with the universe. Every step bringing me closer and closer to Eternal Life until finally…finally, I am there! Oh, I am feeling so inspired!"

"Inspiration is all yours."

"Yes, it is mine! It is all mine! Everything is mine, including you Juju Witch! I am Bugiah, the God of Gods for all Eternity!"

"And now that you have worked out the foundation for your ritual," she said, "I suggest you return to the Palace and concentrate solely on your magic words. Do not return to the Town. The presence of these mortals would only taint your inspiration. Isolate yourself until the day of the Festival. Accept no visitors. Hear no council. This requires your full concentration. If you need anything, consult only your High Priest. Ultimately, it is you, and you alone, who is needed for this great leap forward."

He looked at her and grinned. "You do have magic insight Juju Witch. The way you now fully grasp my importance is testament to this. Yes, I will go into seclusion, as did all the great Gods before me, and from there, I will uncover the magic words. I will meditate fully and without distraction upon the ritual, for I am the God of Gods who makes miracles happen!" Bugiah jumped up from his chair, and stepped outside the cottage.

A crowd had gathered at the bottom of Jeremiah's path. Some of them gasped to see the God of Gods now standing directly before them. Bugiah lifted his arms and proclaimed, "My Townsfolk, look now upon your God of Gods, and worship his greatness. He is about to create for you the greatest Festival you have ever seen! Down! Down on your knees, and bask in his divinity! Take pleasure in your worship!"

Everyone in the crowd immediately dropped to their knees, and watched as Bugiah proudly walked to his carriage then disappeared inside. A second Guardsman followed behind with the red velvet chair. As he placed it inside, Bugiah whispered to him, "Tell them to cheer as I pull away."

The Guardsman then closed the door, and took his place on the footboard. He waved his arm and shouted, "Show the God of Gods your appreciation!" The people, jumping to their feet, broke out in loud cheering and clapping as the carriage pulled away. Many of the younger ones ran after it throwing flowers and ferns. Myanaymiz, standing in the doorway of the cottage, watched silently as Bugiah's carriage disappeared from view. *Work hard false god,* she thought as she turned and went back inside.

———•◦•———

98

"Jotham, let me in!"

When Jotham opened the door and saw Jeremiah standing there, all he could do was stare in disbelief. *What? Is this real?* When it finally sunk in that, yes, he was seeing correctly, Jotham couldn't stop himself from bursting out laughing.

At first, Jeremiah didn't know what was so funny, but then he remembered that Jotham had not yet seen his hair and his beard. "It's really not that amusing," he said.

"I've just…I've never seen you look so…well, so very neat and tidy before." Jotham continued to laugh.

"Alright, alright, just let me in."

Grinning from ear to ear, Jotham stood aside and welcomed Jeremiah in.

"Is Vyx here?" asked Jeremiah.

"No, I suppose he has gone to wherever his God is. He is a very devoted Guardsman."

"The God of Gods is at my cottage, speaking with Myanaymiz."

Jotham immediately tensed up at the thought. "Perhaps, I should go over there."

"No," said Jeremiah. "That is not a good idea. I know how you feel. I want to protect her also, but she has proven to be quite capable of protecting herself…especially against Bugiah. We can't deny that."

"Yes, it is true. She has been full of surprises." Jotham relaxed a little. *Of course, she knows how to handle the situation. I must trust her.* He then stared for a moment at Jeremiah…his hair…his beard…his eyes. Strange, how different he looked. "She told me about you…about you and her," he found himself suddenly saying.

Jeremiah turned red, blushing like a school boy, and making Jotham burst out laughing again.

"I…she…" Jeremiah felt he had to explain, but didn't know what to say about something he didn't really understand.

"Don't worry, friend," said Jotham. "What is either one of us to do? She is what she is, and she does what she does."

Jeremiah smiled, relieved that this had not come between them. "You are very wise for a young man."

"And you are very energetic for an old one." They both laughed this time.

"Would you like some strawberry tea," Jotham asked.

"Thank you, that would be nice," replied Jeremiah. Jotham then disappeared into the kitchen.

Jeremiah stood alone in the workshop and looked around. He could see there were many new pairs of shoes lined up on the shelves. Despite everything that had been going on, Jotham had been working very hard. He looked up at the tallest shelf and noticed the shoes Jotham had made for the God of Gods. "How amazing!" Jeremiah walked over, reached up and carefully took one down. He examined it closely, the shining black glassy look of the heel, the beautiful silver colored leather, the magnificent golden wings.

"Those are, of course, for Bugiah," said Jotham, walking in and placing the tea tray down on his work table.

"I assumed as much. He will be a very well dressed God this year."

"He certainly will." Jotham began pouring the tea.

Jeremiah put the shoe back up on the shelf, and then accepted the cup Jotham was offering him. "Thank you," he said. He took a sip, savoring its fresh pure flavor as it flowed over his tongue, down his throat, and came to rest, warm in his stomach. Jotham had a well deserved reputation for creating the best tea blends in Town, and this was his specialty made from Jeremiah's strawberries. "You brew a fine cup, Tea Master," Jeremiah said, having once unofficially bestowed Jotham with this title.

"Thank you, my friend."

For a while, they simply stood together quietly drinking. Although they had been close friends a long time, there was now a new feeling between them…a strange new bond that had never been there before. It was worth taking the time to silently appreciate it.

Jotham set his cup down upon the work bench. He looked past Jeremiah to the window, and out at the blue sky beyond. Neither cloud nor bird could be seen. All was quiet and still. "It is very strange, isn't it?" he said.

"Yes, it is…very strange," agreed Jeremiah

"Do you…do you feel like things are changing…like you are changing?"

Jeremiah laughed. "Jotham, look at my hair and my beard. Everything is changing."

"Do you feel it's for the better? I think I do. It's for the better, isn't it Jeremiah?"

Jeremiah sighed. "I feel better. You feel better. Everything points to it being better."

"It's not better for Slemi."

"Perhaps the real question is, is it better for us without Slemi?"

Jotham did not have to think about it. "Does it make me a bad man to answer yes?"

"That makes you an honest man. There is nothing wrong with being an honest man. Only be careful who you are honest around."

At that moment, Jotham caught sight of Vyx through the window. "Vyx has returned," he warned. Jeremiah turned just in time to see the Guardsman walk through the open door.

"The God of Gods is now returning to the Palace," Vyx announced. "Glory to the Gods!"

"You are not returning with him?" asked Jotham, hoping to get a hint of how much longer he would be stuck with this Guardsman in his home.

"No, unfortunately, I must remain here a little longer."

"Would you like some tea?" asked Jeremiah.

Vyx hesitated for a moment as he thought carefully about it. At the Palace, a Guardsman's diet was restricted to water alone. But did the same rules apply in the Town? At the Palace, he must wear his uniform, including the veil, outside of his cell at all times, exceptions only under special instructions from the God of Gods, but here, he wore civilian clothes, and his face was uncovered. It was also true that he had already eaten things that were not permitted, and he had slept in a soft warm bed. All in all it seemed that the rules at the Palace did not apply under these new circumstances. Given this truth, the water restriction could not possibly apply either. "Yes, I will try" he said, accepting the cup of tea handed to him. He then put it to his lips and took a drink.

Vyx's eyes grew wide with amazement. "I have never tasted anything so wonderful before!" he exclaimed.

Jotham laughed. "Thank Jeremiah who grew the strawberries."

"But it was you who turned them into tea," Jeremiah said.

"Thank you both," said Vyx, who then quickly drank down the entire thing. "May I have some more, please?" he asked, holding out his empty cup.

Jotham and Jeremiah looked at each other in wonder. Things were definitely changing.

99

Myanaymiz woke Jeremiah with a kiss. "I require your help today," she said. "I want you to call all of the Townsfolk to the place with the old tree…the old tree with the face. Call them there for a picnic."

"A picnic?" Jeremiah was not sure if he heard right. *Am I awake?*

"Yes, a picnic."

"But why? What do I tell them when they ask me why?"

"Tell them it is for the celebration of life. After having to experience so much death, they need to take some time to appreciate life."

"So, first the Master Weaver appears with a haircut, and then he calls them all out for a picnic? You know what they will say? They will say I've gone mad."

"That will be their first thought, but not their last. You will recall that in your Stories of the Gods, there is often mention of healing festivals to counterbalance a series of catastrophes. Tell them it is a healing festival, and you are simply following the ways set down by the Gods."

"But why do you want this? And what will Bugiah say when he hears about it?"

"Bugiah is in complete seclusion as he prepares for the new ritual. As for the other Gods, they are so busy with their vain preparations for the Festival they will not give it any notice. Please, do as I ask. What possible harm could there be in a picnic?"

Jeremiah sat up in the bed and thought about it. *What possible harm could there be? It's simply a picnic…but I know that if Myanaymiz wants it, it must be much more than that.* He ran his hand through his hair. "Alright," he relented. "And frankly, I don't care why you want this. Good things have happened since you appeared… a lot of good things. I am willing to take a chance that you have more good things in mind for the Town. I'll have the Town Messenger inform them of a picnic to be held this afternoon near the old tree. I will tell them we are doing this because such things are written in the Stories of the Gods. They will come." Jeremiah sat up and placed his foot on the floor, ready to find the Town Messenger and get things started. All of a sudden he felt Myanaymiz's hand on his arm gently pulling him back.

"Wait," she said. "There will be time enough to inform the Town Messenger, but for now, I need a good man."

———•◆•———

100

Myanaymiz sat under the tree and watched as the people began to arrive with their baskets and blankets. It quickly became apparent that no one wanted to set up too close to her. They still did not trust the strange Lady from the rock. However, several of the children left their parents' sides and came running over. "Our Lady! Our Lady!" they cried as they surrounded her.

Petal took hold of her hand, "We are having a picnic. Are you here for the picnic too?" she asked.

"Yes," replied Myanaymiz. "I am just waiting for my friends."

"There are your friends!" exclaimed Axis, pointing to Jotham and Vyx who were walking towards them.

"Yes," she said. "There they are."

Jotham sat down close beside her, and kissed her on the cheek. The children giggled.

Vyx who was carrying the basket and blanket remained standing. "You should not kiss her like that," he said. "Everyone is watching."

"Is it against the law of the Gods?" asked Jotham.

"No," answered Vyx.

"Has Bugiah ordered you to disallow it?"

"No."

"Then what is a kiss between friends?"

Petal jumped up and down. "Kissy, kissy, kissy," she chanted as she grabbed hold of the tree and kissed the face carved into it. The children all began to laugh and kiss the tree also.

"Oh tree you are so beautiful!"

"Oh tree! Kissy tree!"

"Kissy, kissy, kissy tree!"

"Now look what you have started," said Vyx, as he set down the basket and spread the blanket on the ground. "A lot of childish nonsense."

Jotham laughed. "This is the same place where we both enjoyed much childish nonsense," he said.

"Thankfully, I do not remember." Vyx sat down on the blanket. He looked over at Jotham and Myanaymiz, and then demanded, "You need to sit here. This is a picnic, and a picnic requires sitting on a blanket on the ground."

"Yes Guardsman, whatever you say," Jotham replied. They then got up, and sat together on the blanket across from Vyx.

"Chase the fox!" shouted Axis, as he suddenly ran away in the direction of a small grove of trees at the edge of the meadow. All of the other children ran after him.

Jotham looked around and could see that more and more people were arriving. "Where is Jeremiah?" he asked.

"He will be here shortly," replied Myanaymiz.

Vyx removed the lamb skin lid from the basket, and began to set out the food. He glanced up for a moment only to see his parents and brother sitting on a blanket not far away. It seemed such a strange sight. There they were having a picnic just like any other family, and here he was, a Guardsman…long ago sent away, no longer a part of them. When he saw his father glance over, Vyx looked down and concentrated once again on organizing the food.

"Why would Jeremiah call for a Town picnic?" asked Jotham. "It's a strange thing to do."

"These are strange times," said Myanaymiz. "But do you not see the Townsfolk? See how much they are enjoying this."

Jotham looked around and knew she was right. The children were running and playing. The adults were talking and laughing. Everyone was having a good time. Just then he saw Jeremiah heading in their direction. "And here comes the Master Weaver," he said.

As Jeremiah walked through the crowd, it seemed that everyone wanted to greet him and shake his hand.

"Hello Master Weaver!"

"What a beautiful day, Master Weaver!"

"How wonderful of you to arrange this picnic, Master Weaver!"

He's strutting! Jotham laughed to himself as he watched Jeremiah making his way through the adoring throng. *He's actually strutting.*

When Jeremiah reached the tree, he smiled and exclaimed, "Hello my friends. It is a brilliant day for a picnic!" He then sat down on the blanket with the energetic ease of a young man. Reaching over he gently touched Myanaymiz's hand and added, "Hello Myanaymiz."

"It is indeed a brilliant day for a picnic," she said, smiling.

"Your hair is wrong, and should be grown out again," said Vyx. "You no longer look like a Master Weaver."

"And you no longer look like a Guardsman," replied Jeremiah.

"It seems that everyone is having a good time," interjected Jotham.

"Yes," said Jeremiah. "A picnic was the right idea." He glanced over at Myanaymiz and smiled.

She smiled back at him and then said, "And after we have all eaten, the real fun will begin."

"What real fun?" asked Jotham.

"You are going to sing them a song," she said.

"A song!" exclaimed Vyx. "He is a Cobbler. He makes shoes. He does not sing songs. Singing songs is beneath a Cobbler. It is for the lowest of the low."

Myanaymiz reached over and touched Vyx's arm. "Jotham is going to sing a song," she said.

Vyx was in shock. *She is doing it again! She is touching a Guardsman! Such a thing is a punishable offence! How dare she? Who does she think she is to reach over and touch a Guardsman…a personal Guardsman of the God of Gods? I must push her away! I must shout at her for this trespass! I must threaten her or…or just punish her outright! I must…*

"It will be alright, Vyx," she said, with her hand still on his arm. "Everything will be alright."

Vyx turned and looked the other way. He pretended not to feel her hand on his arm. *I am a Guardsman!* He pretended not to feel it when she removed her hand. *I am a Guardsman!* He pretended not to feel the cold empty longing left behind. *I am a Guardsman!* He tried hard to pretend that he didn't want more than anything to feel her warm touch again. *I am a…a…a man.*

 Arlene Adamo

101

Jeremiah was stretched out on the blanket…his eyes closed. *Oh, I am full. I have eaten like a God. Have I been asleep? If so, for how long?* He could feel the warm sun on his face, and hear the sounds of joyous laughter all around him. *The picnic was a good idea. The Townsfolk did need a break. I needed a break.*

"Jeremiah," Myanaymiz whispered into his ear.

His eyes opened, and he wished he could simply grab her and pull her to him. He then laughed to himself at the idea of doing it here.

"Jeremiah, it is time to call the people around. Have them come to the tree."

When he sat up, he immediately noticed that Jotham and Vyx were nowhere to be seen. It was then that he heard Jotham call out. "Come on old man! Bring those people forth!" Jeremiah looked up. There sat Jotham high above him on one tree branch and Vyx on another. "Call those people. I have a song to sing," yelled down Jotham.

"From up in the tree, all the people will be able to see and hear him better," explained Myanaymiz.

"And why is Vyx up there too?" he asked.

"Vyx will play the drum." That was when Jeremiah noticed that Vyx was holding the lamb skin lid from the basket in one hand and a stick in the other.

"Am I asleep? Am I dreaming?"

"No," laughed Myanaymiz. "You are more awake then you have ever been in your life. Now call the people, please."

Jeremiah was still confused, however, he did as she asked and unhooked the small ram's horn from his belt. He put it to his lips and blew. It always amazed him how such a loud sound could come from such a small thing. It must have something to do with the curve, or the rings inside. Regardless, this tiny horn was always the one thing that could bring the people together in one place.

When the familiar haunting sound echoed throughout the meadow, everyone immediately went silent. Leaving their blankets and baskets, they all began to move towards the tree.

"Here they come!" said Jotham. "Vyx get ready…and…go!" Vyx then began to beat his drum in a slow precise rhythm.

The people, now gathered together, stared up in disbelief at Jotham and Vyx. The children, on the other hand, were delighted at the sight of the Cobbler and a Guardsman up in a tree. They laughed and began to happily dance around to the rhythm of the drum.

"Ladies and Gentlemen!" cried Jotham. "I am now pleased to bring you Songs from a Tree! Songs that will lift your spirits! Songs that bring you strength and perseverance! Songs unlike anything you have ever heard before! And here to assist me is the great Vyx, Master of the Drum!"

The Townsfolk were dumbstruck.

"Come now, my people! Some applause! Some applause for the Master of the Drum!" shouted Jotham.

The children immediately began to clap and cheer.

"Drum, Master Drummer, drum!"

"Sing us a song, Cobbler! Sing us a song!"

Jotham felt himself hesitate as he looked out at the confused crowd before him. *I, the respected Cobbler, am in a tree about to sing like a traveling outlaw in front of the entire Town. What am I doing?* He then looked down at Myanaymiz. She was looking up at him and smiling so proudly. Had anyone ever looked at him like that before…with such confidence? Jotham suddenly stopped doubting himself. *I can to do this, for myself and for them. Somehow I just know I need to do this no matter how mad it may seem.* He took in a deep

                    Arlene Adamo

breath and announced "This song is called, Her Name is Freedom. I created it several days ago, and now I would like to share it with you." He signalled Vyx to quicken the beat. He then transitioned flawlessly into the new rhythm, pounding the makeshift drum as if he were born to it.

With one arm wrapped around the tree trunk, and the other spread wide as if to embrace the crowd, Jotham began to sing:

When you feel her in the wind
When you feel her in the sun
When you see her in the moon
When you see her in the dawn
Do you know her name?

Her name is Freedom
Freedom, freedom, freedom
The most beautiful name
You will ever hear
Freedom is here

When you hear her in the river
When you hear her in the trees
When you smell her in the flowers
When you sense her on the breeze
Do you know her name?

Her name is Freedom
Freedom, freedom, freedom
The most beautiful name
You will ever hear
Freedom is here

When she wakes you from your sleep
When she calls you to the light
When she softly touches your face
When she kisses you in the night
Do you know her name?

Her name is Freedom
Freedom, freedom, freedom
The most beautiful name
You will ever hear
Freedom is here…

Jotham dramatically drew out the final note, and Vyx slowed his drumming until all was silent. The two men then stared out at the stone faced crowd before them and waited. *Did they like it? Did they like the song?* Suddenly, the children broke out into noisy shouts and applause. This emboldened several of the adults to do the same. It was not long before the entire Town was wildly applauding and cheering.

"Sing it again!"

"More, more, more!"

"Wonderful!"

"Another song! Another song!"

"The singing Cobbler and drumming Guardsman!"

Jotham was overwhelmed by the Townsfolk's reaction. Smiling shyly, he waved in appreciation at the crowd. He then looked over at Vyx and could not believe his eyes. *Is that real? Yes! Yes, it is! The Guardsman is smiling! He's actually smiling…like when we were children!* He then glanced down at Myanaymiz and Jeremiah who were still standing on the blanket below. "Sing again, Jotham" called up Myanaymiz. "Give the people what they want. Give them what they need."

Vyx began to beat the drum again, and the crowd immediately went silent. Jotham smiled at the audience and announced, "This next song is called, *You Made Me Live Again.*"

102

"I'm an eagle! Keeeeerraahh! I'm an eagle." Vyx was flying! Flying over the Town! Flying over his parents' house! Flying over everything! "I'm free! I'm an eagle! Keeeeerraahh!" He swooped down and around the trees, where he could see people from the Town looking up and waving to him. Jotham was there… waving. He passed over Jotham, and gave him a big loud Keeeeerraahh!

As he soared over the cottage roofs, he suddenly spotted Bugiah. The God of Gods was dressed in a black gown, and standing in a dry barren field. He malevolently stared up at Vyx. It was then that Vyx noticed the lasso in his hand. Vyx knew Bugiah intended to throw it around his eagle neck and violently pull him down. *I have to get away! But why am I flying so low? Why can I not fly high? I need to escape!* He saw Bugiah begin to twirl the lasso around and around then snap his wrist and let it fly! As the rope shot upwards, Vyx could see its precise and deadly aim. His heart ached knowing this was the end.

Just before he felt it tighten around his neck, his eyes instantly flashed open, and he immediately sat up! He looked around the room. *A dream! Only a dream!* The light of the early dawn was coming in through the window, and he was shocked to realize he had overslept. *A Guardsman must be up before the sun! This soft bed, it makes me sleep too deeply. It is giving me unacceptable dreams. O' for the cold hard floor of my cell.*

He then got out of the bed, walked over to the window and looked out. *Birds! Look at them. They are everywhere. Making their noise. Flitting. Fluttering. Never ceasing their chaos. Not planning from one moment to the next. So many birds…and all wide awake. A Guardsman must always be up before the birds. Why was I not?*

Vyx was just about to turn around and get dressed when he caught sight of a figure at the edge of the garden. *The Juju Witch!* Myanaymiz was standing near the forest trees. She appeared to be beckoning to him. *What does she want?* 'Come to me. Come to me,' he thought he heard her whisper.

For a moment, he hesitated. *She is dangerous. What if it is a trick?* He curiously watched as many of the birds seemed to be drawn to her…flying near her…even landing at her feet. *Is she commanding them? Does the Juju Witch have such a power? My duty is to find out her secrets. The God of Gods would want me to go speak with her. That is my mission.*

Vyx quickly pulled on a pair of trousers, threw off his night robe, threw on his shirt and slipped into his shoes. He then hurried outside, and cautiously approached Myanaymiz. "What is it you want of me, Juju Witch?" he demanded, stopping a few feet away.

"As you are awake, perhaps you would like to walk with me," she replied.

Vyx took a moment to think about it. *This would be a prime opportunity to gain more information for my God. And if it is a trick, I am not afraid. I am a Guardsman of the Gods. A Juju Witch is nothing. She has no power over the God of Gods' favorite one. I am his favorite one. I am the chosen Guardsman.* "Such an exercise would be fitting. I will walk," he agreed.

Myanaymiz said nothing, but simply turned and headed into the trees. Vyx quickly caught up to her, and began to walk at her side. They continued on silently for a while until finally Myanaymiz asked, "Did you enjoy yesterday?"

"I…The God of Gods would approve. A happy Town is better able to worship the Gods."

"And did you know Jotham was such a wonderful singer?"

"Yesterday, I remembered. I remembered that he used to sing when we were children together. I would have him sing…" Vyx did not want to finish. *Why am I speaking of such nonsense? That is not my duty.*

"Go on. You had him sing, what? Tell me."

"It was only a silly child's game," he replied.

"I enjoy hearing of silly children's games, and you have made me curious. What did you have him sing?"

"When…we played…when we played 'birds'…we would…we pretended to be birds, and I would have him sing songs."

"What kind of songs?"

"Songs about how we were heroes…birds and heroes."

Myanaymiz laughed. "Birds and heroes," she said. "I like that."

Vyx blushed. "As I said, it was a silly game."

"A game is meant to be silly. Otherwise, how is it any fun?"

"Those games…that was before I received my Guardsman training…before I knew better."

"Oh, I see."

As they continued walking, Myanaymiz then asked, "Is drumming a part of Guardsman training because you did an excellent job yesterday? The entire Town was talking about how amazing you were."

"No, drumming is not a part of my training."

"Then your accomplishment was even more impressive."

Vyx held back a smile. He liked to hear her say that, but was it wrong to like it? Did it deter him from his duties? Would the God of Gods approve? There were so many questions, and he was not used to questions. Questions were not necessary for a Guardsman, because the Gods had all the answers he needed. Questions were irrelevant.

As they walked along, Vyx suddenly noticed a strange and crooked tree with broad dark leaves. It was then that he sensed something was not right. He looked around and realized that he didn't recognize anything. This was a part of the forest he had never seen before. Where were they, and why hadn't he noticed they had wandered so far from the cottage? *A Guardsman is always aware. A Guardsman is a master of time. How did this happen so fast?*

　　　　　　　　　　　　　　　Arlene Adamo

Which way is out? A Guardsman never gets lost. He stopped, and looked in every direction. The thick trees and underbrush were confusing him. *Which way do I go?* "Perhaps we should return," he said to Myanaymiz who had stopped alongside him. "I think we have walked long enough."

Myanaymiz suddenly turned, looked him in the eye and asked, "Do you wish to kiss me?"

Vyx was shocked! "What?!"

"Do you wish to kiss me?" she repeated.

"I…Guardsmen do not have such relations," he quickly said. "A Guardsman gives himself over completely to the service of the Gods."

"But this is not relations," said Myanaymiz. "Bugiah has ordered you to find out as much about a Juju Witch as possible. This is a part of your duty. What better way to learn the secrets of a Juju Witch than with a kiss? Words can be deceptive and fall short, but a kiss…a kiss tells everything. In the Stories of the Gods, do they not always relay their secrets with a kiss? It is the same for a Juju Witch. If you want to begin to learn my secrets, you must kiss me."

Vyx went silent as he thought about it. He looked at her face… at her lips. "I…I am not sure if the God of Gods would approve," he said.

"Are you afraid, Guardsman?"

"A Guardsman is never afraid!"

"Then I do not understand. If Bugiah told you to find out everything you can about me, why will you not do your duty and kiss me? You say you are not afraid, but what other explanation is there for your hesitation?" She moved closer to him.

Vyx could feel his body tense up in a way that he had never felt before. Was this fear or something else? *Am I really afraid of this Juju Witch? Look at her. She is so small. Her lips are just lips. What magic could she have over someone as powerful as the personal Guardsman to the God of Gods? She is no threat, and I must do my duty. The God of Gods would wish it.*

No longer hesitant, Vyx then quickly brought his lips down to hers. *Keeeeerraahh!* He was an eagle! He was flying! *How is this possible? I am awake! I am not dreaming! Keeeeerraahh!* Soaring…soaring…so high in the sky no one could touch him! Not even Bugiah. Free! Free to go anywhere! To the stars! To the moon! Anywhere!

No this is not real! This is a Juju Witch spell! In a flash, Vyx found himself knocked to the ground. He looked up at Myanaymiz and shouted, "What did you do to me, Juju Witch?!"

"I believe it was you who kissed me, Guardsman. Did you not enjoy it?"

Vyx jumped to his feet. He franticly paced back and forth in front of Myanaymiz. "Juju Witch, I…I want to…" *I want to do it again. I want to feel your lips. I want to hold you in my arms and kiss you again. I never want to stop kissing you.* "The God of Gods will hear about this," he finally said, then turned and marched away.

"Vyx!" called Myanaymiz.

"Do not try and trick me again! I am not listening!"

"Well, you should listen because you are headed in the wrong direction. The cottage is the other way."

Vyx abruptly stopped, turned and then stomped past Myanaymiz, refusing to even look at her. *Juju Witch, you are nothing but trouble,* he thought as he tried desperately to ignore the longing that remained on his lips.

———•◆•———

103

Myanaymiz stood in Jeremiah's garden studying the beautiful flowering vine that snaked up the side of the cottage wall. The soft ethereal petals of each flower went from a lush rich blue on the inside to pure white at the ends. She put her face close to one of the flowers, and deeply breathed in the sublime fresh scent. *How lovely you are. Once nothing more than a small brown insignificant seed in the earth and now this! You are a miracle! A beautiful miracle!*

Suddenly, someone grabbed her from behind, and lifted her off of the ground. "Hello Jotham," she laughed.

"I wanted to surprise you. Why were you not surprised?"

"After all you now know about me, you have to ask?"

"Fair enough. You know everything."

"Not everything."

"Do you know that I brought you a present?"

"No," she answered, "for some reason that was kept from me."

Jotham smiled and handed her something wrapped in a white rabbit skin. "For you, o' Lady of the Rock," he said with a bow.

"Thank you." Myanaymiz carefully unwrapped the gift. "Shoes!" she exclaimed. "And a very lovely pair of shoes they are." The shoes were beautifully crafted of the softest lamb's skin, and looked as though they had been dipped in pure gold.

"How you have travelled this long without them, I do not know. Shall I put them on for you?" Jotham asked.

"Thank you. That would be very kind." Myanaymiz handed him the shoes, and sat down in the soft grass.

Jotham crouched down in front of her. He carefully placed the first shoe on the right foot. "How does that feel?"

"Very comfortable."

He then placed the second shoe on her left foot. "And this one?"

"Yes, that is very nice."

"Let me help you stand," said Jotham, standing up and offering his hand.

Myanaymiz accepted, and he lifted her to her feet. For a moment, she just stared down at her new shoes. "Yes, they feel right," she sighed, then walked around in a little circle. "They truly are perfect in so many ways," she said. "Thank you, Jotham. You are such a very good man." She then softly kissed him on his lips.

"And do you need a good man, right now?" Jotham asked with a grin.

"I will answer you in a moment," she said. "First you must know that there will be another song show tonight."

"Another?"

"Yes, another. And after that there will be another. There will be a song show every night until the Festival of the Gods. The people will come and enjoy. Soon they will begin to write songs of their own, and will want to sing too. You will encourage this. Everyday there shall be singing and dancing."

"Can the Townsfolk handle that much fun?" Jotham laughed.

"You would be surprised at just how much fun they will want to have. For a very long time, they have waited for fun. It has finally come to them."

"If you say so, I suppose it must be true," said Jotham.

Myanaymiz took his hand in hers. "Now, as to your question, the answer is yes, I need a good man. Shall we take a walk to the meadow near the brook where the grass grows very high?"

Jotham didn't say a word. Instead, he simply smiled, and in silence offered her his arm.

———•◦•———

104

"I delivered the new shoes to the Palace, but the God of Gods would not see me. One of the other Guardsmen accepted the shoes on his behalf. Why would he not see me, Master Weaver?" Vyx seemed lost and confused. It was a peculiar thing for Jeremiah to see.

"I understand that Bugiah is very busy right now."

"But there are things I need to discuss with him…important things." There was a strange sense of sad desperation in his voice.

"What kind of things?" asked Jeremiah.

Vyx was hesitant to say anymore. Why should he discuss the business of the God of Gods with the Master Weaver? "These things are only for the divine one," he replied.

"Oh, I did not mean that I would ever dare speak for Bugiah. I simply wondered about your concerns. And by the way, there will be another song show tonight, and one every night until the Festival of the Gods. Are you prepared to drum again?"

"Why are we doing this again? Would the God of Gods approve?" Vyx asked.

"We cannot bother him with questions at this time, but I am certain he would approve. The shows will help the people prepare mentally for the greater festivities to come. With the deaths of the Gods and of Slemi, they have had many setbacks. This will help heal them, making them better prepared for serving at the Festival of the Gods. Why, look how just one show has already buoyed their spirits. More of the same will make them fit servants indeed."

"Will the Juju Witch be at these song shows?"

Jeremiah was surprised by his question, and the urgency with which he asked it. "Myanaymiz? I would assume so. Why? Has she done something to upset you?"

"A Guardsman does not get upset! A Juju Witch may have such power over Townsperson, but never over a Guardsman!"

"Oh, forgive me Honourable Guardsman. My mistake," said Jeremiah. "Is Myanaymiz the reason you needed to speak to Bugiah?"

"My mission is to report things of interest to the God of Gods."

"And is Myanaymiz a thing of interest for you?"

"The God of Gods has said that the Juju Witch was sent here to serve him. She belongs to him. He should know all that she does."

"And what exactly does she do?"

"She has cut your hair and beard!"

"But Bugiah already knows about that and was not troubled. What else has she done that concerns you?"

"She…she put a spell on me! She put a spell on me with a kiss!"

Jeremiah started laughing. "She kissed a Guardsman?!"

"What is so funny?"

"It's just that you are so…so much of a Guardsman. The idea of a woman kissing a Guardsman is like the idea of a woman kissing a stone. It is very funny."

Vyx did not know whether to be insulted or not. He prided himself on his stone-like qualities. These were what made him such a high ranking Guardsman. And now the Master Weaver was laughing at him for this. The world was no longer making any sense.

"So, were you going to tell Bugiah about the Juju Witch kissing you?" Jeremiah asked. "And if you do, what do you think his reaction would be especially now that he has so much on his mind? Would he thank you for your honesty or would he beat you for showing weakness?"

"I was not weak! She…she put a spell on me!"

"A spell, you say. And is that spell still upon you?"

"No…yes…I don't know."

"Will Bugiah show you mercy even if there was a spell upon you, or would he accuse you of being such a weak Guardsman that a small Juju Witch was easily able put you under her magic? Would he laugh at you? Would he get angry?"

Vyx was silent. He knew the answer. There was no point in trying to deny it.

"Do not worry. I will not tell him," said Jeremiah. "And I do not think any less of you for what has happened. You are still an Honourable Guardsman in my view. Now tell me, will you be drumming tonight at the song show?"

Vyx looked down at his feet. There were no Guardsman boots made of heavy black bull leather to bring him security…to remind him of duty and order. There were only ordinary Townsman shoes made from sheep skin…soft, comfortable to run and walk in, totally and utterly vulnerable in their freedom. "Yes," he answered. "I will be the drummer."

"Good," said Jeremiah. "You are likely the finest drummer in the Town. You should be proud of that."

Vyx wanted to reply, 'I am proud only to be a Guardsman,' but he didn't. He couldn't lie about it. He was proud to be the finest drummer in Town. He was proud how people looked up to him as he sat in that tree. He was proud that they applauded him, and even called out his name. He was proud to be such an important part of the song show. "I will be at Old Man Tree in the evening," he said. "And I will make the people dance."

105

Jotham sat in the grass under Old Man Tree, carefully working on a little flute he had carved from a juniper branch. He was trying to get the sound chamber just right. *Tweet, twoot.*

"It sounds very good," said Jeremiah, walking up behind him.

"I don't know. There's something that is off…just slightly…just enough to bother me."

"You have become a very meticulous musician."

"I suppose a meticulous Cobbler makes for a meticulous musician also."

Jeremiah sat down beside him. "Have you seen Myanaymiz today?"

"Yes, I saw her earlier, but she said she had something to do. I gave her a present…a pair of shoes. She was very pleased." Jotham looked down at his flute and smiled.

"That was kind of you. I don't think she has really been treated well since coming to the Town. First, there was Slemi…and there was even you and I. I don't think we were all that kind at first. It's good that you have given her shoes. You are the first to give her a proper gift."

"You gave her the gown."

Jeremiah laughed. "That was an accident. It wasn't a real gift… not a gift from the heart."

"Well, I hope she enjoys her shoes."

"I'm sure she will."

Jotham held up the flute and peered into the sound chamber. "I think I see the problem," he said. He inserted the carving tool, and carefully scrapped the inside. A tiny fleck of wood fell out. "There. Let me try it now." *Tweeet Twooot Tweeet.* "Perfect," he said. "Now, it is perfect."

"You are a very talented musician. I wish I were as musically inclined."

"Perhaps one day you will discover the hidden music within you."

Jeremiah laughed. "After the arrival of Myanaymiz, I believe that anything is possible. But look now, I see some Townsfolk appearing around the bend. Are you ready for another one of your inspiring song shows?"

"I've never felt more ready for anything in my life."

106

Vyx was crouched in the garden doing his traditional Guardsman strengthening exercises. "A Guardsman is obedient to the Gods. A Guardsman is strong for the Gods. A Guardsman gives all he has to give to the Gods. A Guardsman lives only for the Gods," he repeated over and over again as he stretched his body into various positions to put as much of a strain on as many muscles as possible.

"It is not easy being a Guardsman," said a voice behind him.

In a single move, Vyx turned and jumped to his feet! "Why are you sneaking up on me like that?" he demanded.

Myanaymiz smiled. "I did not sneak up on you. I merely walked into the garden. You were so involved in your exercises that you did not see me."

"I could have killed you. I am trained in moves of sudden death. You are lucky that my mind is quick enough that I could stop myself from automatically breaking your neck."

"And do you want to kill me?"

"I do not want anything. I serve the Gods and the Gods alone. If you threatened the Gods, it would be my duty to kill you."

"Oh, I see."

Vyx turned away and resumed his stretching exercises. "A Guardsman is obedient to the Gods. A Guardsman is strong for the Gods. A Guardsman gives all he has to give to the Gods. A Guardsman lives only for the Gods."

"I have a present for you," said Myanaymiz.

Vyx became quiet and still. Did he hear her right? "A present?" he asked.

"Yes. Allow me to go and get it. I left it just inside the cottage door." Myanaymiz hurried over to the open door. She disappeared inside, but then quickly reappeared holding something round in her arms. She walked over to Vyx.

"Here it is," she said, setting it down at his feet.

Vyx looked at the strange object. "What is it?" he asked.

"Can you not tell? It is a drum."

"A drum?" Vyx crouched down and looked carefully at it. *Of course it is a drum.* He ran his fingers over the taut sheepskin. "Where did you get it?"

"I made it. I gathered up materials from different Townsfolk, and then I put it together. Do you like it?"

Vyx tapped his fingers on the drumhead. *Such light taps yet such a large sound.* He then began to pound out the rhythm that was in his head. *Pah pa-pah pah pah…* The sound of the drum bounced off the forest trees, echoing throughout the garden. Vyx smiled.

As he continued to drum, he glanced up and noticed Myanaymiz watching him and smiling. He abruptly stopped. "That is enough for now. It seems to be a good enough drum," he quickly said.

"Are you going to thank me?" Myanaymiz asked.

"Thank you?"

"Yes, thank me for giving you a present. I do not think a Guardsman would receive many presents, which would make it even more important to thank the giver."

A Guardsman does not receive any presents. "I suppose…I suppose that is the traditional thing to do if you are Townsperson. As I am currently in Townsperson garb, I will then say, thank you. Thank you for the drum."

"You are welcome."

Vyx suddenly found himself looking up into her eyes. *What color are they? I cannot tell.* His eyes then wandered down to her mouth and he thought about the kiss. *If I kissed her again, would the same thing happen? Or would it be different? Maybe another kiss would change me into a real eagle, and I would fly away. Is that the secret of the Juju Witch, to transform? Will she transform me if I stand too close for too long?*

"I must go now," Myanaymiz said, turning and then quickly disappearing out the garden gate.

Vyx was now left crouching alone in the garden. He looked at the drum again. *A present? The Juju Witch gave me a present?* He tapped his fingers lightly on the drumhead. *The sound is wonderful! Much better than that old basket lid and stick.* He then lifted his hand high, and let his palm come crashing down to test the strength of the workmanship. BOOM! It didn't tear. It didn't give way. It was strong. *This is a good drum.* He happily picked it up, and headed in the direction of Old Man Tree.

———•◆•———

           A r l e n e   A d a m o

107

When the people began arriving, Jotham was surprised to see how many had brought musical instruments with them. Most of the devices looked brand new, quickly crafted for a night of music, but some of them seemed quite old and well used. This surprised him. *They secretly have musical instruments? What other secrets is this Town hiding?*

They also came with songs they wanted to sing or have Jotham sing for them. Eventually Jotham had been handed so many pages of songs that he began to wonder if the song show would last all night and into the morning.

"We should begin soon," he said to Jeremiah, handing him the songs for safe keeping, "but where is Vyx?"

Jeremiah looked around. He suddenly spotted Vyx making his way through the crowd. The Townsfolk seemed very excited to see him, and as he passed by, they didn't hesitate to say hello or praise his drumming. It seemed he was no longer the fearful Guardsman in their eyes. At least for tonight, he was the Town's beloved drummer. "Here he comes," Jeremiah said.

"Vyx!" called Jotham. "Are you ready to begin? The people are waiting to hear us, and now we have even more musicians!"

Vyx walked up to Jotham and Jeremiah. Under his arm, he carried his new drum.

"Where did you get that?" asked Jeremiah.

"It was a…the Juju Witch. The Juju Witch gave it to me."

"Myanaymiz gave you a drum?" If he didn't know that a Guardsman was incapable of lying about such a thing, Jotham would not have believed him.

"Yes," replied Vyx. "It was a present."

Jeremiah and Jotham laughed.

"Why do you think that is so funny?" Vyx was visibly annoyed with their reaction.

"I am sorry," said Jotham. "It is just that Myanaymiz does such strange things, and I've never heard of anyone giving a Guardsman a present before."

"Well, she did. She made this drum herself. She made it for me."

"If Myanaymiz made it, it must have a good sound," said Jeremiah.

"It has a very good sound," Vyx replied.

"Shall we put it to the test?" asked Jotham. "Climb up a few branches of Old Man Tree, and I'll hand the drum up to you.

Vyx then gave Jotham the drum, and began to climb the tree. "I have a feeling that this is going to be an incredible show, and already have a new song for it," said Jotham as he watched Vyx reach the third branch.

"It will be a magnificent show," said Vyx, reaching down to grab the drum. Jotham stretched up and handed it to him. As Vyx lifted the drum he added, "After all, it has the best drummer in the Town."

Jeremiah and Jotham looked at each other, amazed that a Guardsman would say such a thing.

"Alright, best drummer," smiled Jotham who now began to also climb the tree, "let us give this Town a show they will never forget."

⸻

     Arlene Adamo

108

Myanaymiz stood alone in the garden, looking up at the evening sky. It was not yet dark, and only a single star was visible. *O' star…lone star. Do you feel like me? Star alone. Do you feel like me? Waiting for your companion in the twilight…surrounded only by clouds…clouds passing you by…never seeing…dull blind clouds. Do you feel like me as I wait, alone, for my Lord? …my shining bright Lord!*

In the distance, she could hear the sounds of the song show. She could hear the beat, beat, beating of the drum she had made for Vyx. She could also hear many other instruments playing. *Many have come to create music. Music is healing. Music is freeing. Music helps slay the blind beast within.*

Still looking up at the sky, Myanaymiz let out a heavy sigh. *O' my Lord. My Lord, I know You will come soon…but I also know that, for now, I must join the people of the Town. It is their time to be with me, and my time to be with them. They need my help. I must think of them for now. Before I can leave, I must first move them forward.*

She then turned and headed in the direction of the song show.

———•◆•———

109

Vyx sat in Old Man Tree pounding his drum. Jotham, on a branch just slightly higher, sang as loud as he could. "Feeling like I could fly, Feeling like I a-a-am the sky..." Down below many people played along on their musical instruments. Some danced and some slowly swayed. The meadow was alight with both torches and frivolity.

Jeremiah sat quietly a short distance from Old Man Tree. He had never seen the Town like this before. It was as if they had been asleep a very long time, and now they were finally waking up. The smiling! The laughing! The joy! Something good was happening! He looked up at Jotham and Vyx, and was reminded of how he used to see them climb that tree when they were boys...although not quite as high, and not having half as much fun. He laughed to himself.

Many of the children were now gathering at the base of the tree. Several of them, wanting to be just like Jotham and Vyx, had begun to climb into the lower branches. A few carried with them their own roughly crafted musical instruments tied onto their belts or clutched tightly in their teeth. As he watched, Jeremiah saw that Twill was among the group. Twill had lost his sight to disease as an infant, but that never slowed him down. He was fearless, and always kept up with the other children as best he could. He was so fearless that his parents constantly worried about him following the other children to the river bank or the edge of some cliff. The image of Twill falling was always something fresh in their minds, and now, here he was, intent on climbing like the rest of them.

Jeremiah began to feel concerned as he watched Twill quickly reach the fourth branch from the ground. The ones who had climbed the highest stopped there. This was as far up as they were willing to go, but not Twill. He kept climbing. The others could see how high they were, but for Twill it was all darkness. He could not be sure just how far he was from the ground.

Jeremiah quickly began to make his way towards the tree when he saw that Twill had now reached a point where the branches grew further apart. He hoped the boy would stop there, but he didn't. He would feel his way up the trunk to the next branch, stretch up his arms around it and pull himself up. Jeremiah quickened his pace. Meanwhile, Twill's parents had also noticed and were pushing their way through the crowd. "Twill! Twill!" they called, but he did not hear them over the music.

Suddenly, it happened! Jeremiah saw Twill's foot slip! The boy wildly tried to balance and reach out for the branch above him, but he could not grab what he could not see. It all happened so quickly yet seemed to happen in slow motion. The falling backwards! The flailing arms and legs frantically searching for anything solid! The scream! Everything so strangely slow until…THUD! He landed flat on his back.

Jotham and Vyx immediately stopped playing. Jeremiah ran over to where Twill's parents were now kneeling on the ground next to their son. The boy's eyes were wide open, and he was not moving.

"Twill!" wailed his mother which made Twill start to scream.

"Do not touch him," Jeremiah instructed the parents.

Twill's parents were frantic. "Oh Twill! Oh Twill!" cried his mother, as she helplessly stared at her son.

Jeremiah began to search for any signs of injury. "We must be careful," he said. "His back may be broken." He could see no blood, and no obvious broken bones. "Twill, listen to me. Can you move your legs?"

Twill did not answer. He only continued to scream.

"Calm down. Calm down," said Jeremiah, but this only seemed to make him cry even louder.

Suddenly, Jotham was at his side. "Let me find Myanaymiz," he said. "She can help." He then disappeared.

Jeremiah had managed to quiet Twill a little by the time Jotham had returned with Myanaymiz. The child was no longer screaming, but would not stop whimpering. They now all knelt at Twill's side.

"I think his back may be broken," explained Jeremiah.

Myanaymiz placed her hand on Twill's stomach. "His back is fine," she said. "He is bruised and sore, but he is in one piece."

"How does she know this?" asked Twill's mother. "Who is she to examine my son's injuries?"

Jeremiah simply waved for the mother to be silent. He then asked Myanaymiz, "Are you certain he is fine? Why will he not stop crying?"

"He remains frightened by what has happened. That is all." Myanaymiz then gently stroked the boy's face, and told him, "It is alright, Twill. You are alright." Twill immediately went silent and closed his eyes.

"What has she done to my boy!" cried the mother.

"Quiet woman," said Jeremiah. "Your boy is fine."

Myanaymiz then placed her hand softly over Twill's eyes. "It is alright…it is alright…it is all light. Now, do as I tell you and open your eyes, but do it very slowly," she said, taking her hand away.

Twill ignored what she had said, and opened his eyes quickly. "Ahhh!" he screamed as he quickly squeezed them shut again.

"My son! My son!" shouted his mother. "What have you done to my son?"

Myanaymiz ignored the mother and said to Twill, "Try again, but this time open your eyes slowly."

Twill's eyelashes fluttered a little, and then he slowly, carefully opened them. His eyes then grew wide with wonder. A huge smile crossed his face. "You are so beautiful, Lady of the rock," he said.

The boy's parents stared in disbelief. Could Twill really be seeing the Lady? "Can you see me?" Twill's mother asked of him.

Twill turned his head and looked at her. "Yes," replied Twill. "I see you, Mother. Your hair is the same color as your dress."

Twill's mother began to sob.

"Do you see me?" asked his father.

"Yes, Father. I see you too. I see everyone here. I see the tree. I see the stars in the sky. I see the moon. And I see that strange looking man staring at me."

Jeremiah looked up to see what strange man Twill was speaking of, and there at the front of the crowd stood Vyx. Gone was the smile of the Town's drummer. Now, his face was stern and frozen… it was once again the stone-hard face of a Guardsman.

110

"I must go tell Bugiah," said Vyx.

Jotham, who had intercepted him on the road, stood in his way. "You must not go!"

"She made a blind boy see! The God of Gods needs to know about this."

Jeremiah hurried up to them, and stood beside Jotham. "You are right," he said to Vyx. "Bugiah would want to know about this, but is now the best time? He is in seclusion working on his greatest miracle, and you would insist on disturbing him? It is no emergency, and the God of Gods already knows the Juju Witch has powers."

"But he does not know the Juju Witch has this kind of power. This kind of power is the power of the Gods."

Jotham laughed. "So you want to go and disturb the God of Gods when he is busy with his greatest work to tell him that a mere Juju Witch has the power that belongs to the Gods alone? I suppose I will say goodbye now, because I shall never see you again."

"I am a Guardsman. My duty is to the Gods."

"Yes it is," said Jeremiah. "But that includes being able to anticipate what the Gods desire? It is only a few days from the Festival, and they are all deep in sacred preparations. Would they want you to disturb them with something that would likely only be addressed after the Festival anyway? Bugiah is in divine meditation. He is busily working on his most glorious achievement ever. Do you really want to bother him now when it would make more sense to tell him when he arrives in Town for the Festival? Why,

　　　　　　　Arlene Adamo

Bugiah would probably refuse to see you anyway, just as he did when you delivered his shoes. And it is possible that you could be severely punished for trying to bother him a second time."

Vyx thought about it. It was true that a Guardsman must fore-see the desires of the Gods, and also that the Gods were currently busy with some very important matters. The God of Gods would want to know about the Juju Witch…but would he want to know about it now?

"The people have been enjoying your drumming," Jotham said. "I think they would feel very disappointed if you should go up to the Palace of the Gods, and then never return for some reason."

Vyx looked at Jotham and felt a stabbing pain in his right arm…some old nerve damage, and a reminder of one of Bugiah's more severe beatings. *I must do what is best for the Gods. I am a Guardsman.*

"Since the God of Gods has indicated that the Juju Witch is here to serve him," Jeremiah said, "think of how pleased he will be when you tell him of her power. But as we both know, Bugiah is no ordinary God. He is the God of Gods, so he must always be addressed with only the greatest thought and consideration. You simply cannot march up there and demand a meeting. Think about it a while longer, Vyx. Perhaps observing the Juju Witch some more will give you additional insights. And if you think about it, the God of Gods would surely prefer that all the information be available at once than to be burdened with unanswered questions and multiple interruptions. His divine time is very precious, and you will likely have far more information for him later when he arrives for the Festival. Also at that time, you will be guaranteed that he will be in very good spirits. You know how much the God of Gods enjoys the Festival."

Vyx took in a deep breath as he carefully considered what the Master Weaver had said. *It is true that this is a particularly holy time of divine meditation for the God of Gods, and he did refuse to see me before. Also, perhaps it would be wiser to learn more about the Juju Witch before rendering a report. And my drum…such a good drum, and I have left it near Old Man Tree. What if the children should get hold of it? They could accidently break it.*

Suddenly, it all became clear. "Master Weaver, I see your point," he said. "I have not yet learned the extent of the Juju Witch's power. I must learn all I can before I report to the God of Gods. As it is late, I will pick up my drum and then return to the cottage. Tomorrow, I will go and talk with her. I will have all the necessary questions prepared by that time." He then abruptly turned and headed back in the direction of Old Man Tree.

Jeremiah sighed in relief. "That was very close," he said.

"Why did she do that?" asked Jotham. "So boldly. In front of everyone. In front of Vyx."

Jeremiah shook his head. "You would have to ask her that question." He then smiled. "But she did it, didn't she? She made a blind boy see. Have any of the Gods ever made the blind see before?"

Jotham sighed. "No," he said. "None of the Gods has ever made the blind see, but when they find out about it, that is what worries me."

"I know, my friend. I know."

<hr>

111

"What is wrong, Jeremiah?"

Jeremiah was sitting at his loom weaving. He looked up to see Myanaymiz standing in the bedroom doorway. She was wearing one of his sleeping robes.

"I could not sleep," he answered.

"You are worried for me," she said, as she walked over and stood behind him. She then pressed herself against his back, draping her arms over his chest.

He gently caressed her arm. "Yes, I'm very worried."

"You do not have to worry."

"But do you understand how powerful Bugiah and the Gods are? They can have you killed. Bugiah need only give the order, and Vyx himself would kill you. Can you not see that?" Jeremiah swiveled around on his stool, and looked up into her eyes. He felt like crying.

"Oh Jeremiah, do not worry! My Lord is with me. He will keep me safe."

"But you said that you were waiting on your Lord. How is He with you?"

"I am waiting, but also He is here. He is a part of me, and I am a part of Him. He will not let any harm come to us."

Jeremiah stood up and wrapped his arms around her. "If He does not come, I will protect you. I will die for you if I have to."

"You are such a good man," said Myanaymiz, "but no one will have to die for me. My Lord will come. He will come, but not now.

Now is the time we have together. So let us enjoy the gift that we have been given."

Jeremiah could feel the beating of their hearts together. "Tell me again that you will be safe," he said. "I want so much to believe it."

Myanaymiz stroked his soft beard and whispered, "I will be safe. You will be safe. Everything is just as it should be. My Lord has made it so." She then kissed him on his mouth. "Now come back to bed. Our time together is short, and we must not waste it."

 Arlene Adamo

112

As Vyx headed for Jeremiah's cottage, he thought about what he would do when he got there. This time he was determined to take full control of the situation, and learn all there was to know. *I will demand the Juju Witch divulge every last one of her secrets. The God of Gods would expect nothing less of me. She will explain how she made the blind see. I will make her explain. And she will not trick me. A Guardsman is more powerful than the spells of a Juju Witch. I am a Guardsman. I am the God of Gods' favorite.*

Up ahead, he noticed a group of people walking along the road towards him. To his surprise, they suddenly turned up the Master Weaver's front path. As he got closer, he could see that there was a large crowd of Townsfolk gathered in the front garden. *What is this?*

When he reached the path, he couldn't see anything because of all the people standing in his way. "I am the Guardsman. Let me through," he demanded. Vyx was confused when they did not obediently part. "I am the Guardsman! Move aside!" he commanded, now pushing his way through the crowd.

Eventually, he found himself in another group of people who were sitting on the ground. They were all staring intently at the Master Weaver's cottage. Vyx looked in wonder at the strange scene near the open doorway. It was Myanaymiz they had come to see. She was standing on the threshold as a line of people slowly filed past her. As they passed, she would speak to each one then gently touch them. *What is this about?*

Carefully stepping between the people sitting on the ground, Vyx made his way closer to the cottage. When he found himself standing not far from the door, an old man suddenly stopped him. "Look! Look, Drumming Guardsman! Look at what she has done to my hand!"

Vyx looked at the man's hand, but could see nothing. "It looks like an ordinary hand," he said.

"Yes!" exclaimed the man. "It is an ordinary hand! Before our Lady touched it, it was withered and the fingers could not bend. Now it is healed! It is whole again. She has restored me!"

Vyx looked at Myanaymiz as she gently placed her hand on the shoulder of the next person in line. *She is healing them!* He quickly pushed his way up to where she was standing. "Juju Witch, you should not do this! You have no permission from the God of Gods!" he demanded.

Jeremiah, who had been standing nearby, tried to protectively get between Myanaymiz and Vyx. "Honourable Guardsman…" he began, but before he could say anything more, Myanaymiz interrupted him.

"It is alright, Jeremiah. I will handle this." Jeremiah then stepped back, and she said to Vyx, "The people are being prepared."

"Prepared? Prepared for what?"

"They are being made whole for the Festival of the Gods. Do you not wish the Festival to be a grand success?" she asked, as she moved closer to him.

Vyx found himself staring into her eyes. *Those eyes! What color are they?*

"It is very important that the people be prepared, and such things are written in your Stories of the Gods. I am doing what I must, Vyx."

Prepared, she said…the people are being prepared. She is the Juju Witch, here to serve the God of Gods. She has established the song shows to prepare the people for the Festival. It would be reasonable that she would do more to prepare the people. She is here to serve the Gods. The God of Gods will be pleased that she is fixing the Townsfolk. They will be better able to serve the Gods this way. "Yes, I see," he replied, never turning away from her gaze.

"Good," said Myanaymiz. "Would you like me to fix your arm? I know it does not hurt right now, but it will hurt later. You know it will. Shall I fix it so that it never hurts again?"

Vyx looked down in confusion at his arm. *How did she know? A Guardsman never shows his pain. I have never let anyone know about this.* "I…my arm…?"

Before he could say anymore, Myanaymiz reached over and gently placed her hand on his right arm. Immediately, he felt the heat shoot deep into his flesh, down into his fingers, and up into his shoulder! From his shoulder, it traveled like liquid lightning down his very spine leaving him feeling weak, and yet so powerful at the same time. *What? How? It is so…so strange!* Myanaymiz took her hand away. His entire body was left tingling from her touch.

"You will notice the difference over time," she said. "It will no longer hurt. You are restored."

I am…I am healed? Vyx looked in amazement at his arm, and then into her eyes. "Thank you," he said, without thinking about it.

Myanaymiz smiled at him. "You are welcome, Guardsman. And I am looking forward to tonight's song show, for now you shall beat that drum with a passion you have never known before."

———•◆•———

113

Jeremiah was resting under Old Man Tree. Myanaymiz was leaning against his shoulder. He no longer cared about anyone seeing these small demonstrations of affection between them. Myanaymiz had brought so many good things to the Town, what bad could they possibly say about her? What would they care when they were too busy enjoying themselves and being happy to be judgmental?

Above them, Jotham and Vyx led the crowd in a rousing rendition of one the songs that had become a Town favorite. "Will you love me? Love me, love me, love me. I am hungry…o' so hungry for your love…"

"They are having such a good time," said Myanaymiz.

"Yes," replied Jeremiah, "they are. But now Jotham has reached the last song of the show, and they will not want to go home to their beds. You have turned this entire Town into a bunch of naughty children."

Myanaymiz laughed. "Before you tell everyone to leave, I would like to talk to them. There are things I have to say."

"What kind of things?" asked Jeremiah.

"It is like a story, but more than a story."

"But the Town is only allowed to hear the Stories of the Gods."

"Jeremiah, are you really going to try to convince me otherwise?"

"Sorry," he said. "I do not mean to tell you what you should be doing, but eventually, you know Bugiah will come out of seclusion. He will not like what is going on. I'm still…I'm still afraid for you."

Myanaymiz reached over and grabbed his hand in hers. "Stop worrying. It is a beautiful night. Jotham has sung magnificently. Vyx played the drum superbly. The people have danced and laughed and felt joy. Now, it is time for a story. As soon as Jotham is finished, blow the horn for them to remain, and I will tell them a story they will never forget."

114

Bugiah sat at the table, staring at the sheet of paper in front of him. At the top of the page was stamped his crest, a golden tusked boar with its head down ready to charge. The rest of the page was blank. *It shouldn't be this way. There should be words written here…many words…words of magic for the new ritual.*

Another morning had passed, and he had nothing. Over and over again he tried to induce a trance to reveal the words, but each time he felt like he was reaching the Point of Enlightenment, he would then find himself only in a dark and empty silence. Nothing for him had ever been this difficult before, and his frustration was mounting.

"Where are the words…the visions?" he suddenly shouted aloud, pounding his fist on the table. "I am Bugiah, the God of Gods! I am the wind! I am the sun! All things must come to me when I demand."

He got up, walked over to the mirror and stared at his image for reassurance. "God of Gods, who does not bow to you?" He smiled admiringly at his image. *I am a beauty! A God of beautiful, magnificent symmetry. Such power in my eyes, such a proud and noble nose, such…* His eye, suddenly, caught sight of something new. "What is this?" He stared in amazement at the two faint lines in his forehead. *Where did you come from? Streaks? Strikes? Scratches? Furrowed brow? Furrowed like a common Town field?* "I am immortal!" he screamed at the lines. "You are not there! Be gone!" The lines only seemed to deepen with his command.

He turned away from the mirror. "High Priest!" he shouted. "High Priest, come in here!"

The High Priest was the only one allowed to see Bugiah during his seclusion. It was his job to remain outside the door during all waking hours, ready to serve whenever called. "My God," said the High Priest as he hurried in then bowed down on one knee.

"The words? What are the words? For days I have tarried. I have kept in seclusion, and given up many of my comforts. I have prayed to those who came before me. I have done all that I am supposed to do, and yet, still, the words do not come to me! Why priest? Why? I am the God of Gods! Such things are not beyond such as me!"

"Yes, my God. You are the God of Gods. All things are possible with you."

"So where are the words? Tell me! What more must I do?"

The High Priest felt that dull familiar ache in his stomach. He knew Bugiah had very high hopes for this new ritual, and if he didn't help him find the words, he could find himself dead or even worse. Thinking quickly he answered, "If I may, my God, I would suggest that you identify the signs. As in the days of the Stories of the Gods, signs are of great importance, and are meant as a way for the Gods to navigate towards eternal life. The signs are sent from the Other Side to the God of Gods. You need only look for them. All things are possible through you, o' my God."

Bugiah clapped his hands together. "Yes, of course! Signs! I shall look for signs! And there are signs all around me! The God of Gods is graced by signs constantly! I need only recognize the right ones!" He looked around the room. "Signs, signs…what are the signs?"

Just then there was a knock on the outer door. The High Priest quickly got up then disappeared. When he returned, he carried a silver food tray. "Your midday meal, my God," he said, bringing it over to the table.

"My meal! That's it!" said Bugiah. "What is my meal?"

"I am happy to report, my God, that it is one your favorites… honey glazed pigeon."

"Pigeon! Why, that is the sign! My first magic word is pigeon… no bird…no not bird…wing! Oh glorious, glorious me! Wing! Of course…wing…flying…flying on the wind. This is the first word." Bugiah rushed over to the table, and quickly scribbled it down on the empty sheet of paper. He then stood up straight, and looked proudly down at what he had written. "Wing!" he said again. Turning to the High Priest, he commanded, "Go now! The signs are coming to me. It is best that my connection to all that is divine be not hindered by the presence of your mortality."

"As you wish, my God," said the High Priest, feeling greatly relieved as he backed out of the room.

Bugiah stared down at the single word on the piece of paper. "Wing…but what next? What other signs are here?" He looked over at his plate…the red squash, the green lentils, the brown sauce…"Gravy? That's it! Gravy is a liquid like water. Wing… air…gravy…water. No, not gravy, but something related. Gravy comes from the juices of the body…blood is the life giving juice of the body. It is the blood of Gods that flows through my veins, and gives me the insight and the power for this great undertaking. Blood is the next word…a word of power!" He quickly wrote down the second word underneath the first. "Wing, blood! Oh, how exciting this is! Exciting and exhausting! Two magic words so quickly. It is far more than I have done in days. And all in a matter of moments! But I should not work so hard. I must not exhaust myself. I shall eat, and then nap, and then I shall look for the other signs. The signs will come to me, and reveal the rest of the words…words that will be the key to the great ritual…the key to finally opening the secret door to Eternity! And I shall be the one to open that door because I, Bugiah, am the greatest God of Gods to ever live!"

———◆———

"Now is the time for something different and new. Tonight, I shall share with you a story," said Myanaymiz who stood in front of the crowd seated comfortably on the ground. She spoke carefully, and with pauses that those in front could loudly repeat her words in unison for those in the back to hear. "This is a very old story…"

"We are only allowed to hear the Stories of the Gods! You should not tell us this story!" shouted Vyx's brother Konn who was standing off to the side.

Myanaymiz looked over at him and smiled. "That was before, not now. Now, we are in special times, and special times call for special measures. This story will help prepare you for what is to come. It is a good story, and when you hear it, you will enjoy it."

"Let her tell the story!" shouted someone in the back.

"Yes, I want to hear a new story," yelled another.

Many people nodded in agreement, and no one spoke up in support of Konn.

With no further objections, Myanaymiz stepped closer to the torchlight so that the people could see her better. "This is a very old story… as old as the rivers…as old as the mountains…but it is also new and fresh like the rain in springtime," she said. The Townsfolk felt strange exciting chills run up and down their spines as the chorus echoed her words throughout the dark meadow.

"It is the story of two men," she began. "One was poor, and had worked hard all his life with little to show for his great effort. The other was rich. He owned many things including the fields that the poor man tilled. He was the one who appeared to benefit the most from the poor man's work.

Now it happened that one day, a stranger suddenly appeared in their midst. The rich man saw that the stranger was beautiful and said, *I want her for my own.* So he set about to impress her with all that he had. He told her, *Come and see all of my riches for I am a great man.*

So the stranger went with the rich man, and looked upon his fields. It was then that she saw the poor man. *Who is that who tends the fields and grows your food?* she asked.

That is the man who does the work, the rich man replied.

And if he does the work, what do you do? asked the stranger.

Why, I am the owner. I do not work. I own the fruits of his labor, he answered. *I am a great man, and great men do not work. I command the worker. I can tell this man to stop, to go, to run or to walk, and he will do it. I suppose, I own not only the fruits of his labor, but the man himself.*

The stranger sighed then looked him in the eye and said, *This man tends the fields with care and commitment, whereas you tend nothing. You care for nothing. Only an empty heart cares for nothing. And more than that, nothing here belongs to you—not the fields—not the crops and certainly not the man. Everything you believe you have is only borrowed from me. You have nothing and you do nothing. Do you not know me? I am the true owner.*

It was then that the man suddenly recognized the rightful owner. *Yes,* he reluctantly agreed. *Everything is borrowed.*

Even your mortal life, the stranger said. *Your mortal life is borrowed only for a short time.*

It was then that the rich man became frightened, and he decided that he must kill the rightful owner so he could claim everything for himself.

But the owner knew the wickedness that was in his mind. She knew that he planned to do her harm and said, *I know what is in your heart, but do you not know that your heart too is only borrowed?*

With that, she squeezed her fist tightly as if to squeeze his heart, and the rich man fell down…dead.”

All of the Townsfolk were amazed. What kind of story was this? They had never heard anything like it before. The children immediately began to clap and cheer. The adults then quickly joined in. The entire Town was astounded at the wonderful and strange story!

Jotham put his arm around Myanaymiz and whispered into her ear. “You are so-o-o dangerous. I love you.”

116

Myanaymiz sat at the edge of the river. Her shoes were beside her, her gown was pulled up to her thighs, and her bare feet were dangling in the water. She gazed at the myriad of tiny suns sparkling on the water's surface…a moving universe full of suns. *Where is my Sun? Where is my Lord?*

She then looked up into the sky, and saw a small yellow bird with black tipped wings. It circled about then disappeared from view behind a tree. *Where did you go little one?* Suddenly, it reappeared, swooped down and fluttered around her. She held out her hand, and it perched itself upon her finger. "Do you bring a message from my Lord?" she asked. The bird was silent, and simply looked about at nothing in particular the way birds do.

Myanaymiz stared at the tiny creature. How lovely were his yellow feathers. The lines so perfect…so intricate. And how delicate and vulnerable he seemed. To think that such a fragile creature flies through this world every day. A world full of hidden dangers…sudden winds, heavy rains, strong hungry animals. And yet, here he is flying, soaring bravely, living in the face of terrible things. "You are courageous and beautiful," she told him.

"It is only a bird," said a voice behind her, making the little bird fly away.

"Hello Vyx," she said, not turning around.

Vyx came over and squatted down beside her. He stared at her, but she did not look at him. Instead she looked at her feet as she slowly moved them in circles just under the surface.

"Juju Witches can sometimes enchant wild animals. I know that. I did not know they could also enchant birds."

"I did not enchant the bird. He came to me because he wanted to. Is it the duty of a Guardsman to tell a bird where to fly and where to land?"

Vyx just grunted and shook his head. He then suddenly asked, "And does it frighten you that I will tell the God of Gods everything?"

"Do you want me to feel frightened?" she replied.

"I want only what is best for the Gods."

"So you have said on many occasions."

Myanaymiz kicked her feet and gently splashed in the water. She then put her head back to feel the sun on her face and neck. "It is a wonderful day, is it not?" she asked.

"Kiss me again!" Vyx suddenly demanded.

Myanaymiz slowly turned her head and looked at him. "No," she replied.

"As a Guardsman, I order you to kiss me. I want to experience the strangeness of it again…to add to my report for the God of Gods."

"No," said Myanaymiz. "That is not what I do. That is not who I am."

Vyx was confused. "But you did it before. Why will you not do it again?"

"Before is not now."

"You speak in riddles, Juju Witch."

"And you do not seem to know my name."

Vyx stood up. He was angry. "I do not understand you!" he exclaimed.

Myanaymiz looked out at the river before her, searching for the little yellow bird, and hoping he would return. "You do not understand much of anything, Guardsman."

Vyx stomped away in anger, but a few yards on he stopped, and looked back at her. She continued to sit facing the river, never giving him even a parting glance. *Why will she not kiss me again?*

He ran his fingers over his lips. The feeling of her kiss still burned in his memory. *She cannot deny me. I will find a way to make her kiss me. I am a Guardsman of the Gods, and she must do as I command.* He then abruptly turned and marched off towards Town.

117

Jotham sat at his work table busily working on a new pair of shoes for a man whose twisted foot had been made whole by Myanaymiz. He was carefully sewing the sole to the upper portion when Vyx suddenly stormed into the cottage, and plopped himself down on a stool on the other side of the table.

Jotham glanced at him then went back to his work. After a few moments of uncomfortable silence, he finally asked, "Do you have something on your mind, Vyx?"

Vyx glared at him. *That long yellow hair! Do Juju Witches like long yellow hair?* He then thought about his own black hair cut so very short. "What do you do to make the Juju Witch kiss you?" he demanded. "I know she kisses you. Do not deny it."

Jotham smiled as he continued to work on the shoe. "I won't deny it."

"How do I make her do it to me?"

Jotham was confused. "Why would a Guardsman want a Juju Witch to kiss him?" he asked.

"It is not that I want it. It is for the Gods…for my report to the God of Gods."

"Oh, I see. And what do you expect to learn from a kiss?"

"She has already kissed me once before. I want her to do it again."

Jotham set down the shoe, and looked at Vyx in surprise. "She kissed you? A Guardsman?!"

"And why would she not kiss a Guardsman?"

"Well, because you are…you are a Guardsman."

"Guardsmen are men."

"Yes, but they are Guardsmen. Isn't it true that you are not allowed to touch a woman in that way?"

"This is true, but she is a Juju Witch. The rule does not apply. Also, the touch was for the greater purpose of serving the Gods."

"I see."

Vyx suddenly pounded the work table with his fist. "Tell me, Cobbler! How can I make her do it again?"

Jotham looked at him silently for a moment and then said, "Why would you think you could make Myanaymiz do anything? She is very independent, and has a mind that is clearly her own. She does what she wants. Not I, nor anyone has command over her."

"So, why does she kiss you? Why does she want to?"

"I don't know…perhaps she likes me…maybe…maybe she even loves me."

"Why?"

"Why does anyone love anyone else? Possibly, it's because of the way I treat her."

"I have not harmed her?"

"Vyx, it requires more than simply not harming a woman. For instance, you always call her 'the Juju Witch.' She may not like that."

"What do you call her?"

"I call her by her name, Myanaymiz."

"What else? What else do you do that makes her want to kiss you?"

"I gave her a present."

"What present?"

"The shoes she is wearing. I gave her those shoes. Also…"

"Also what?"

Jotham blushed. "She seems to like me because she feels I am a good man."

"I am a good Guardsman."

"Yes Vyx, you are. But it is not the same as being a good man."

"What does it involve to be a good man?"

"Let's see…I suppose it involves being kind…also considerate. There's generosity and caring. Thoughtful and respectful…respect is very important. All of these are qualities of a good man."

Vyx was silent for moment then asked, "What about strength?"

"Strength can be a part of it, but alone, it is not enough."

"Do you think that if I had not become a Guardsman, I could have been a good man?" Vyx asked.

Jotham was surprised at his question. He thought carefully about it and then answered, "When we were boys, you were a good friend to me. You had all of the qualities that would make you a good man. Perhaps those traits are still a part of you, buried somewhere beneath your Guardsman training."

Vyx did not say a word. Instead he simply got up, turned and walked out the cottage door. As he padded along the road, he looked down at his soft civilian shoes. *I am a Guardsman,* he reminded himself. *A Guardsman is devoted only to the Gods. A Guardsman does whatever is required to protect the Gods. A Guardsman's life belongs to…* He didn't finish the thought, but instead found himself stopping and looking up into the bright blue sky. At that very moment, a large majestic bird suddenly flew overhead. Vyx did not know what kind of bird it was, but he watched intently as it as it dipped and soared, and then finally disappeared into the tall and distant trees. After it was gone, he continued to stare up at the open sky imagining what it would be like to be up there…carried on the wind in that limitless space. *O' to be a bird and fly! To fly! I am an eagle. I am Vyx. I am a man. I once kissed a woman whose name is Myanaymiz.*

———•———

118

A large group of children seated on the ground had squeezed themselves in at the front of the crowd. They wanted to be as close as possible to the woman they called 'our Lady.' "We want a story. We want a story," they began to chant.

It wasn't just the children waiting in anticipation for the story. After enjoying a wonderful night full of joyful singing and dancing, everyone was now eager to hear another fascinating tale. "Jeremiah, please let them know that it is time to begin," said Myanaymiz. Jeremiah then blew the horn to call the Townsfolk to order. Quickly, they all settled into place, and waited quietly.

Myanaymiz smiled out at the crowd and then announced, "This story is called Glass Town." As before, those near the front repeated her words aloud for those in the back, making them echo across the meadow. "It is about a Town where all of the people were made of glass," she told them.

Made of glass? Many of the Townsfolk 'oohed' and 'aahed' at such a strange and fanciful idea.

"As you may imagine, life could be very difficult for people made of glass, and every day they lived in terrible fear. What if they should get a chip or a crack? Would it be noticeable? Would it lead to something more serious? And then there was, of course, the ultimate fear of being smashed into a myriad of pieces."

Some in the crowd winced at the thought of being so vulnerable.

"The people of glass were ruled by a King who was not made of glass. He was made of stone…stone that could easily crush glass.

I am the great King of Stone, he would declare. *Obey me, or I will crush you!*"

Many of Townsfolk gasped at the frightening words of the King.

"Of course," continued Myanaymiz, "the people of glass were very afraid of their stone King. Although, they were never allowed to see him crush anyone, they were required to view the aftermath. One by one they would be forced to file past, and look upon the tragic mound of shards. It was a terrifying sight, and a reminder of what would happen if they did not obey him."

A few in the crowd nodded their heads. "Obedience is a good thing," someone mumbled.

"Just on the outer edge of Glass Town, in a small shack made of soft leaves and feathers, (for all the people of glass had houses made of soft leaves and feathers), lived a little glass girl named Steen. She was an only child to her glass parents, but also a worry to them. You see, Steen was a very curious child who was often getting into trouble for her curiosity. While the other children spent their days playing games together, she preferred to spend most of her time alone, thinking and creating things out of found objects. Many in the Town called her Strange Steen, and not in a very nice way at all.

One day, Steen was walking through the forest when she suddenly found a straight strong branch lying on the ground. A powerful wind had broken it from the tall tree above. *This is the straightest branch I have ever seen,* she said. So she picked it up, and carried it with her.

A little further on she saw a stone in a perfect triangle shape. She was not supposed to pick up stones as obviously, in a world of glass people, it would be strictly forbidden, but she picked it up anyway, and carried it with her.

A little further still, she spotted a long piece of strong vine that she thought might be useful for something. So she picked that up, and also carried it with her.

Steen then went to the river, and sat down on the bank. She looked at the three things she had found…the branch, the rock and the vine. *What could I make with these?* she asked herself. Suddenly an idea came to her…a brilliant idea…a bold idea…a strictly forbidden idea! Steen decided to make a hammer!

As you may imagine, a hammer in a world full of glass people was unthinkable to everyone…everyone but Steen. So she took the strong vine, and used it to tie the triangle stone to the branch. When it was complete, she held it up, and examined her handiwork. It looked strong and sturdy. She swung it through the air, nearly knocking herself over. How exhilarating! A hammer! A forbidden hammer!

Now, Steen knew that she must hide the hammer. She could not let anyone know she had made such a thing. So she looked around until she found the perfect place…under the hawthorn bush. No one would ever accidently find it there. People were afraid of those thorns. They believed them to be strong enough to chip glass. So she carefully tucked the hammer away underneath those thorny branches.

Everyday Steen would return to play with the hammer. She would swing it this way and that. She would slice through the wind, breaking off tree branches. She would smash it through the grass, cutting out large swaths. She would slam it down on empty shells, shattering them to pieces. Then she would hide it again under the hawthorn bush.

One morning, as she was just about to run out the door to play with her hammer, her mother stopped her. *The King is speaking today,* she said, *and everyone is required pay homage to him. That includes you.*

Steen did not want to go. She did not like the King or his speeches, but she knew what was required of her, so she went along with her parents to the palace wall.

At the wall, the King walked out onto his balcony, and stared down at the crowd. He did not launch into one of his usual speeches. Instead, on the stage below him, a King's guard shouted, *Hear ye hear ye, someone has been overheard questioning the authority of the King! Today is a Day of Punishment!*

                    Arlene Adamo

Everyone was immediately filled with terror. A Day of Punishment meant certain death for someone, but who would it be this time?

Steen was not afraid like the rest of them. Instead, she felt angry as she watched one of the King's Guards march into the crowd, and pull out a young boy. He then dragged him by the hand onto the stage where the child stood trembling and crying with fear. His mother, being held back by another guard, was desperately pleading, *Please he's just a boy! Have mercy!* Tears were streaming down her face as she struggled to break free of the guard's grip.

The terrible scene was too much for Steen. She had felt anger before, but something new was rising within her. It was a furious anger so intense, she knew she could not possibly stand idly by and watch the boy be killed. *I will stop this!* she thought. *I will do something!*

Steen then left the crowd, and ran to the hawthorn bush. She reached in and grabbed her hammer, hoping it would not be too late by the time she returned.

Hurrying back as quickly as she could, she was relieved to see that the boy was still on the stage, receiving his formal sentencing. No one noticed the hammer she held in her hand as she pushed her way through the crowd. Steen did not know exactly what she would do when she reached the King, but she thought about the many times she had swung against the wind, and the many tree branches she had broken. When she reached the wall, she quickly climbed a snaking vine to the King's balcony. The guards were too busy focussing on the boy and his mother to notice her. When she jumped onto the balcony, the King was so surprised that he had no time to call out. *You are no King!* she yelled then swung her hammer. SMASH! The King shattered into a million pieces!"

Myanaymiz went silent as she waited for the Townsfolk to understand. Suddenly someone called out, "He was glass! The King was glass like the rest of them!"

"Yes," shouted another, "he lied about being made of stone! The King was a liar!"

"What happened next?" asked a woman in front.

Myanaymiz smiled and said, "At first, everyone was frozen with shock. They simply could not believe what they saw. Everything they believed to be the truth had been proved false. The King, they had feared as a great power, was just an ordinary person like anyone else. As it all began to sink in, many of the people now felt very ashamed that they had treated Steen so badly. They could see she was a hero who had saved them. After this, Steen was raised to a place of honour in Glass Town, and they passed a law to never again follow the rule of a King."

The Townsfolk were amazed at the wondrous story! This was even better than the last one! They all broke out into cheers and applause.

　　　　　　　Arlene Adamo

119

Vyx stood in the dark outside of Jeremiah's cottage. He had wanted to talk to Myanaymiz…to see her…to try and trick her into kissing him again. After the story was over, and everyone was leaving the meadow, he tried approaching her, but either Jeremiah or Jotham were always in the way. Now, she was in the Master Weaver's cottage, and the lights were out. He reached up with both hands to the tree branch above his head, lifted himself off the ground, and began to swing back and forth.

"I did not know that Guardsmen played in the trees at night."

Vyx dropped to the ground and swung around. "Myanaymiz!"

Myanaymiz silently walked past him and over to the garden bench. She sat down then asked, "Do you wish to sit here next to me, or do you prefer to swing from the trees?"

Vyx felt his heart quicken. He wanted to run to her…to be close to her, but he held himself back. *A Guardsman must always maintain control.* Instead, he marched over, and sat as far away from her on the bench as he could. He then silently looked off in the other direction.

As time awkwardly dragged on, and she did not speak, Vyx knew he must say something soon. Before opening his mouth, he reminded himself of what Jotham had told him about being a good man. *I must say something that she would consider thoughtful.* He turned, looked at her and said, "The Townsfolk enjoyed the story."

"But did you enjoy it?" she asked.

"I am a Guar…" Vyx stopped himself in midsentence. If he was going to get her to kiss him, he must be very careful of what he was to say. "Yes," he answered. "It was a strange story, but I enjoyed it too."

"That is good."

Vyx could see the outline of her face in the moonlight, but not her eyes. He was a little glad of that. Seeing her eyes could distract him…hamper his ability to focus. He took in a deep breath. *Now say something else she will like.* "You look like a good meal," he said.

Myanaymiz laughed. "What do you mean by that?"

Suddenly realizing he had said the wrong thing, Vyx felt embarrassed. "A meal is good," he tried to explain. "Guardsmen do not get good meals at the Palace. I have had good meals here in the Town. A good meal is a good thing. It was a compliment."

"Oh, I see. Then thank you, Guardsman," she replied.

Vyx immediately felt better. His plan seemed to be working.

"As you do not get good meals, I suppose then, it is true that Guardsmen do not get much of anything. Is this correct?" she asked.

"Our lives are very strict," he explained. "That is the way it is. The way it has to be."

"Who says?" she asked.

"The Gods say."

"Well, if I were a God, I would do it all differently. I would make it the law that my Guardsmen would eat the best meals, sleep in the softest beds, wear the smoothest silks and take afternoon naps in the warm sun."

Vyx surprised himself when he laughed out loud. He couldn't remember a time when he had ever done that before. It felt strange…strange but good. "I think I would like to be your Guardsman," he found himself saying.

"I would love to have a Guardsman as strong and as brave as you," she said. She then did something that caught him by surprise. She leaned over and kissed his mouth.

Vyx did not hesitate. He passionately grabbed her in his arms and kissed her back. "I…I cannot stop," he then whispered into her ear. "I cannot let you go."

"I never asked you to," she replied. "I never asked you to let me go."

———•◆•———

      Arlene Adamo

120

Jeremiah and Jotham sat together under Old Man Tree. All around them the Townsfolk were dancing, singing and playing their instruments. Vyx sat in the tree, pounding his drum to the collective rhythm.

"Tomorrow is the Festival of the Gods," said Jotham. "Are you worried?"

"Of course I am," replied Jeremiah. "Once the God of Gods comes and sees what has been happening…what will he do?

"Myanaymiz keeps telling me everything will be alright."

"Do you believe her?"

"Sometimes, yes, but other times, I'm not so sure."

"Where is she now?" asked Jeremiah.

"She is over there, dancing with the children," said Jotham, pointing in the direction of the road.

Jeremiah could see her in the distance moving and swaying in the moonlight. He sighed. "She says she is leaving with her Lord soon. If she goes, I will miss her."

"As will I," replied Jotham.

"Also Vyx," laughed Jeremiah. "He has grown very close to her over the last few days."

"I have noticed. I have also noticed that he is much more pleasant to live with."

Jeremiah laughed again. "That can be said of all of us."

———

121

What was it in the air? That strange sense of calm…of peace… the moon so bright it was putting the stars to shame…the shadows of the trees so mysterious and inviting…the flickering torch lights so alive in their dancing. Had there ever been a night like this before? The revellers, now tired but happy, were beginning to assemble around Old Man Tree. Tonight had been the best song show yet, and part of them never wanted it to end, but it was time for a story. They loved the stories, and afterwards, when they went home to sleep, the memory of the stories always brought them good dreams.

Myanaymiz stood at the base of the tree surrounded on three sides by torchlight. Once it looked as if most everyone was in place, Jeremiah then blew the horn to signal that she was about to speak. Quickly, the crowd quieted until the only sounds heard were the distant love songs of the crickets in the darkness. It was then that Myanaymiz began. "My people," she said. "Tonight there will be no story."

"No story?"

"Did she say 'no story'?"

"But we want a story!"

"Tonight instead, I would like to speak to you about something of great importance. I wish to speak to you about who you are, and your place in this world."

"About us?"

"Why would she say such a strange thing?"

"We know who we are."

"You are the Townsfolk," she said, "but have you ever really thought about what it means…what it truly means?"

"What is she talking about?"

"Since I have come to know you, I have seen who you are. Above all you are a very hard working people. You work hard for what you have. And you work hard for what you share with those you call the Gods."

"Share with the Gods? But all belongs to the Gods."

"What does she mean 'those you call the Gods'?"

"You till the fields. You tend the sheep. You weave the cloth. You make the shoes. It is generous of you to share with those who do nothing."

"Is she talking about the Gods?"

"Yes, it is true. The Gods do nothing."

"Ssshhh!"

"You are good people. You are fine people. The One and Only God loves you."

"Who is she talking about? Does she mean the God of Gods?"

"I don't think so. The God of Gods does not love us. We serve him. This God she speaks of is different."

"Let no man tell you that you are unworthy. Let no man tell you that you must serve him because you are less than what he is. Let no man tell you that you are not precious. You belong to God, and all that belongs to God is precious."

"We are precious?"

"We belong to God?"

"Yes, I am precious!"

"This world is meant for those who are precious to God. All who are precious should be able to sing, dance, play music, tell stories and discuss things freely. Freedom is air. Freedom is food. Freedom is water. The way to God is through freedom and truth."

"But what of the Gods," someone called out from within the crowd. "Who are the Gods, to this God you speak of? Are they His divine children?"

Myanaymiz shook her head and said, "No. Those whom you call the Gods are not Gods. They are not divine. They are men and women just like you. They were born, they live, and they will die. What makes you believe they are more? Think about it. What miracles do they perform? Can anyone here tell me even one thing they do that is evidence they are Gods? Why, in your everyday work you have created greater things. Just look at what your Master Weaver does. Look at what I am wearing. Has even one of your gods ever created anything this wonderful? You are the ones who grow the food, who dig the wells, who build the houses and roads. It was even Townsfolk, centuries ago, who built the Palace of the Gods. Tell me, who are the creators here, those who do nothing or those who create?"

She waited for an answer, but there was only silence from the crowd.

Vyx, who was standing close by, suddenly ran over to her. "What are you doing?" he pleaded. "You cannot say such things!"

"Here is a Guardsman," said Myanaymiz to the Townsfolk, "a Guardsman who has seen the gods up close many times. Tell us, Guardsman, what have you seen that makes these people Gods? Can you explain to any of us why we should call them Gods?"

Vyx looked at her in utter disbelief. "I…they…why?"

"You see! Even the Guardsman cannot answer as to why these people are considered Gods." Myanaymiz then leaned over and whispered to him, "Bugiah has hurt you long enough. I will never allow him to hurt you again."

Vyx stood frozen in shock and confusion. *I am a Guardsman. I protect the Gods. What do I do now?*

Myanaymiz turned back to the crowd. "Tomorrow is the Festival of the Gods. It shall appear to proceed as it always has. You will all follow the rules, and do what is expected of you, but know this, tomorrow everything will change. The truth about your gods will be revealed. It will be the end of your servitude."

Jeremiah looked at Jotham, "Am I dreaming? Did she really say those things?"

"Yes, she really did say those things," Jotham replied, smiling.

Myanaymiz then, without another word, walked into the crowd. As the people parted to let her through, they said nothing. What she had just told them was so shocking…so earth shattering that they were only able to silently watch her walk by. She had healed them, and brought them so many good things, but how were they to accept what she had just told them? It went against everything they understood about their world.

When Myanaymiz reached the edge of the crowd, they all watched in wonder as she calmly crossed the road and then, without looking back, instantly disappeared into the darkness of the forest.

"Should we follow her?" Jotham asked Jeremiah.

"No," Jeremiah answered. "She did not ask us to, and she seems to know where she is going."

"…and tomorrow?"

"For that, I suppose we will have to wait and see."

122

J otham and Vyx showed up early at Jeremiah's cottage. Jeremiah was already up, and dressed for the Festival. "She is not here," he told them before they even had a chance to ask. "She did not return last night."

"I am worried about her," said Jotham.

Jeremiah looked at Vyx. "Will you tell the God of Gods what she said?" he asked.

"I...I am a Guardsman."

"Are any of us who we thought we were before she arrived?" asked Jotham.

Vyx shifted uncomfortably. "Perhaps she has gone already with her Lord."

"I don't believe she has," responded Jeremiah. "Her plan was to be here at the Festival. Also, she would not have left without saying goodbye. She would not do that to me...to us."

"So what should we do now?" asked Jotham.

Jeremiah looked at Vyx. He was definitely not the same hard-hearted Guardsman he once was, but had he changed enough that he would not betray Myanaymiz? When face to face with Bugiah, he may not be able to help himself. "We shall do as she told us, and proceed with the Festival of the Gods as would be expected. After all, is there anything else we can do?"

"No," said Jotham. "That is all we can do for now. We must obey the Gods." *Hopefully for the very last time.*

———•◆•———

123

The people dutifully lined the road just as they had done every year. At the head of the procession were four Guardsmen in full uniform, followed by twenty colorfully painted horse-drawn wagons that later would carry the offerings back to the Palace of the Gods. The High Priest, clutching the sacred Book of the Festival to his breast, walked behind the wagons. Every now and then he would have to do a little skip to avoid a pile of hot manure. After the Priest, came the Gods on horseback in their brilliant and colorful gowns. The pomp and ceremony of this year's Festival seemed unprecedented, as they rode along on their beautifully decorated horses covered in dyed feathers and silk ribbons. Following them, marched four more Guardsmen and, finally, at the very end was Bugiah.

It was true that Bugiah was looking more magnificent than he had ever looked before. The Townsfolk could not believe the beauty of his incredible gown or the wonder of his golden winged shoes as he rode along on his new dapple grey steed with his back straight, and his head held high.

As Master Weaver, Jeremiah's place was to walk directly behind Bugiah. The Townsfolk, lining the route, would then join in one by one behind him until everyone was a part of the procession.

Jeremiah stared up at Bugiah's back. *Look at him…more arrogant and puffed up than ever before, and more dangerous. How could this possibly end well?* He put concerted effort into every step as he tried not to let his unsettled feelings show. With each group of people he passed, his eyes searched for Myanaymiz. *Where are you? I need to know that you are still here, and that everything will be alright.*

The procession slowly moved along the road towards the place beside the river where the Festival was being held this year. That is where the Townsfolk had spent days setting up altars with all of the offerings. They had taken extra care to ensure everything was perfect for the Gods, but after last night, and what Myanaymiz had told them, they could no longer be certain what to expect. Mixed with the usual excitement was a peculiar pall in the air…a mystifying shroud over everything. The celebration was proceeding just as would be expected, and yet there was the something strange they could sense…something waiting just around the corner…something that told them this would be unlike any Festival they had ever experienced before.

 Arlene Adamo

124

"Guardsman Vyx!" called out Bugiah as he proudly stood facing the crowd, his back to the river. Vyx appeared out of the middle of the throng, and hurried over to kneel before his God. "Guardsman, have you missed your God of Gods? Do not worry. Tomorrow you will return to your regular posting at the Palace. Now tell me, where is that Juju Witch?"

Vyx did not know what to say. *Tell him what she said. You are a Guardsman. Your loyalty is to the Gods. Tell him everything. The song shows. The singing. The dancing. The blasphemy. The kisses…her sweet, sweet kisses.*

"I am here." Everyone turned to see Myanaymiz approaching along the river bank. The Gods, who were clustered to one side of Bugiah, parted to allow her through.

Jotham sighed with relief when he saw her, but that quickly changed to fear. *What is going to happen now? How can she protect herself from Bugiah's wrath? How do I keep her safe?* He was barely able to keep himself from running to her.

"Good!" exclaimed Bugiah. "Come here Juju Witch, and observe whilst I perform the greatest ritual ever conceived by a God."

Myanaymiz stopped several feet away and watched silently.

Bugiah then raised his arms, and all of the Townsfolk and Guardsmen obediently knelt to the ground. Myanaymiz and the Gods were the only ones who remained standing. "Worshippers of the Gods, you have done well," he declared. "I see your offerings. These offerings are good in the sight of the Gods." He swept his hand across indicating the many altars surrounding the crowd which were piled high with wood for fires, foods, textiles, wines, precious stones and much more. "I accept your offerings, and give you the divine blessings of the Gods."

"We are grateful to serve the Gods," the crowd replied in unison just as they had done every year.

Bugiah lowered his arms, and stared with satisfaction at the people kneeling before him. "Now," he announced, "I shall do something no God has ever done before. I, Bugiah, the greatest God to ever live, shall open the Eternal Gates before your very eyes! I shall resurrect all of the Gods who came before me! I shall usher in the Golden Years! Because of what I will do, you will no longer fear the Deluge of Death, and shall instead live, until you die, in glorious servitude to your eternal Gods."

Jeremiah looked over in concern at Myanaymiz. She did not appear worried at all, but merely smiled at him as though nothing was amiss.

"High Priest!" Bugiah called out. "Come here and pray!"

The High Priest got up from the ground, and rushed over. He then dropped down to his knees again, and silently began to pray.

Bugiah reached to the scabbard at his side, and pulled out the sword that had been handed down to each God of Gods throughout the ages. He held the glistening steel blade high in the air and shouted, "Gods who came before me, know that I am the God of Gods Eternal! Know that I am the one and only King…King of the Gods!"

Turning around to face the river, he then walked to the very edge of the bank. He stared out over the sparkling water and declared, "I will command the winds! I will command the direction of the rivers! I will tell the trees to grow, and the flowers to bloom! I am Bugiah!" Raising the sword with both hands up over his head, he then violently plunged it down into the water's edge! Still clutching onto the hilt with both hands, he called out the magic words. "Wing of blood, dust of ember! I am Bugiah and I proclaim the Eternal Gates open!"

The crowd was perfectly silent with anticipation as they waited for something to happen.

Bugiah kept his hands firmly on the sword. *Where was the spectacular show of force? The loud boom and flash of the Eternal Gates?* He turned his face upwards and shouted again, this time directly into the sky, "Wing of blood, dust of ember!" *Still nothing?* "Wing of blood, dust of ember! Thunder! Lightning! I command you!" he shouted even louder. Everyone looked up at calmness of the bright blue sky with its soft fluffy clouds. "Thunder! Lightning! I, Bugiah, God of the Gods, command you!" he screamed as loud as he could, but still there was nothing. Bugiah glanced over at the other Gods who stood staring at him, confused and eagerly awaiting their eternal inheritance.

What is wrong! Where is my miracle? Bugiah was trying to think fast. What had he missed? Suddenly, he remembered. *It's the dance! Of course the dance! I'm forgetting the dance.* "With this dance, I will command you!" he shouted. Bugiah then began to dance around in a small circle. His feet came down rhythmless and clumsy upon the river bank. He looked up at the sky with the full expectation that he would soon see the dark clouds rolling in. "Wing of blood, dust of ember," he shouted, bringing down his right foot hard upon a flat stone. Instantly, a searing pain shot up into his foot. He screamed out in shock and agony. The small nail Jotham had secretly placed in the sole of his shoe had found its mark. Bugiah stumbled then awkwardly wobbled as he tried to regain his balance. He reached out to grab onto something…anything, but there was nothing to hold onto. His arms flailed in the air as he fell unceremoniously into the water. The children instinctively burst out laughing, and their parents immediately filled with dread.

The High Priest ran in to help. He reached down to take the hand of his God of Gods, but was only rewarded with an angry pull that sent him flying into the water also. From land, the Townsfolk watched nervously as Bugiah slowly crawled up onto the bank. He then stood up and began to limp towards them. His face was hard and lined with rage. No longer caring about the pain in his foot, he only wanted to make someone pay for his humiliation and suffering.

The children were no longer laughing. They were now terrified. Some of them tried to seek shelter behind their still kneeling parents. Others froze in fear. Bugiah, dripping wet, slouched towards where he thought the loudest laughs had originated. "You would dare commit blasphemy, and laugh at the God of Gods?" he shouted as he reached out and picked up Petal who was standing closest to him. Lifting her up by her shoulders, he scowled into her tiny frightened face and hissed, "What good are you? Such a useless insignificant thing, and such a stupid creature to laugh at the God of Gods! You should not have even been born! You have no place in this Town!" With that, he suddenly threw her, like a rag doll, onto a nearby pile of precious stone offerings. There was an awful sound as she hit the rocks. Petal's mother screamed as she and Petal's father ran over to the still body of their child.

Jeremiah did not know what to do. He looked over at Myanaymiz, but she was already walking towards Petal's mother who was on the ground clasping her little girl to her breast. "My baby!" the mother cried. "My baby is dead!" Blood from the back of her child's head was staining her best white Festival gown.

Everyone watched in shock, not knowing what to do. Myanaymiz did not hesitate. She walked right up to the grieving mother, held out her arms and said, "Give her to me."

"Juju Witch, stay away from my people!" Bugiah screamed in anger.

The mother looked at Myanaymiz, and then down at her battered, bleeding child.

"Do not hand her that child!" shouted Bugiah.

Petal's mother only dared to glance at Bugiah who she could see was glaring intensely at her. She knew he would have her tortured and killed that very day if she did not do as he ordered. There was no excuse and no mercy for those who disobeyed the God of Gods.

Arlene Adamo

She then looked again at Myanaymiz. Here was a woman who had been so distrusted by the Townsfolk when she first appeared out of nowhere. She had said many things that upset people, and even went so far as to challenge the Gods. When she started to demonstrate her power some had called her a 'dog', the backwards spelling of 'god.' Even now a few had doubts, and whispered unpleasant things despite all she had done for them. Would ignoring the God of Gods, and trusting Myanaymiz be a decision she would regret?

As Petal's mother continued to stare into that face…into those eyes, she remembered how she once asked Petal why she wanted to go see the strange woman. Petal told her, "Mother, Our Lady has the sky in her eyes…the sun and the moon and the stars. It makes us laugh and dance and feel good. It helps us grow big and strong. If you wish me to grow big and strong, then I must go."

Suddenly, there was no question about it. She knew there was only one choice…one real chance of hope. Petal's mother handed over the small limp body to Myanaymiz.

"You will all die!" screamed Bugiah as he watched in outrage. No Townsperson had ever dared refuse his order before.

Myanaymiz held Petal gently in her arms. She looked down at the tiny bruised face. "Petal," she softly called. "Awake Petal, awake." There was complete silence as everyone waited and wondered what would happen next. Even the birds in the trees and the river seem to have become quiet. All was still. *Could the Lady who made the blind see, and healed the sick and the lame, make Petal come alive again? Did she have the power to defy death?*

It was Axis who first noticed something. "Her hand moved!" he cried out.

Everyone stared at Petal's hand which hung lifelessly from her body.

Did the boy really see it move?
Don't bodies move after death?
Is it only the death nerves he saw?

But then it twitched! They all saw it! It twitched again and then again!

"The boy is right! She moved!" called out someone from the crowd. The fingers then began to slowly wiggle. Next, it was the arm. The arm rose up...it rose up and Petal softly rested her tiny hand against Myanaymiz's cheek.

"The bleeding has also stopped!" shouted Jeremiah who could not believe what he was seeing.

Petal's eyes then began to flicker. They opened, and she looked up at Myanaymiz. A huge smile crossed her face. "Oh my Lady!" she said. "Will you take me to dance under Old Man Tree? The Cobbler can sing, and the Guardsman can play. We will have a wonderful time!"

Petal's mother gasped. "Petal! Oh my dear Petal, you are alive!" Myanaymiz set the child down who was then quickly embraced by her weeping mother.

The Townsfolk, still kneeling on the ground, were frozen in silence. How were they to comprehend the great miracle they had just witnessed? Never had they seen anything like this before! No one knew what to say or do.

Finally, it was Jotham who spoke first by suddenly jumping up and shouting, "She has defied death! Myanaymiz has defied death!" The Townsfolk then leapt to their feet as they began to cheer and clap.

Bugiah was livid! "How dare you get off of your knees before me!" he screamed.

"But she has raised the dead," said Jotham, defiantly. "Have you any idea what that means?"

Bugiah knew exactly what that meant. "No one but the God of Gods can raise the dead!" he shouted. "I will kill you for saying this...and for the shoes, Cobbler, but first I will kill the Juju Witch so you may watch her die!" Bugiah tore off his shoes, and ran back to his sword that was still imbedded in the river's edge. He was just about to pull it out when he suddenly stopped. A strange sensation had begun to take hold of him. It started out as a tiny tingle then quickly began to grow in intensity. In an instant, it was all over him! A million insects crawling everywhere…eating into his flesh…weakening him…a legion of unbearable bites! He looked down, and clutched at the gown of strange moving shapes and colors. "This gown!" he cried out, suddenly aware that he had been duped. "This gown has not been woven by the Master Weaver! It has been woven by the Juju Witch!" He tried to pull it off, but it seemed to be stuck to his skin. Sinking down to his knees in agony, he looked over at Jeremiah and cried, "Weaver, what have you done! You too will die for this! Guardsman! Guardsman!"

Vyx obediently ran over to his God of Gods!

"Guardsman! Take my sword and kill the Cobbler! Kill the Weaver! But first, you must kill that Juju Witch!"

Vyx bowed before his crippled God, then reached down and pulled the sword from the river's edge. He turned towards Myanaymiz and stood staring at her.

Myanaymiz did not move or say a word. She only calmly stared back at him. Petal was now clinging to her gown and weeping.

"Kill her!" shouted Bugiah.

Vyx took a step in her direction, but then stopped.

"Not my Lady!" cried Petal. "You cannot kill my Lady!"

"What are you waiting for!" screamed Bugiah. "Go and kill her!"

What am I waiting for? I am a Guardsman. A Guardsman is… I am a Guardsman of… I am…what? What? What color are your eyes? I am YOUR Guardsman! A lightning fast swing! A flash of silver blade! CRACK! In an instant, Bugiah's head was gone! His body fell over, SPLASH, into the water! Further out in the river, everyone could see his severed head being grabbed by the current. They all watched in shocked disbelief as it bobbed along then quickly disappeared into the white rapids.

"Noooo!" screamed out one of the Gods. "The Guardsman has murdered the God of Gods!"

The other Guardsmen quickly jumped into formation, and began to move in on Vyx. "Stop," commanded Myanaymiz. When they did not obey, she then raised her arms to the sky and called out, "Thunder! Lightning!"

There was a loud BOOM and a blinding FLASH as the lightning hit the ground between the Guardsmen and Vyx. "If you touch him," she warned, "you will all die!"

Completely shocked, the Guardsmen carefully backed off. Never before had they ever seen one of the Gods command lightning. This Lady had a far greater power…greater than Bugiah… greater than any of the Gods!

The Gods now began to weep like frightened children. What were they to do? Bugiah was gone, the Guardsmen had been rendered useless, and the Juju Witch had taken control. Nothing made sense any more. *But we are the Gods! We are the all powerful Gods!*

Upon seeing the Gods so afraid and weeping, one of the Townsfolk called out, "Our Lady is right! They are not Gods. They cry. They are afraid. They are human just like us."

Everyone stared in wonder at those they had so fearfully revered only moments before. *Are these really our Gods? The same ones who such a short time ago seemed so large and powerful riding in on their steeds? Is this the real truth? Who are they? Who are we?*

Some of the Gods had now dropped down in despair to their knees, their gowns getting dirty, their faces wet with tears. None of them dared even glance in the direction of Bugiah's headless body. They could not bear to look upon it.

Axis suddenly ran up to one of the Gods who was still standing, and kicked him in the shin. "Owww!" the God screamed, and everyone began to laugh.

"You are not Gods," said Axis. "Our Lady was right. It was all lies."

"Listen to me," Myanaymiz suddenly called out, making everyone turn and stare in awe at the beautiful sight before them. The sparkling of the precious stones behind her, the glistening of her gown, the shimmer of her skin, the silver glow of her hair, she and everything around her were covered in the reflective kisses of the sun. "Townsfolk, listen to me! You are no longer slaves! You are free! No longer will you be forced to worship these ordinary people as gods. No longer will you work hard, but never enjoy the full fruits of your labor. No longer will you be forced to live in fear. You will be free to dance, and to sing and to live. This is a new day…a new beginning. You will begin to build your new world…a better world…a fairer world…a balanced world. It has been a long night…a long time coming, but the dawn is finally here. Move forward, never look back, and always make wise and good judgements for the welfare of all."

———•◆•———

125

"My Lord will be here soon," said Myanaymiz as she stood together with Jeremiah, Jotham and Vyx on the road leading out of Town.

"Do you have to go?" Jotham asked sadly.

"I was only here to wait for my Lord. My waiting is almost over." It was then that Myanaymiz noticed a tear in Vyx's eye. She walked over and put her arms around him. He grabbed her and held her tightly. "It will be alright," she tried to reassure him. "You have a new life ahead of you now, full of all kinds of new things to experience and learn."

"But I don't want you to go!"

"Oh Vyx, you know I must. In your heart, you know it is time," she said.

Myanaymiz then stepped back from Vyx and turned to Jotham. "And you, Outlaw Singer who makes a fine pair of shoes, you have much ahead also. The Townsfolk will need you and your songs more than ever now." She hugged him, and softly kissed his lips.

Next she turned and looked at Jeremiah. "And what of an old man like me?" he asked her. "What is ahead for someone like me?"

Myanaymiz lovingly stroked his beard. "You still have a long life ahead of you. The Town will need your guidance and your wisdom as they build their new society. There are wonderful things ahead for you also, Master Weaver."

Jeremiah sighed, and then gently kissed her on the cheek. He was just about to say something more when he suddenly noticed a strange light up ahead on the road. At first he thought it was a trick of the eye…only the reflection of the sun, but then the light quickly began to grow larger and brighter. It stretched out taller and taller as it took the shape of a full grown man. From head to toe this Man of Light glowed with such a beautiful and amazing intensity, Jeremiah could do nothing but stare. All words had left him. The Man of Light stood only a few yards away, but at the same time He seemed as far away and as unattainable as the stars. Jeremiah thought he could see the outline of His eyes. He could certainly feel their powerful gaze upon them all. Never had he felt such a thing before! It was then that he suddenly became aware of his own deep intense desire to go to Him. Jeremiah wanted desperately to be close to the Man of Light! A strong instinct was pleading with him to go…begging him, but Jeremiah's feet would not move. He sensed the frightening power before him…a power greater than lightning…a power greater than the sun! His heart wanted more than anything for his feet to move, but his feet knew better then to approach such a power as this.

"Is…is that your Lord?" Jotham asked Myanaymiz. He too was overwhelmed, and had just barely been able to get the words out. Vyx had been rendered completely speechless.

Myanaymiz sighed and called out, "Oh my Lord! At last, You are here! You have come for me! You have not forsaken me!"

She then looked at her friends and said, "Remember that I love you. I love all of you. And I have left with you some secret powers that you will discover over time. Do not forget me. And tell the children stories about me. But I will be back one day. I will return to you again, and on that day I will bring your son that you might see him." Then without another word, Myanaymiz turned towards the Man of Light.

Jeremiah, Jotham and Vyx watched as the Man opened his arms, and without hesitation, Myanaymiz ran straight to him. Instantly, she was wrapped up within His glorious luminescence, and the three men were amazed they could no longer see her. Myanaymiz seemed to have melded with the Man, becoming Light also. Now, there remained only a single brilliant Light.

Jeremiah smiled. *By what miracle has a wondrous Star wandered from Heaven and ended up here, upon our simple Town road. How blessed we are to be a part of such a thing as this.*

The Star then rose up a little from the ground and, for several seconds, simply hovered there as if in one last goodbye. Vyx sighed and under his breath whispered "Thank you for everything. I will not forget you." The Light then grew brighter and in a blinding flash, they were gone!

The men now stood silently staring at the empty road before them. Just like she always said she would, she had left. Jotham wiped a tear from the corner of his eye. "I will miss her," he sighed.

"We all will," said Jeremiah.

Vyx stared at the empty place in the road where they had disappeared and asked, "When she said she would come back with 'your son', who was she talking to?"

Jotham smiled. "She leaves us the way she came…with an unfathomable riddle."

"Perhaps," said Jeremiah, "she was speaking to all three of us. She has certainly shown us some very strange and wonderful things."

"A son from all three of us?" laughed Jotham.

"In any case," said Jeremiah, "I will wait with anticipation for her return, but for now gentlemen we have a new Town to build. We have people who have lost everything they ever believed to be true, and will be in need of guidance. Are you ready for a new beginning?"

"I am," said Jotham. "I am ready for a new Town and for a new world. What about you Vyx?"

"The new Town will need a loyal Guardsman," Vyx smiled. "A Guardsman of the Town."

Jotham clapped him on the back. "Then let's go get started. The Townsfolk were expecting a Festival, and there are still altars full of wine and food just waiting to be enjoyed. I think it is time to have a new kind of Festival…The Festival of the Townsfolk, and

I believe I even have a new song for the occasion. It's called *My Heart Waits for You*."

"It sounds like a song that needs a drummer," said Vyx.

"Yes, it will indeed," laughed Jotham.

As the three men turned and headed back towards the center of Town, Jeremiah asked his two companions, "Did I ever tell you about the story I once heard as a child? It's about a Lady…a Lady who came from a rock…"

www.ingramcontent.com/pod-product-compliance
Lightning Source LLC
Chambersburg PA
CBHW070055120726
47909CB00002B/398